Deadline

Michael Litchfield

ROBERT HALE · LONDON

Typeset in 10½/13½pt Palatino
Printed in Great Britain by St Edmundsbury Press,
Bury St Edmunds, Suffolk.
Bound by Woolnough Bookbinding Ltd.

For those special people in my life – Michele, Luke and
Savannah

Also a big thank-you to my editors, who are
always so professional

Luke Templeman was living proof that there really is life after death.

Templeman had not been in the university-dominated city of Oxford since the day seven men and five women – all good, true and trusty, according to Western mythology – unanimously convicted him of murdering his wife.

Traditionally, cops don't fare well in gaol. Templeman was no exception. Hell would have been a knees-up by comparison. The governor of Belmarsh had to confine him to the hospital wing to give him a sporting chance of survival. After that, metaphoric death improved, mellowing into purgatory, though a couple of medical orderlies, paid by the godfathers of the prison mafia, cut him twice.

His appeal against conviction failed, all three judges upholding the trial verdict, thus his misery continued.

Two years to the day after being robbed of his freedom, a small brown package was received through the post by his London firm of solicitors. The receptionist, whose job it was to open the mail every morning, fainted the moment she emptied the contents of the package on to her tidy desk. In addition to a message, composed on a computer or word processor, was a human finger.

The anonymous message read:

Your client, Mr Templeman, has suffered long enough. Now let's have some fun. Let the game of cat and mouse begin. Come catch me, Mr Templeman, if you can. It's playtime!
J and H

Home Office pathologist Professor Grant Parsons quickly confirmed that the severed finger had been preserved in cold storage and, beyond all scientific doubt, had been amputated from the corpse of Charley Templeman, Luke's estranged wife, whose body had never been found. Conclusive proof had come from advanced DNA profiling.

Within a week, a judge had released Templeman, pending a full-scale hearing. A month later, three appeal judges quashed Templeman's conviction. That was the day of his resurrection. He had risen, beating death rather than cheating it – to him an important distinction – but the emotional roller-coaster was far from over. In many ways, the ride was only just beginning.

Now his ambivalent return to Oxford had his pulse jumping. He was met at the railway station by Detective Inspector Mike Hardman, florid-faced and paunchy, with a rubbery build that gave a bounce to his step.

They shook hands cordially on the concourse, nothing contrived.

'Good to see you again,' said Hardman, the sentiment swathed in sincerity. There was something adhesive and bonding about their white-knuckle flesh-pumping.

'Let me take your bags.' Hardman spoke like a jolly farmer who had just enjoyed a bumper harvest. 'You look blitzed. The wheels are out front, on double yellows. If I've been stung with a fine, it's your treat, OK?'

Hardman was doing all the talking, fuelled by nervous energy, as garrulous as a doorstep salesman afraid that the slightest hiatus might lose him closure on a lucrative sell.

Before Templeman could protest, Hardman had picked up the two canvas travel bags and was leading the way purpose-fully to his unmarked Rover police car.

'Good flight?' He continued to make conversation, peering over his shoulder, without once losing the rhythm of his rolling stride.

'Any flight that ends the right way up, wheels down, is a good one,' said Templeman, with all the feeling of a nail-biting flyer. 9/11 had changed his attitude irrevocably to defying gravity and defining danger.

'I've booked you into the Randolph. Nice and handy; as if you need telling that.'

'Everywhere changes.'

'But not *everything*. Cities are like criminals. They may change their appearance, but they keep their bad habits, their basic character.'

In another five minutes they were outside the neo-Gothic hotel in Beaumont Street, opposite the grandiose Ashmolean, the oldest museum in Europe.

'Bad memories?' Hardman asked, carelessly.

'What do you think?'

'I think it was a stupid question.'

No comment was expected from Templeman. None was forthcoming.

Templeman took charge of his luggage and checked himself in, telling Hardman he would meet him in the lounge for a drink 'in five'.

By the time Templeman returned, having deposited his bags in his room, without unpacking, Hardman had staked his claim on a window table.

For a full minute they sat facing one another without speaking, suddenly comfortable in each other's company, like a couple who have learned to rub along together, after the novelty shine and nervousness have worn off. No more sales patter from Hardman. It was a done deal; he knew that. Templeman was hooked. He had flown the Atlantic for this. He was on a mission, taking up the irresistible challenge.

The justice system, to which Templeman had been betrothed for so long, had betrayed him when he had needed its reciprocation most. He was bitter; of course he was. No amount of financial compensation or belated vindication could ever begin to soothe the soreness of his soul. His hurt went to the very core of his chemistry, but above and beyond everything else he was a hunter; that's what Hardman and his top brass had relied upon. The murderer of Charley Templeman, a celebrated criminal defence lawyer, was big game. For Templeman, with all his emotional and personal involvement, the chance to bag this quarry was a prize he would have rowed – swam, even! – the Atlantic for, never mind flown.

A waitress took their order. Templeman asked for coffee and a bottle of non-carbonated water. He had dehydrated during his overnight red-eye to Heathrow and was determined to avoid alcohol for at least a couple of days. Not so Hardman. Since the finger-in-the-post development, he had been drinking as a matter of maintenance. Although it was only noon, his breath already smelled of a spit-and-sawdust bar. It was time for a top-up, hence his request for a pint of draught beer. And just before the waitress left their table, Hardman amended the order to include a whisky, 'straight up'. The slight tremor of the detective inspector's fingers was noted, but not remarked upon, by Templeman.

'How's Simone?' Once again it was Hardman leading.

'As good as new.' Templeman had been tutored by the barrister defending him in his trial in the technique of verbal economy.

'Fully mended, then?'

'She's been fully recovered a long time.' There was a glazed, faraway look in Templeman's melancholy eyes now, more than a symptom of jet-lag.

Simone Tandy had been Templeman's partner when they were detectives with Scotland Yard; Templeman an inspector, Tandy a sergeant. They were having an affair during a high-profile murder investigation, when Tandy collapsed, not from stress but due to a brain tumour. Undergoing delicate surgery was her only hope of survival. Ironically, she had survived her ordeal far better than her lover had come through his nadir.

After brain surgery, Tandy had recuperated in the country at the horse-racing stables run by Templeman's parents. By then, Templeman had separated from his wife, nicknamed 'The Sorcerer' in legal circles for her supernatural powers in court, defending the rich dross of society with spectacular success.

Soon after Templeman moved out of his matrimonial home to live with Tandy, his wife initiated divorce proceedings, warning him balefully by text: *My God, you're going to pay for your cock-up! This is going to be the costliest screw-up of your lousy life!* If he had indeed made a mistake, he compounded it by keeping the text in his mobile's memory as a marriage memento, rather than deleting it immediately after reading. Inevitably, it returned to haunt him, especially as he stood in the dock at Oxford Crown Court, answering to the charge of murder. The motive came by mobile. New technology was proving itself to be as double-edged as the medieval sword.

One week after sending that text, Charley Templeman went to Oxford to defend Alan Gent, a small-time gangster accused of shooting a shopkeeper during a hold-up. The shopkeeper was shot when refusing to hand over the day's takings from the cash register. The trial was scheduled to last two weeks and Charley was staying at the Randolph Hotel. After the second day of the trial – a Tuesday – she dined at the Randolph with her junior counsel and Gent's solicitor, both women. Following dinner, Charley said she needed to 'walk off' her meal. She went alone, while her companions migrated to the bar. Charley Templeman was never seen again. Neither dead nor alive.

Bank records revealed that, on the evening of her disappearance, Charley drew out fifty pounds in cash from a wall machine in Cornmarket Street, a mere hundred yards from the hotel, at 9.15. She and her professional colleagues had finished dinner around nine, so she had used her bank card within minutes of setting out on her stroll. None of her clothes or toiletries had been taken from her room. From that day, her several bank accounts had remained untouched. It was not until the following morning, after Charley failed to appear in court, that she was reported missing.

Luke Templeman had been in Oxford that fateful Tuesday evening. When interviewed by Thames Valley detectives about his reason for being in Oxford, he explained that he had received an anonymous call earlier in the day from a man claiming to have 'inside' information about an unsolved

Scotland Yard investigation. Templeman, in those days a detective inspector with the Yard, told the Thames Valley investigators: 'The call came late morning, not on my mobile but through the switchboard. The caller refused to give his name, but insisted he had information that was gold-dust; that would break the back of a long-running case. You know as well as I do how the game's played. Those kind of calls aren't unusual. Nine out of ten are from cranks, but it's worth wasting time for that tenth call, the one that really delivers. So I went ... to the Turf Tavern at nine o'clock.

'I know Oxford pretty well. I was brought up near Lambourn, where my father trains racehorses. Oxford's an old stamping-ground of mine. The caller said he was fifty years old, almost bald, short and stocky, and would be wearing jeans and a floppy jumper, emblazoned with the slogan 'Elvis Lives' across the back. Whoever he was, he didn't show.'

Within a few weeks of Charley's disappearance, the Thames Valley police concluded that she must have been murdered. Suicide was ruled out. She was at the pinnacle of her career and earning a king's ransom every time she stepped into court, her coliseum, where her opponents were made to feel that they were being fed to the lions. And although her marriage had broken down irrevocably, her colleagues reported that she had shown no signs of depression. Suicide candidates did not go to elaborate lengths to kill themselves in places where they hoped they would never be found. Suicide was an elaborate two-fingered salute to the world. Without a body, there was no gesture, no point.

Luke Templeman had the motive. He had the text. He was in Oxford at the material time. He had not mentioned the alleged mysterious caller to anyone else. This was a call that was never made or received, the prosecution was later to claim. The defence argued that Luke had no reason to admit being in Oxford that evening if he had anything to hide.

It was a classic 'no body' murder trial, characterized by orthodox prosecution and defence tactics. Against clear direction from the judge to acquit, the jury had demonstrated its independence by convicting. The appeal court had been loathe to overturn a jury verdict without substantial new evidence or proof that there had been misdirection from the trial judge. There was neither.

Then came the finger and now, after all that trauma, Templeman was back in Oxford, the city of dreaming spires … and, for this man, haunting nightmares. He was free, yet shackled to a macabre mystery that would enslave him all the way to the grave unless he found the key to its solution, which in turn would release him. Now free, though still very much a prisoner of his past, he was staying in the hotel where his wife had last slept, where, for all he knew, he could be sleeping in the same bed. There were still many ghosts to be exorcized. Nothing would ever expunge the injustice. Even the arrest and conviction of the real killer could not compensate Luke for the wasted years. They were gone for ever. Somehow he had to focus only on the future, applying creative editing to his memory.

When Templeman began his sentence, Tandy vowed to use all her detective training and skills to establish his innocence, but he had vetoed this, insisting she go to the United States to start a new life, which she had reluctantly done, launching her own PI agency in Naples, on the west coast of Florida. Luke joined her immediately after his release. Tandy was ecstatic. They celebrated. But within a few days, Luke was brooding. He was sore; a man with a score to settle.

Three days ago, Hardman had phoned him to say, 'I have a proposition. We need your help. *I* need your help. We'll cover all your expenses, put you in a decent hotel, and give you the chance for revenge. With a bit of luck, it might get something rotten out of your system, once and for all. Sure as hell we want it out of ours. I'm putting this to you not only with the full authority of my chief constable but also the home secretary.'

Luke didn't act on impulse. He replied, 'Give me twenty-four hours.'

When talking it through with Tandy, she told him, 'You know and I know what you have to do. Go do it.'

The following day, he was on the overnight flight from Miami to London. That was yesterday.

Hardman drank some more. The nectar nursed his nerves.

'How much are you aware of what's been happening here since you took off?'

'I follow the news. *Took off* sounds as if I did a runner.'

'I didn't mean it that way. Words aren't my forte.'

Templeman smiled. Self-deprecating cops were rare. Special, even, because they tended to be the best.

'I know you've been having a rough time.'

'Three murders in six months. All women. All in the city of Oxford. All on my watch. All attacked from behind, clubbed unconscious with a blunt instrument, then strangled with a stocking. And then the note ... always the damned note.' A suffusion of sweat had erupted around Hardman's white shirt-collar.

'*Note?*'

'Now that's something you won't have read about. Jesus! I need another drink.'

Twitching, Hardman looked around for a waiter. There wasn't one in sight, which agitated him even more.

'I'll fetch it myself. How about you?'

Templeman held up a hand, at the same time saying, 'Count me out, but you go ahead.'

Hardman was back in five minutes, his replenished beer glass already half empty.

'You were saying something about a note,' said Templeman, reining him in.

Hardman dried his lips with the upper surface of his hand. 'After each killing, a note, yes.'

'To the police?'

'To me, personally, as lead investigator. The message that came with the finger triggered a bad enough media feeding-frenzy. You can imagine the carnival they'd have if they got wind of the subsequent three piss-taking notes. Press and public haven't yet linked Charley with this year's trio. No reason why they should without knowledge of what we're sitting on.'

'What did these notes say?'

'"You'll never catch me without the help of the main man. You'd better send for Templeman. Don't insult me with the B-team. I deserve to be in the ring with the best."' Hardman was reciting, as if every word had become etched on his soul, never mind his brain.

'Always the same?'

'Never a variation.'

'Handwritten?'

'No, a print-out from a computer or word processor.'

'Posted in Oxford?'

'Always.'

'Still no trace of Charley?'

'Nothing since the finger.'

That made Templeman grimace.

'There's a sicko on the loose out there, Luke, and it's now a political hot potato. And I'm the one in the oven, feeling all the heat.'

Hardman had been with Scotland Yard, a team player with Templeman at the time of Luke's arrest by the Thames Valley cops. Hardman, like all the other Yard detectives, had never accepted Templeman's guilt. Therefore the cama-raderie between them had never been trashed. Hence Templeman's willingness to co-operate with Hardman, despite his transfer to Thames Valley that had accompanied promotion from detective sergeant to detective inspector. When Templeman had heard of Hardman's move from London to Oxford, he had commented, 'The devil always recruits the best.'

'Three women have been murdered—' Templeman started to say.

'Four,' Hardman interjected.

'Three excluding Charley. No attempt has been made to conceal their crimes. Quite the reverse, in fact. Yet Charley's body remains missing. Nevertheless, you're convinced there are four murders and one perpetrator.'

'Absolutely.'

'My successful appeal was extensively covered by the media, in the papers and on TV.'

'And I have a collection of all the cuttings and footage, Luke.'

'Millions of people, therefore, know in detail the history of Charley's disappearance and the grisly finger-in-the-post delivery.'

'I know exactly what you're hinting at, Luke, but, believe me, we don't have a copycat here. You see, there's nothing to copy. There's no original. Until Charley's body surfaces, no-one has a clue how she died. What I'm sure about is that your trial and absolution inspired – if that's the right word – this sicko.

'Something I haven't told you: each note was signed off "J and H", the same as the one to your solicitor. No handwritten signature. J and H were part of the typed text, just as before.'

'J and H,' Templeman repeated. 'Are you thinking these murders could be a team effort? A duo?'

'It has to be a possibility. Scary, isn't it?'

'Scary' wasn't the word Templeman would have used; 'interesting' would have been more his choice.

'How soon after the murders have the notes been arriving?'

'Always within forty-eight hours.'

'You must be pretty desperate to turn to me.' Templeman's self-effacement was tinged with a tease.

'This is a city on the edge, Luke.' Hardman was too fired up for humour. 'A city in the grip of fear. One more body and we'll have panic and hysteria to contend with. We have two universities, with undergraduates totalling in excess of 20,000, more than half of them female. The parents of girl students are withdrawing their daughters in droves; the beginning of an evacuation that will bleed this city dry if it becomes a haemorrhage. The colleges are Oxford's lifeblood, its culture and heritage. The vice-chancellors of both universities have written to the chief constable *and* the home secretary. The home secretary, herself an ex-graduate of Balliol, has reacted aggressively behind the scenes, firing off several snotty missives to our chief con, casting doubt on the ability of Thames Valley officers to catch a pet rabbit, let alone a prize sewer rat, such as our scribe psycho. A motion of no confidence in the region's police force has been tabled by a group of councillors for debate at the next meeting of Oxford City Council. Neighbourhood Watch committees are threatening to put vigilantes on the streets after dark. Everyone's feeling the heat, especially *me*. The kicking, as usual, gets more vicious as it works its way down the chain of command. You know the drill. I'll be honest with you, Luke, it's getting to me in a big way. I'm not sleeping. I'm eating all the wrong stuff, nothing but junk food. This has become my oxygen.' He held up his beer glass. 'I walk the house at night. My wife has turfed me out of her bed: she says I keep her awake because I'm so restless and that's true. This could bust up my marriage.'

Templeman had always been a good listener, an attribute that was now being tested.

'It was my idea to approach you. The chief con expected you to snub the offer, but I pointed out that we'd worked well together in the Smoke and you had no beef with me. He agreed there was nothing to be lost by trying to entice you on board. After all, our killer was involving you in each murder. In a strange way, you're as much his target as the woman victim every time he strikes. To be honest, it's getting much too Freudian for me, but perhaps you can make some sense of it. Anyhow, from our point of view, the gamble paid off. You bit and here you are. I knew you'd be unable to resist. After all, unless we're grossly mistaken, this guy was responsible for messing up your life big-time.'

'Refresh my memory over some of the basic details, Mike. What was the date of the last murder?'

'June 2nd, three weeks ago.'

'And the one before that?'

'April 1st, Fool's Day.'

'And ...'

Hardman pre-empted the question that Templeman didn't have a chance to ask. 'January 15th. A cluster of three within five months. We have a busy maniac on the loose. He's into a rhythm. On a roll, like a gambler who has to keep going until his luck runs out.'

'No particular significance in the dates, as far as you're aware?'

'Except April 1st. Perhaps that was chosen to symbolically make fools of us. Nothing more than that, I guess.'

Templeman did some mental arithmetic. Charley vanished on 15 July four years ago. It was a year after that before he was charged. Another six months elapsed before his trial, followed by two years in gaol. He had been out around six months.

'I can follow the windmills of your mind,' said Hardman, as troubled as Templeman. 'I know what you're thinking. If the perp started with Charley, he went three and a half years before striking again, then compressed three murders into a five-month period. There's no discernible pattern, right? How was he able to exercise such restraint over himself between Charley and January 15th this year, then erupt into an orgy of murder?'

'Perhaps his original plan was for me to rot in gaol. After all, I'd abandoned all hope until he broke cover. Have you considered the possibility that he may have killed elsewhere while I was behind bars?'

'It had occurred to me. I've made a nationwide check on all unsolved murders.'

'And?'

'There aren't any that really fit. Of course, he could have changed his MO and we don't yet know how Charley died, but psychopaths don't, as a rule, alter their style. You could argue that their MO is almost involuntary.'

Templeman evaluated some more. 'There's always the possibility that he was unable to reoffend for several years because he was in prison for some other offence, or was working overseas.'

'That's a possibility,' Hardman conceded.

'Though doubtful.' Templeman quickly rubbished his own conjecture. 'Where would Charley's body have been stored while he was in gaol? I can't believe that it could have been preserved in such pristine condition, undetected, as evinced by the finger, while he was locked up all that time. The same applies if he was confined to a psychiatric institution or abroad.' Templeman slapped his sides. 'Enough of the negativity. To begin with, I'll focus on what we know, rather than what we don't. I'll need to see everything you have.'

'That's already been taken care of. I've got copies of all the case files in my car. I'll fetch them for you.'

'I'll come with you, give you a hand.'

Copies of documents relating to the murders had been stacked in four cardboard boxes. Together, the two men carried the boxes to Templeman's room, lining them up on one of the decent-sized twin beds.

'Grief! I can't believe how out of shape I am,' Hardman complained breathlessly. 'A year ago I was a twenty-a-day smoker. I decided I must quit and that was my New Year's resolution. Now I'm smoking sixty a day. I'm not sure which'll come first, bankruptcy or lung cancer. These murders will be the death of me.' And then, 'Have you given any thought to a game plan?'

Templeman stroked his prickly chin thoughtfully. 'First of all I'm going to read through all this little lot,' he said, pointing to the boxes. 'Then I'm going to take a look at the crime scenes, just to get an atmospheric feel for each incident. I'll walk the route taken by each woman during the last steps of their lives. Maybe something will occur to me, though probably not, but at least it will be a way in for me.'

'Whatever you're comfortable with. You do it your way, that's the whole idea. After all, you're the one the nut wants to play with.'

'That raises a tricky issue. Do you intend letting the killer know I'm back in town? If you do broadcast that fact, you realize the danger, don't you?'

'It'll encourage him to kill again quickly, just to taunt you as well as the rest of us, to put you to the sword.'

'Precisely.'

'But he's going to keep on killing, whatever we do or say, until he's caught. You can bet your life on that.'

'Accepted, Mike, but by keeping our heads down, maybe we can buy a bit of time.'

'The press and politicians are behaving like packs of hungry wolves, so I'm afraid there's no chance of any respite or a quiet life, whatever we do.'

'It's your call, Mike.'

'On balance, I agree with you, that it's best to keep your presence a secret for as long as possible. It will allow you to poke around away from the spotlight.'

'Agreed, then.'

'I'll leave you alone, Luke, to get on with it in your own time and tempo. I'll wait to hear from you.'

Before parting, they exchanged mobile numbers.

'I take it I negotiate through you at all times.' Templeman checked the ground rules.

'Unless you have any objection.'

'Of course not. Best, though, that we sort out procedures now, to eliminate recriminations later.'

'Anything you want, at any time, just ask.'

Hardman had the bedroom door open and was straddling the threshold when his mobile vibrated in a side pocket of his crumpled jacket, prompting him to stop mid-stride and step back into the room to take the call.

'Yeah. You what?! Read it to me. Hellfire! I'm on my way.'

Hardman's face had gone from rubicund to bloodless in the time it took him to utter those twelve staccato words.

Templeman feared the worst. 'Not another body?'

'Not quite. Not yet. Another note, though, but preceding the event this time, signalling a change of tactics. The killer has turned tipster, forewarning of what is to follow. Advance notice of his intent to kill again.'

Although he was finding it hard to stay awake, Templeman was determined to avoid sleeping during the day in order to shake off his jet-lag as quickly as possible. As soon as Hardman had thundered off like a tornado about to uproot everything and everybody in its path, Templeman decided to throw himself into his homework without delay. He began with the box relating to the 15 January murder of Gloria Swift, an environmentalist campaigner who had become a successful author of books for adolescents. Swift, a forty-three-year-old divorcee, had lived with her three children in a large Victorian house – a former vicarage – on the Banbury Road, in the northern, most expensive belt of the city, a dormitory for the highest paid professionals. Her husband, Malcolm Jefferson, a lecturer in medieval history at St John's College, was ten years her senior.

Demonstrating her independence from day one of their marriage, Gloria had declined to relinquish her maiden name, a stand that had met with the approval of her husband, himself very much a modernist. It was only after she had been married a couple of years that Gloria launched her writing career, coinciding with her first pregnancy. Her books were not an immediate success, although she had secured a publisher at only the third submission. Appreciating the importance of branding, from designer accessories to toilet paper even, she made the colleges of *her* city very much the backdrop to all her novels. Gradually she forged a niche for herself upon that narrow shelf between children's swashbuckling adventures, far-fetched juvenile fantasy and adult fiction.

Because of her husband's position, she socialized mostly in academic circles and this limited her need for research. Ideas popped into her head at college cocktail parties, from anecdotes – apocryphal and otherwise – Malcolm regaled her with over dinner at home, and breathless conversations she overheard among students in the city's many coffee shops, quaint restaurants and pubs of character.

By the time she was thirty-six, her books were selling all over the world, having been translated into more than twenty languages. Success had come at a not-so-uncommon price. While on promotional tours and book-signing sessions, her husband was shagging their twenty-two-year-old Swedish nanny. Gloria had returned from Germany a day earlier than scheduled and caught her adulterous husband in abandoned coitus, as if copulating for his country in the bedroom Olympics. She promptly kicked out both of them, giving them five minutes to dress and telling them to return the following day for their belongings, which would be heaped on the front lawn for collection. The subsequent divorce was messy, naturally, and Gloria stung Malcolm for every penny to which she was entitled, plus a little more as retribution. That was five years ago.

Since then, Gloria had used her writing as therapy and had also increased her involvement with Green campaigners, lobbying aggressively for smoking to be banned in all public places and for private vehicles to be excluded from Oxford's congested city centre. She argued for all major companies to be compelled by law to provide a fleet of bicycles, instead of cars, for their employees. The need for more recycling of rubbish was another cause she had robustly championed.

This was the background, the build-up. Now Templeman came to the day of her death.

She had kept to her routine of writing in her study, on the ground floor, between eight o'clock and noon. Her son, Damian, aged sixteen, cycled to St Edward's School. Her daughters, Edwina and Georgina, aged thirteen and ten respectively, were driven by a neighbour to their private school, St Hildred's. A group of mothers ran a rota for the morning and afternoon school run.

At one o'clock, Gloria kept a lunch date with two fellow female members of the Green Party to discuss tactics aimed at stopping millions of tons of London garbage being transported from the capital by train every day and dumped on Oxfordshire in a landfill site in the picturesque southern part of the county. The renewal of this contract was to be debated in a week's time by the executive committee of the Oxfordshire County Council. That lunch wound up at around 3.15 in The Mitre Inn and Restaurant in High Street, next to Lincoln College and almost opposite University College, where US President Bill Clinton and his daughter, Chelsea, had both rounded off their higher education. The three women had shared one bottle of white wine. Apart from water and coffees, they had not had anything else to drink.

Gloria was home for the return of the children at 3.45. While Damian and Edwina did their homework, and Georgina played in her bedroom with toys she had received for Christmas, Gloria made calls to her literary agent and publisher. All told, she was on the phone for longer than an hour.

After tea at around six, Gloria caught a bus back into the city centre, a distance of about two miles, to attend a poetry reading in the Bodleian Library, an event that started at 6.45. Three celebrated poets from London, whose work had been published by mainstream publishers, read examples of their most recent compositions – not yet available to bookshops – to an audience of about seventy people. Gloria was known to most people there, many of whom later testified that she had stayed to the end of the readings at about nine o'clock. Instead of leaving immediately, she had lingered a while, circulating. Just after 9.15, she called home on her mobile and spoke briefly with Damian, who was looking after his sisters. Gloria asked if there had been any problems. Damian assured his mother that everything was 'under control' and that his sisters were in bed. Georgina was already asleep and Edwina was reading. Gloria explained that she was calling from outside the Bodleian in Broad Street, which connects with St Giles, where she would soon be catching a bus home. 'I'll be indoors before ten,' were her last words to her son.

When she hadn't returned by eleven o'clock, Damian took himself to bed, not the least concerned for his mother's safety. Gloria had a very active social life and her son assumed that she had bumped into a friend – or friends – and gone for a drink, or maybe even supper in one of the numerous late-night bistros peppered around the cosmopolitan city centre. He made no attempt to reach his mother on her mobile and was asleep well before midnight.

Gloria's body was discovered at 8.50 the next morning, floating face down in the River Thames south of Folly Bridge, still well within the city boundary, but in the opposite direction from her route home. The body was wedged against the western bank, opposite college boathouses, near allotments and playing fields. It had been a very dark and cold morning, explaining why the body hadn't been noticed earlier. A towpath, running alongside the river, was heavily used by cyclists and walkers, especially people going to and from work and eager to avoid the pollution from traffic fumes that poisoned all life in the Abingdon Road area. Daylight didn't push through the blockade of black clouds until 8.30 and the grim discovery was made by houseboat owner Harold Thurlow, who was heading downstream with his wife, Lucy. Thurlow, a retired lock-keeper, had been at the helm at the stern of his long, slim boat, *Quite Contrary*, while Lucy was down below, under cover, cooking breakfast. The frothy wash from the boat had dislodged the body, causing it to drift away from the bank. It was as Thurlow looked over his shoulder, attracted by a squadron of airborne swans flapping furiously towards him, that he spotted 'a human kind of shape bobbing about' in the wake. As he cut the throttle and manoeuvred the houseboat into the side, his wife joined him to find out what was happening. As soon as they were near enough to the towpath, Harold Thurlow jumped ashore and ran back to investigate. Minutes later, he was calling the police from his cellular phone.

Gloria Swift had suffered head injuries, but had died from strangulation. She was dead before entering the water.

When Damian discovered that his mother's bed hadn't been slept in and he couldn't get any reply from her mobile, he tried to call his father for advice, but Malcolm Jefferson was in the USA, a guest of Princeton University, where he was giving a series of lectures on medieval Britain in return for a considerable fee. The five-hour time difference meant that when Damian punched out his father's mobile number at 7 a.m., it was 2 a.m. in Boston and Jefferson was asleep, with his phone on recharge, a fact that had immediately eliminated the ex-husband as a suspect.

Since his divorce, Jefferson had been renting a spacious flat in St John's Street, behind the Ashmolean Museum. The Swedish nanny had not gone with him, but he wasn't living alone in resentful exile. He shared his flat with a much younger female lecturer in contemporary art. Not surprisingly, they were known humorously around their colleges as A&M – Ancient and Modern. Gloria Swift had told her friends that her divorce was very civilized because she had never spoken to her husband since the day she caught him in flagrante delicto.

Despite extensive police inquiries, including prolonged exposure in the local press, there had been no positive sightings of Gloria between her walking northwards away from the Bodleian Museum towards St Giles and her being washed up south of the city in the Thames. That was just one of the myriad teasing mysteries. What had occurred to deflect her off-course, to turn her away from homeward-bound?

Pinpointing accurately the time of death had been another problem because of the icy weather and the impact of the chilly water on the body. However, a consultant pathologist at the John Radcliffe Hospital had concluded that Gloria was still alive at 10 p.m. and was 'probably' dead by 2 a.m – a four-hour window of opportunity for untold horrors, but she hadn't been raped or tortured. Sexual gratification and deviancy didn't appear to have been the motive.

Several portrait photographs of Gloria Swift, in addition to grisly scene-of-crime shots, had been photocopied and included among the documents of witness statements, officers' reports and medical findings. Before defacement, she had been handsome, with an obvious penchant for dressing sensibly, conservatively even. Doughty and durable were the images that made an impression with Templeman, yet the latter of those qualities had already been rubbished. Certainly she had been no stereotype temptress, no siren of the streets, not the usual prey of perverts. Something was wrong, horribly off-kilter, not making sense, not adding up, Templeman was agonizing, when his mobile began chiming to the sound of cathedral bells, not so jarring as most of the crass jingles. It was Hardman.

'We've got seven days.'

'For what?'

'To stop the death toll from rising.'

'What does the note say?'

'Hold on, I'll read it to you.'

Templeman could hear the rustle of paper.

'You ready?'

'Go ahead.'

'"You guys aren't getting anywhere. I keep telling you there's no hope for you without the Main Man. Just to help you along, I'm going to give you another corpse for your collection on July 1st. A Friday. Party night! The higher the body count, the more chance of a mistake, so you should be grateful that I'm raising the stakes and increasing the risk factor. Once again, Oxford will be the location. The countdown has begun. The clock is ticking. Your nightmares begin all over again."'

'Now what do you propose doing?'

'Apart from hitting the bottle?'

'And praying.'

'I'm relying on you.'

'That's an onerous responsibility.'

'Our serial killer has faith in you. He believes you're the Main Man, his nemesis. For fuck's sake, prove him right, Luke!'

That evening, Templeman decided to dine in The Mitre Inn, where Gloria Swift had lunched on the day of her death. Most of the other diners were students – many with their parents – and academics. The Mitre, dating back to the fourteenth century, enjoyed a regular university clientele. Memorabilia of Lincoln College, including pendants, shields and faded black and white photographs of bygone rowing eights, graced the wood-panelled walls.

Templeman tried to visualize Gloria sitting at one of the tables – perhaps his – in animated conversation with her political friends, unaware that she was already into the final, premature throes of her life. The weather would have been very different then, of course, back in bleak mid-winter. Now the overhead fans whirred and doors were left open to promote ventilation on such a sultry evening.

At nine o'clock, with his jacket over his arm and the collar-button of his shirt undone, Templeman dodged traffic as he crossed the High and headed towards Carfax Tower and St Aldate's, to his left, which took him sharply downhill past the austere Gothic City Hall, a hamburger and hot dog vendor's van outside Christ Church, and Thames Valley Police Station – not a place near to his heart.

After crossing Folly Bridge beside The Head of the River pub, he ventured on the towpath alongside Salters boatyard, a long-time landmark of Oxford, where one could hire pleasure-craft or book rides on sightseeing tours by water. After a dog-leg turn, the towpath ran straight into the distance, parallel to the Abingdon Road. The college boat-houses were about 400 yards ahead, on his left, the other side of the Thames. He passed several courting couples, entwined in each other's arms and too wrapped in their own dreams to even notice him. Swans sailed past silently, haughty and disdainful, like tall-mast ships in miniature. Lights glowed from all but one of the boathouses. The sound of music, laughter and clinking glasses floated across the river, lingering in the air like pollen. Rowers – men and women – chatted spiritedly as they removed oars from the rowlocks of their racing shells at the water's edge. A few stood on the slipway, between boathouse and river, swigging beer from tankards, soaking up the kind of gilded summer evening they would romance about in their dotage.

Templeman knew that he must be very near the spot where Gloria Swift had been seen floating. How had she got there? he asked himself. Could she have drifted down from Folly Bridge? Yes, but very unlikely, he answered his own question. Oxford was a restless, neurotic city. Because of its dispropor-tionate student population, it never really slept. And the whole area from Folly Bridge, up St Aldate's, into the High, Queen's Street and Cornmarket Street had a fast pulse-rate of activity through the night as well as by day. No one would have been able to unload a body from a vehicle on the Abingdon Road, anywhere near Folly Bridge, and heave it over the stone parapet into the Thames without being observed by a dozen or more people.

Templeman looked around and soon came across a rough, unlit dirt and gravel track that was wide enough for a vehicle. It meandered away from the river, so Templeman decided to see where it led. He soon found himself sandwiched between college playing fields and the grounds of a four-star hotel. After a few more twists and turns, the sickly, yellow street lights of the Abingdon Road appeared directly ahead of him. Instantly and instinctively, he knew in his bones that this was the route the killer had taken to dump Gloria Swift's body. The track, part of university property, provided direct access from the Abingdon Road, a main artery carrying constant traffic around the clock. But the track was seldom used and virtually never at night. After all, it went nowhere, except to the river. It didn't afford access even to the hotel or playing fields.

Turning northwards on the Abingdon Road, Templeman headed back towards the city centre and the Randolph. What had he achieved? Nothing of substance; nothing that Hardman and his team wouldn't have latched on to during the first twenty-four hours of their investigation. But it was a beginning, a constructive introduction, like the first day of a new job – finding the loo and the coffee machine, the essentials.

The moment he reached his room, the irresistible pull of sleep began drawing him towards its black tunnel, but before he allowed himself to succumb to slumber there was a call he had to make. It would be 6 p.m. in Florida and Simone would be anxious to hear from him, if only to be reassured that he had landed safely.

Simone answered their home phone in Naples on the third ring. Luke was soon giving her a synoptical account of his day, then asked, 'How's things on the home front?'

'Just negotiated a major assignment, acting for Nancy Carter. While you were in the air, her daughter, Tammy, was abducted. You don't know Nancy, but she's a big fish around here. Last year she hired me to collect evidence for her against her cheating husband. He was having a ball with virtually every bimbo in the state. Now they're separated and she's divorcing. Tammy went to a beach barbecue yesterday evening and didn't return.'

'How old is she?'

'Nineteen. I know exactly what you're thinking, but think again. Seven o'clock this morning, Nancy got a call.'

'Saying what?'

'"We have your daughter. Go to the cops and we send you her head in a parcel, special delivery, after raping her enough times to make her feel like a pin-cushion – before she ceases to feel anything ever again." She was instructed not to do anything until contacted again. After half an hour of hysterics, she called me. She wants me to mediate on her half.'

'Be careful. If anything goes wrong, the cops will throw the book at you.'

'I advised Nancy to go to the cops, but she won't hear of it. For a start, she fears the kidnapper – possibly plural – will carry out the threat. Secondly, she's determined to retain control of any rescue operation, which wouldn't be possible if the FBI took over. They would almost certainly prevent her from paying a ransom, whatever her inclination. Thirdly, she doesn't trust the cops to handle the situation subtly; it would be an all-guns-blazing, *Dirty Dozen*, Clint Eastwood reaction.'

'Even so, protect your own rear.'

'I taped our conversation, my advice and her instructions.'

'Good girl! Still, I don't like the idea of your being without cover.'

'I won't take any chances.'

'Don't lie. You *will*, if you believe it's necessary.'

'Trust me.'

'I have little choice.'

Then they briefly discussed the latest note from the Oxford serial killer.

'Do you believe it's genuine, that it will happen?' said Simone, grimly.

'Oh, it'll happen.'

'How can you be so sure, so defeatist?'

'Because this is someone who sees himself as a perfectionist, the best-ever serial killer and a man of his word to boot. To renege on his pledge would be dishonourable.'

'That's sick.'

'Of course it is; that's a prerequisite. Having made a promise, he'd regard it as abject failure not to deliver; a loss of face.'

'Have they brought in a profiler?'

'I haven't got around to discussing that, but it's such standard procedure these days that I should imagine it was one of Hardman's initial reflexes.'

'How is he?'

'Cracking up.'

'I wish I could be with you.'

'Sounds to me as if you've got more than enough on your plate. We can't afford to neglect our core business, the business you built up while I was lapping up holiday-camp luxury.' His bleak humour about his time in prison was strained and demonstrated that the memory still hurt, despite his boyish bravado.

'Are the police going to put out a public warning?'

'I think they're going to have to, but there are drawbacks with that.'

'More problems with *not* doing it, I'd say.'

'Hardman has kept the last three notes a secret from the public.'

'That's understandable, but you now have a very different situation. This is advance warning. Women have a chance to save themselves by staying home that day, by not venturing out after dark, or if they do, at least making sure they're in a group and are escorted home.'

Their transatlantic conversation ended with Templeman promising to call her again, 'around the same time', the following night.

Struggling to keep himself awake, Templeman called Hardman, mobile to mobile.

'Yeah?' Even the one word was slurred.

'It's Luke.'

'Luke! I thought you'd be dead to the world by now.'

If anyone was lifeless, it was Hardman. Templeman could hear a pub's cacophony in the background.

'My body has gone into shutdown mode but my head won't quit. Can we have a brain-stormer?'

'What with?' Hardman managed to joke, and then, 'I'm game. I'll come to you at the hotel.'

'Seven o'clock?'

'Seven it is. Early birds catch the worm.'

'If only!'

The last time Templeman went to bed, he was in Florida, with a panoramic view of the Gulf of Mexico, even as he reclined. Now he could see no further than the net curtains and if he did peep beyond them, then the concrete and stone of the Ashmolean Museum would be in his face, like an over-bearing colossus, its interior charm hidden behind a forbidding edifice.

Templeman's limbs felt leaden and his muscles ached, as if he was stricken with Grade A influenza. The temptation was to surrender to gravity and allow his body to flop on to the bed, not bothering even to undress, but he knew that he would regret it in the morning. Despite his overwhelming fatigue, he would shower first, scrub away that soiled feeling, wash air-travel grime from his hair and then douse himself with redolent splash-on lotion.

He was in the bathroom no longer than fifteen minutes and when he returned to the bedroom, he didn't immediately notice the red light blinking on the bedside phone, alerting him to a message having been left for him. Someone had called and the noise of the shower had prevented him from hearing the ringing. Naturally curious, he pressed the button for his voicemail to play.

'So they've taken my advice at last and recruited the Main Man. How very wise of them. Now I might get some real competition. Time is against you, though. And I never miss a deadline. Never.'

The emphasis was well and truly on *deadline*.

CHAPTER 4

Templeman and Hardman resembled two wrecks washed up by the same rough night. Sleep had jilted Templeman at the altar, an inevitable consequence of the mischievous voicemail message. Hardman was simply hungover, an inevitable consequence of the liquor and demons that came out to play and torment in his head after dark.

They were slumped opposite each other at a table in the Randolph's restaurant. Both craved for fatty, greasy food, reflected in their breakfast orders. But before anything else, they needed coffee, black, strong and very sweet – preferably injected straight into their bloodstream.

'There's a development I don't understand,' Templeman began tentatively.

Their unfocused eyes hardly had enough power to receive images from one side of the table to the other.

Templeman then briefed the inspector about the anonymous phone message. Twitching and blanching, Hardman asked Templeman to repeat, 'word for word', what he had just said. This wasn't going to be easy for either of them.

When Templeman had finished for a second time, Hardman's face was a spectacle of denial.

Pinching the bridge of his nose and closing his eyes, Hardman said, disbelieving, his throat clogged with phlegm, 'This can't be, Luke. You only landed at Heathrow yesterday morning. When you got that call, you'd been in Oxford less than twelve hours. How the blazes could the killer know you're here? It doesn't make sense. This is driving me nuts.'

Hardman opened his eyes, as if hoping he was waking from one of his myriad nightmares, that he was home in bed and not with Templeman in the Randolph. The one time a nightmare would have been to his advantage, there wasn't one in sight. Just what people say about police officers, he mused, his sense of humour not having forsaken him completely.

'How many people *officially* know I'm here?'

The coffee arrived in time to help them both reboot their brains.

Hardman used his fingers as back-up for his mental arithmetic.

'The chief, his deputy, DS Ray Lamont—'

'Who's he?'

'Number two on my team. Then there's me, of course.'

'*Of course!*'

'That's it. A grand total of four.' Hardman had fingers to spare.

'Nobody in the loop at the Home Office?'

'Well, yes, the home secretary, as I told you, and no doubt some of her underlings, but they're hardly likely to be gossiping and jeopardizing their own integrity, now are they?'

'What about within the city and county councils?'

'Nope.'

'Is there anything in writing, on paper or a computer file, that someone else might have been able to access?'

'Nothing. Everything's been debated and decided by word of mouth, and deliberately for security reasons contained within the cabal of four, not counting the Whitehall prats.'

'Who booked this hotel for me?'

'I did it personally.'

The caffeine was fast-acting. Almost immediately, Templeman felt virtually alive again. Virtual life had its virtues, especially compared to real death.

'OK, let's toss this about, Mike, now that the shock is wearing off.'

'Not for me, it isn't.'

'I've had a few more hours – albeit sleepless ones – to get used to the idea that I've been rumbled. There is a positive side to it.'

'There is?'

'If last night's caller really was the killer, and there's no reason to assume otherwise, then he may well have made his first big mistake.'

'Because the hotel will have a recording of his voice?'

'Which will be as good as any fingerprint once you have something to compare it with. Your scientists will have no trouble these days matching a voice to a recording, conclusively enough to be accepted by a judge as admissible in court. It could be that he's becoming careless and over-confident in his bid for recognition and notoriety.'

'Do you really think that's what he's after? Star-billing?'

'If he isn't, he'll be the first serial killer not to be.'

'But how the hell ...'

'How *he* found out about my being in Oxford is unimportant, unless it helps to uncover him,' Templeman reasoned, breaking Hardman's circuit. 'Doubtless he's hoping we'll be unnerved.'

'If that really is his intention, he's succeeded.'

'But only in the short-term and at a price. His voicemail is on record for posterity; that won't go away. He's also revealed that he knows I'm in town, working with you. Once again, that may give him a short-term edge, making him appear smart, way ahead of the game, the choreographer of the show, pulling all the strings, with us – *you*, in particular – his marionettes.'

'And how does that help us in the long-term?'

'He might well live to regret sharing his knowledge so readily, but my guess is that he couldn't resist it, which indicates a possible flaw in his character.'

'Which is – apart from the fact that he believes it's his mission to single-handedly reduce the world's population?'

'He's impulsive. He isn't as detached and unemotionally methodical as he reckons himself to be and would like us to believe he is. Now that *we know* that *he knows* I'm here, we don't have to be quite so circumspect. We can reappraise our approach accordingly. It's almost always possible to convert a negative into a positive.'

'Even so, I'll never rest until I track down the leak. There has to be a mole somewhere, however impossible and implausible that seems right now.'

'Not necessarily. The guy could be so conceited that he was convinced you'd be cornered into doing his bidding, by enticing me over.'

'If that's the case, he really *is* pulling the strings.'

'But it doesn't mean you have leaky plumbing back at the ranch. If I was going to be in the Oxford area, how many places are there, realistically, where I might be putting my head on a pillow?'

Hardman, his shoulders slumped and his whole demeanour deflated, shrugged. 'I guess not *that* many.'

'And the Randolph would top the list. He could have been calling all major hotels and motels daily, simply saying, "Put me through to Mr Templeman's room, please." When they replied that there was no guest by that name, he'd ring off and repeat the procedure elsewhere, until he got a hit.'

'Perhaps,' said Hardman, uncertainly, desperate for a cigarette, but smoking wasn't allowed, so he sought comfort from more coffee and then his grilled breakfast, which served as a welcome distraction from the more unpleasant food for thought. 'I'll get a copy of that voicemail before I leave the hotel and have the lab boffins work on it, see what they turn up.'

'It's a start and considerably more than you had this time yesterday.' Templeman tried to be upbeat.

'Six days to go,' said Hardman morosely, like a masochist inflicting pain on himself, while simultaneously shovelling egg, bacon and sausage into his mouth, as if trying to prove that cholesterol held no fear for him. Nowadays, he was alternating between binge-drinking and binge-eating, with chain-smoking sandwiched between.

'I was talking with Simone last night.' Templeman

attempted to steer the inspector away from the killer's schedule to their agenda.

'You homesick already?'

A pair of sizzling kippers passed on a plate en route to another table, their dead eyes showing more life than Hardman's – and Templeman's, for that matter.

'Not homesick, just making sure the hurricane season isn't making a premature show and we still have our roof intact,' Templeman lied inoffensively. And then, 'Simone wondered about a profiler.'

'In connection with what, a hurricane?' Hardman struggled for flippancy.

Templeman could tell it was going to be one of those Mad Hatter days.

'No, this case, the Oxford killings.'

Hardman talked as he chewed. 'We've had the lot: profilers, psychics, fairground fortune-tellers, tea-leaf and tarot-card readers, and mystics. You know my opinion of the lot of 'em.'

'I don't, actually.'

'They suck. Not one of 'em told me anything that I couldn't have read in a cheap crime novel. We're looking for a loner, a social misfit, an under-achiever, possibly a mummy's boy, aged between thirty and fifty, trapped in a routine, boring job, considering himself under-appreciated, unable to sustain a relationship with the opposite sex, a fantasizer who can communicate with animals much easier than with people. That was it. Who needs the mumbo jumbo of so-called experts to tell us that? Not me! My old mum knows all that junk – from paperbacks she reads on the bus to and from bingo. Jesus! Next we'll have highly paid specialists to tell us what kind of nut we're looking for who gets a thrill from starting fires. A guy with a box of matches!'

Templeman sympathized. 'Detection is becoming more scientific by the day. Soon we mere mortals will be totally redundant. Machines will do it all, with robots making arrests and giving evidence in court, cross-examined by prosecution and defence counsel, who will also be automatons.'

'It's not the progress of science I'm against but the proliferation of the pseuds, the pretentious prats.'

'They're nothing new in our trade, Mike.'

'But not in today's numbers and not so accepted by the Establishment. It won't be long before someone making an emergency call will be asked by the operator, "Which service do you require – police, fire, ambulance, shrink or sorcerer?"'

They were digressing, so Templeman rerouted the derailed dialogue back on track.

'I've been going through the Gloria Swift papers.'

'What do you make of it?'

'There's something funny about it.'

'No one's laughing around here.'

'*Funny* as in atypical.'

'Go on.'

'Wrong age group. Wrong type. Wrong everything.'

'For what?'

'For a serial killer's prey.'

'I've thought about that a lot, Luke.'

'And?'

'It hasn't got me anywhere. This guy has never raped his victims. There hasn't been a jot of evidence to suggest a sex crime. So, if sex isn't the motive, there's no logical reason why he should target only leggy, busty, young man-eaters.'

'Even when a serial killer doesn't appear to have carnal intentions, the crimes nearly always have powerful sexual connotations.'

'Where's this come from, Miss Marple? Next you'll be suggesting I should roll the dice to see if it might be Colonel Mustard, with a piece of rope, et cetera, et cetera.'

Templeman was unfazed. 'Prostitutes, the demi-monde, are the stereotype victims of serial killers, right?'

'Right.'

'However, they don't need to be *actual* whores, simply fulfilling the role in the eyes of the beholder, but Gloria Swift doesn't figure in that category, not anything like; not by any stretch of the imagination, warped or otherwise.'

'Nor any of the other victims. Charley, for instance.'

God, yes, Charley! How could I possibly have omitted her from the equation? Templeman berated himself.

'After all, it started with Charley,' Hardman reminded Templeman, who was ashamed that such a prompt was necessary.

'I'll devote today to the other two cases. After dinner yesterday evening, I took myself along the towpath, from Salters boatyard, to the strip of river where Gloria Swift's body was fished out. What's the current theory on how she got there?'

'We reckon she was dropped into the water very near where she was recovered.'

'She hadn't floated downstream?'

'Not according to my reckoning.'

'That tallies.'

'With what?'

'My theory.'

'Which is?'

'There's a sinuous track, linking the Abingdon Road with the towpath near that point. It struck me as the obvious way the killer got the body to the river without being conspicuous.'

'I think we're all agreed on that.'

'That time of year, in seasonal winter weather, I'd expect good prints to have been left from the tyre treads.'

'There were – especially from squad cars, scene-of-crime vehicles, coroner's office cars, the paramedics' ambulance and our own film unit. Anything left by the killer in terms of tyre and footprints were obliterated by the tram-lines of our own people. Great, eh!'

'Par for the course, I'd say. One of the witness statements, in particular, aroused my interest.'

'Which one?'

'The name escapes me, but it would appear that, of all the people interviewed, she was the last to see Gloria Swift alive.'

'That would be Fiona Bridges. She was outside the Bodleian, talking to one of the poets, as Gloria walked away alone from the museum towards St Giles.'

'I think the actual phrase she used in her statement was that Gloria Swift was heading off into the night with a "swaying walk".'

'Something like that, Luke. I'll take your word for it – after all, it's only hours since you read it and some weeks since I did.'

'The *sway* must have been quite distinctive and pronounced for this witness, Bridges, to include it in her account.'

Hardman poured himself more coffee, added four cubes of white sugar, and stirred desultorily, in sluggish reverie.

'One of the lads took these statements, a young DC.'

'While you concentrated on the big picture?'

Hardman searched for sarcasm but there was none reflected on Templeman's hawkish, undernourished face.

'Of course I read all the statements,' said Hardman, watchfully. As if having to justify himself, he continued testily, 'I must admit there was nothing in that statement that particularly grabbed me.'

'Was she a lush?'

Hardman was taken by surprise, as if ambushed.

'The thought never occurred to me,' he admitted, without guilt. 'I don't imagine that question has ever been put to anyone. Her friends – the two she lunched with at The Mitre – were specific about the three of them sharing one bottle of wine. That hardly projects the image of someone with a drink problem.'

'True,' Templeman said, dubiously. 'Unless she was a secret, closet tippler, of course, and did her utmost to keep it from her friends.'

'In that case, how would *anyone* know?'

'Maybe people had their suspicions. Problem drinkers can't keep it from their families for ever. Her children might well know, certainly the son, the oldest one, though it could be that he'd be reluctant to acknowledge the fact publicly. For all we know, it could have been a contributory factor in the marriage breakdown.'

'I doubt it somehow. From all accounts, Malcolm Jefferson

had always been a serial adulterer, which at least has the merit of making him a little less dangerous to women than a serial killer.'

'Couldn't that have driven his wife to drink?'

'Even if it did, I fail to see the connection with her death.'

'It might explain abnormal behaviour.'

'Such as?'

'Why she deviated from her schedule, why she didn't catch a bus home straight away.'

'We don't know that she didn't, not for sure. We have no leads that point to where and when she encountered her killer. Although none of the drivers of buses going northwards from the city centre recalled her being one of their passengers, it's far from conclusive. It's entirely possible that she was attacked and abducted in the Banbury Road as she walked from a bus stop towards her home.'

'The Banbury Road is well lit and well used, even at that time of the evening, surely?'

'There are dark, secluded spots,' Hardman said sullenly, unyielding.

'But no reports of anything suspicious?'

Hardman let his body language give the answer.

'I think I'll have a chat with Fiona Bridges.'

'Be my guest,' said Hardman, without resentment. 'That's what you're here for – to kick old stones around and hopefully unearth something we've overlooked and freshen up our investigation. I'll be grateful for crumbs, believe me.'

'Where are Gloria's children living now?'

'Where they've always lived. Their dad has moved back in with them.'

'Has his current lover, the lecturer in contemporary art, gone with him?'

'Malcolm Jefferson could never be without a woman. Monica Dawson has been surrogate mother to the kids since the murder.'

Templeman made a note of the live-in lover's name.

'Gloria's death was rather opportune for Jefferson,'

Templeman observed cynically. 'He got back his house, his kids, and maybe a lot of other possessions; money even. I don't suppose there's any chance of a hole in his alibi?'

'No chance. It's as watertight as a submarine in dry dock. Anyhow, why would Jefferson wish to harm Charley and the other two victims, even if he did welcome his ex-wife's death – and there's no evidence to suggest that he did.'

Everything went full circle to Charley, if one accepted that she was the serial killer's first hit and, even without her body, that seemed a fact beyond refutation.

'One last thing for now,' said Templeman, as they emptied the coffee pot and the last drops of their discussion. 'You're going to have to issue some kind of public warning in view of the seven-day notice of the next strike.'

Hardman began massaging the bone above each eye with thumb and finger. It was more than a mannerism communicating concentration. Prolonged stress, lack of sleep and his unhealthy lifestyle had all conspired to trigger an acute attack of sinusitis, but he couldn't spare the time to consult a doctor for a prescription for antibiotics, so he had to make do with palliative, over-the-counter painkillers, which he shouldn't have been combining with alcohol. Three days of dark facial growth and a night slumped in his office chair had left him resembling a tramp who had been donated a scarecrow's suit. At least Templeman had managed a shave and a shower, and had the benefit of freshly laundered clothes, plus trousers that had spent the night in the press provided in the room.

'How can we broadcast an alert without the media going over the top, making a feast of it, that, for some poor soul, is going to be the last supper?'

'You can't.'

'Thankfully, the final decision won't be my call. I've got a mid-morning head-banging session with bald Badger and his poodle lapdog.'

Humphry Badger was the county's chief constable and Hector Renton was his 'lapdog' deputy.

'They're having a breakfast meeting with the leaders of the

county and city councils,' Hardman elaborated, dripping with derision. 'What they call breakfast would be our lunchtime. That little hegemony will be calling the shots over what statement – if any – should be made. For once, I'm more than happy to be usurped.'

'You'll still carry the can if it backfires,' Templeman warned, simultaneously wishing he'd tethered his tongue.

Hardman twitched even more now. If he had an ulcer, then Templeman had just sprinkled salt all over it.

'You're right, of course,' said Hardman, his retort vinegary. 'Heads they win. Tails I lose. Sod the lot of 'em! A plague on all their houses!'

To avoid listening to another rancorous rant, Templeman said abruptly and peremptorily, 'Time to give the day a kick-start.'

'Hitting the ground running, as they say, eh?'

'Two more cases to squeeze in before bedtime. Compulsory reading, though hardly light entertainment.'

Hardman snatched a look at his wristwatch three times in quick succession, having become shackled to the clock by the harrowing hands of time.

'I was never much of a student, but I now know the truth of history repeating itself. If it didn't, we wouldn't have serial killers.'

'Ah! But history also demonstrates that we never learn, that we repeat our mistakes, Mike. That applies to killers, too; that's the positive spin, *our* edge.'

'I've a dreadful feeling in my water that our perp is going to stand history on its head. Six days and counting!'

Fatalism somehow suited Hardman.

Caroline Marsh, aged forty-two, unmarried, mother of a twelve-year-old daughter, Samantha, a regional organizer with the giant trade union Unison, and vociferous champion of women's rights, especially equity in the workplace. These were the primary biographical bullet points of the April Fools' Day victim.

Templeman sat in his hotel room, TV murmuring mid-morning blather in the background, familiarizing himself with the details of the last two murders.

Marsh had gone to a trade union conference in Birmingham on 1 April. In the morning, just before 8.30, she purchased a return ticket, having left her red Toyota sports model in the long-stay car park. She arrived back in Oxford, by train, a few minutes before 10 p.m. CCTV cameras filmed her exiting the station concourse, appearing to be unaccompanied. There was no footage of her that evening in the car park, a mere 200 yards from the station, over a footbridge crossing the busy Botley Road. Her Toyota was still there when her body was dredged from the river.

What had happened in those 200 yards to stop her reaching the sanctuary of her car and driving home? Something that would solve everything, Templeman predicted to himself.

On the morning of 2 April, Marsh's body was seen floating in the Thames, between two moored houseboats, at Osney Lock. This was a taciturn stretch of the Thames, further upstream from where Gloria Swift had been ditched. The loch was no more than a quarter of a mile south of the station and could be reached along quiet side streets of old but quite attractive terraced houses, behind which lay an ugly, modern industrial estate.

Marsh's injuries were consistent with a repeat crime that mimicked the Gloria Swift murder. She had been struck hard with a blunt weapon behind the head and then strangled with a silky ligature, more likely a stocking than a scarf. Once again, there had been no sexual assault and the time of death had been estimated at between 10 p.m. and midnight. The pathologist had been helped in this respect by the arrival time of the train into Oxford and the fact that the buffet manager on that service from Birmingham remembered serving Marsh with food and a drink, which she had paid for with a credit card. Barclaycard's records showed that Marsh had bought a burger and a gin and tonic. The burger had only been half-digested. Traces of alcohol were still in her liver.

Hardman's team had appealed for every passenger on that train from Birmingham on 1 April to come forward, but no more than a dozen had done so. A number had been traced through credit-card transactions: they had bought tickets at Birmingham for Oxford, or stations beyond, during the half-hour before the train departed. Of course, many of the passengers on that five-coach, full train would have paid by cash and joined the train before Birmingham, while others, like Marsh, would have been using the return portion of their tickets. All those who contacted the police, or were tracked down, were shown photographs of Marsh, but no one recalled seeing her on the train or alighting. The same procedure had been followed with barrier staff at Oxford railway station, but the response had been a collective shake of heads. As one railway employee told detectives plausibly, 'We examine tickets, not faces. Thousands of passengers pass through here every day. I could tell you about an odd-looking ticket, but I probably wouldn't notice if a woman walked through the barrier carrying her head under her arm – unless, of course, she owed money on her fare.'

Templeman identified with that statement. It was honest,

gently self-deprecating and, most of all, it resounded with the ring of truth. Could anyone travel on a packed train for two hours unnoticed and then spirit away into the night ether at a bustling railway terminus? The answer was unequivocally yes, Templeman accepted. Crowds had always made the best hiding places.

Two days after the murder had come the trademark, taunting note, which had gone straight to the lab boffins. The killer, although certainly barmy, was no fool. He had used a self-sealing envelope, thus avoiding having to lick it, which would have left saliva and a DNA ID that would prove crucial as soon as there were suspects. Indeed, it could even finger the killer before there was a single suspect, if the perpetrator had a criminal history and his DNA identification was stored on the database.

The police response to this crime had been standard and, in that respect, beyond reproach. Statements had been collected and collated methodically. Marsh's ex-partner had been interrogated. Graham Hunt had been in London for a science award-presentation dinner at the Hilton International Hotel in Park Lane. There were more than twenty distinguished academics who could vouch for his presence in the Hilton until midnight. The interviewing of Hunt, right from the outset, was never anything more than a showcase. Whatever his relationship with his ex-partner, there was nothing to connect him with Gloria Swift and Charley. And if he was single-handedly attempting to reduce the female population of Oxford, why kill the one person who inevitably would focus attention on himself? Hardman, just like Templeman, had seen Hunt as a non-runner right from the off.

Hardman had pressed all the right buttons. Scotland Yard had helped, looking deeply into the current lives of the enemies Marsh had made as a teenager growing up in an anarchic neighbourhood of London. Dead ends in every direction.

Templeman's appetite for more information was now insatiable and he read on, without pause, to the last – so far – of the chinks in the expanding murder chain: Laura Fleming, aged forty-nine, a councillor on Oxford City Council, who wrote a weekly acerbic column in the daily *Oxford Mail* newspaper. Laura had been married twice and had a child from each marriage. Her first child, a boy, was now grown-up and working as an economic adviser in Whitehall with the government. Her daughter, from her second marriage, was at Bournemouth University, taking a course in media studies. Laura's second marriage, from all available evidence, seemed to have passed the litmus test of time and tolerance.

'Theirs was a chemistry that worked,' Simon King, the editor of the *Oxford Mail*, had told detectives. 'Laura talked to me a lot about her husband, Walter. She appreciated his constant support and encouragement, not only in politics but also in journalism. She was unquestionably the most outspoken councillor in Oxford – and thereby a thorn in the flesh of many for her provocative weekly column. She revelled in irreverence, which earned her a well-deserved faithful following among our readership. Despite her barbed, uncompromising language, she was respected as well as feared.'

Laura's second husband, Walter Fleming, was a professional musician and played lead violin in the Thames Valley Symphony Orchestra. Their home was in the Woodstock Road, part of the city's prosperous northern girdle. Here was the first readily apparent common denominator between any of the victims. Gloria Swift had also lived in the affluent, leafy northern sector. Templeman made a note in his yellow legal pad. It was probably irrelevant, but it was a start and at least made him feel as if he was doing something constructive, if not exactly making progress. Charley hadn't lived anywhere near Oxford, let alone in the north of the city, Templeman reminded himself. She was a total outsider, just like himself, who had been in the city on business, taking part in a trial; a transient, her only tenuous tie with Oxford being that she had been a law student there many years previously, as he had been. Surely a case of being in the wrong place at the wrong time?

Laura Fleming's battered and strangled body was taken

from the Oxford Canal, in the city's Jericho quarter, on the sunny morning of 3 June. The subsequent post mortem examination, although not conclusive, suggested that she had departed this life about 'an hour or so' before 2 June handed over the baton to 3 June.

What of her last known movements? Templeman thumbed through papers until he came to the germane documents.

On 2 June, a Wednesday, Laura had dined at home with her husband before going to her study to apply the finishing touches to her newspaper column that always appeared on Fridays, meaning that it had to be with the editorial staff of the *Oxford Mail* by first thing on Thursdays. Normally, she e-mailed her column to the newsdesk, but her server was down, so she printed her contribution and decided to deliver the hard copy by hand that evening.

Walter was rehearsing for a forthcoming concert in his own den when Laura tapped on the door at around 9.30 p.m. According to Walter's statement, she had said, poking her head around the door, 'I'm just going to drop off my copy at the *Mail* office. I shouldn't be longer than half an hour. I won't bother with the car. I'll cycle; that'll give me a bit of exercise.'

Her bicycle was recovered from the canal only a short distance from where her body had been floating. The alarm was raised by Walter when his wife hadn't returned by 1 a.m., after repeated attempts to make contact via her mobile phone, which was still in the rear pocket of her jeans when she was found. None of her clothes were missing, nor did any of them seem to have been tampered with. The mobile hadn't been used after she left home and was still switched on when examined by forensics for clues.

The offices of the *Oxford Mail* were located among light industry factories on the Osney Mead industrial estate, no further than one hundred yards to the west of the lock where Caroline Marsh's body had ended up, a fact that immediately intrigued Templeman. Another report revealed that CCTV cameras on the industrial estate had captured Laura arriving outside the electronically operated gates, where she had fed an envelope into the newspaper's postbox. Street lighting was more than adequate and a number of the industrial premises were floodlit. CCTV cameras also showed her cycling away from the *Oxford Mail* at 9.47 p.m. She was keeping to the roads, avoiding the short-cut towpath that would have taken her past the lock on the way to the Botley Road.

Laura Fleming had been within a hundred yards of the spot where the previous victim had been disposed of, yet the killer hadn't been inclined to get rid of her there. What does that tell me? Templeman asked himself as he prowled around his room like a frustrated, captive big cat, eager to be out in the wild, catching prey. Maybe nothing. Just maybe a little something. The odds are that Laura crossed paths with her killer after leaving the industrial estate. But by the time she reached the Botley Road on her way home, she would have been on the main inner-city highways – unless she'd been lured off-course, which also seemed to have happened to Gloria Swift.

The canal in Jericho ran close to the railway lines and wasn't far from the station – in fact, it could be reached in just a matter of minutes from the Botley Road by a footpath, which had the River Thames on its other side.

By lunchtime, Templeman was following that footpath towards Jericho. Two freshly painted, lovingly cared-for houseboats chugged unhurriedly towards him from the north. External flower arrangements brightened both boats. A dog was sitting upright on its haunches on the roof of the leading vessel. A bronzed woman, in a bikini, sunbathed atop the second craft. The allotments across the river were as quiet as a graveyard. Templeman soon approached a right-hand curve that took him to the canal and Jericho, while the Thames snaked its own independent way to the left.

Jericho occupied the territory to his right, immediately giving him a very different perspective of Oxford from the other districts of the city he knew. Houseboats were lined up awaiting servicing and repair at a boatyard. The atmosphere of that entire Jericho canal frontage was one of men messing about in boats. Most of the houses were terraced and red-brick, the homes of industrious artisans and the less affluent young couples with their feet having just reached the first rung of the property ladder. In this melting pot of Oxford, it was still possible to imagine the city when its inhabitants considered themselves river people, described by author Jan Morris as 'like Mississippi mudlarks'.

By the time Templeman headed back to his hotel, dodging the cavalcade of student cyclists, three thoughts dominated his deliberations.

1. The river seemed to have been an important element in the trio of killings that started in January. The killer had not tried to hide the bodies. Taking them to the Thames or the canal each time for dumping exposed him to increased risk of chance observation, unless he had good reason to feel especially safe and protected there. Could the killer be living on a houseboat? Had all three victims been invited back to his floating home, possibly for a drink? If so, they would have known him quite well – socially and/or profession-ally. None of the three was the kind of woman who could be lured into potential danger by a stranger or someone about whom they knew very little. Maybe he had some kind of obsession about waterways?

2. Had the killer chosen three very different sites of waterway to leave the bodies in an attempt to confuse the police about the area where he lived? In other words, he could live near or in the Abingdon Road (south of the city centre), in the vicinity of Osney Lock (to the west) or in Jericho (west central).

3. All four victims – that was including Charley – were powerful, independent and successful women, a far cry from the hapless, inadequate stereotypes that serial slayers targeted by tradition. Was this signifi-cant? Templeman believed that it was. Very much so. Pivotal, even.

From his room, Templeman used his mobile to catch up with Hardman, who sounded encased in a vacuum when he answered with a pithy, 'Yes, Luke?', having recognized the caller's number on the screen of his handset.

'I'm ready for a talk with Fiona Bridges. Can you fix it for me?'

'This afternoon?'

'Any time. Sooner the better.'

'I'll have Ray make the connection for you.'

Detective Sergeant Ray Lamont was Hardman's trustworthy workhorse.

'How did this morning's pow-wow go?'

'Badly. Degenerated into a verbal brawl. Correction. It started as a verbal brawl and got increasingly worse.'

'Why was that?' Templeman's question was unnecessary.

'You'd have thought I was doing all the frigging killing around here. They put the boot in with their mouths. I'm as frustrated as they are – one of the finer points they chose to overlook.'

'We've all been there,' said Templeman, sympathetically, offering camaraderie, which came cheaply, if not glibly.

Not the least mollified, Hardman said, 'They're demanding a miracle. Walking on water won't be enough for these bastards. Have you any reliable genies among your contacts? You know, one you can polish out of an oil lamp who will grant any wish. Good, solid detective work is no longer sufficient, apparently. In fact, it's positively pissed on from those up high. Sod CID, Badger and Renton believe they command a DOW – Department of Wizardry. They've been reading too many of their kids' Harry Potter books. They're expecting nothing less than sorcery from me and you.'

'You'd better tell them I had my magic wand stolen by Father Christmas.'

'More than my life's worth, old mate. Humour is the last taboo in this place.'

The reference to 'in this place' and the continuing background void – no clink of glasses – indicated that Hardman was within the police station precincts and not seeking refuge – yet – in the devil's nectar.

'What was the decision on action to warn women about the killer's proposed schedule?'

'Badger's going to make a statement on TV this evening. A sort of big deal, state-of-the-nation address. Pompous and pukey. It'll go out live on the *Six O'Clock News*, then be repeated later tonight and throughout tomorrow on the regional channel. I've been instructed to stay away from the cameras. That's fine by me. As far as I'm concerned, the top brass are welcome to the media circus. Mind you, if it back-fires, they'll expect me to be their bullet-catcher. The shit will be kept off their fan.'

Templeman was glad to be away from institutionalized buck-passing.

As if by way of an afterthought, Hardman asked, 'No further contact from our letter-writing, message-leaving psycho?'

Hardman's question guided Templeman's eyes to the bedside phone, which he hadn't looked at properly since returning from his site visit to the canal in Jericho.

How could he have possibly missed the blinking red light, alerting him to another voicemail message?

'Nothing so far,' Templeman replied honestly, though fearing that this was a truth with a very short shelf-life.

Templeman immediately recognized the voice.

'*You disappoint me. I really thought you'd be a worthy adversary. But you don't seem to be taking the game seriously. This is no time for going on long strolls, even if they are down Morbid Lane. The canal in Jericho is as busy as a motorway by day, yet so silent at night. Silent Night! Except for the occasional death-rattle, of course! Bet you didn't come across Charley there! Seek her here, seek her there, but still she doesn't appear! I'll have to think of a very special resting place for your Charley. No R.I.P. for her yet, though. Not while she still has work to do.*

'*If you really are to be worthy of my respect, I suggest you cut out the walks and get down to business. Another day gone, another day less to save the next chosen one. Oh, yes, the selection process is over. I have made my choice. I'm watching her closely – and also you, of course!*

'*Isn't this fun? Aren't we both having a ball? No? Oh dear, you're falling well short of my expectations. No matter, the show must go on, as those showbusiness luvvies would say.*

'*Please do your best, though it will never be enough. However many public warnings are given, the chosen one won't listen. They never do. They believe they're too smart to be ambushed by sudden death. Conceit and self-delusion are my allies. They never let me down. We're invincible buddies.*

'*Time marches on. I must get on with preparations, putting the final touches to my strategy. And, of course, you'll soon be back from your walk into the wilderness. No nearer to an answer than you were when those fools on the jury believed that you were responsible for my artistry. Never trust a human!*'

Templeman instantly informed Hardman about the new voicemail, opening the conversation, 'I spoke too soon.' Hardman's initial response was a characteristic, 'Holy shit!' 'Calm down,' Templeman urged him. 'It's another mistake he's made. This message was considerably longer than the first. This should give your speech experts and profiler plenty to work with. It seems to me that he's bursting at the seams to demonstrate how clever he is. He's revealed that he's aware of my movements. He must have followed me to the canal in Jericho. I didn't get a whiff of him, but that's not significant. I wasn't expecting to be tailed, so I wasn't exactly taking the usual precautions. But it means he must have been hanging around the hotel. Perhaps there are CCTV cameras on the premises, though I doubt it: that might be regarded as intrusive and likely to scare off guests. It's worth a question to the management, though. The encouraging thing is that he's taking chances, leaving voicemail messages as well as written notes, and venturing into the open.'

'I don't share your optimism,' Hardman said cheerlessly. 'I hear all that you say, but I guarantee he's only giving us what he knows will be useless information.'

'But we now know what he sounds like.'

'Exactly! Because he knows it won't help us.'

'It's not what he *knows*, it's what he *thinks*; let's not confuse the two,' Templeman emphasized. 'Giving us *anything* unnecessarily is a mistake, an unforced error. It signifies that he's a chancer and he can't resist a gamble.'

Hardman still wasn't convinced. 'I'll have Ray collect the latest voicemail tape from the hotel – as soon as he comes off the phone from making arrangements for you to get together with Fiona Bridges. The hotel manager has been very co-operative, not to mention discreet.'

Fiona Bridges represented the articulate and friendly face of Oxford. Her home was a large, rambling place on an avenue that curled its way lazily from the Banbury Road to the sleepy River Cherwell and the atmospheric Boathouse restaurant, which had its own slipway, where punts and rowing boats could be hired.

'You're expected,' Bridges greeted Templeman, as if she were the maid rather than the mistress. 'You're some kind of consultant with the police, aren't you?' This was a rhetorical question, not requiring an answer. 'I don't think I'm going to be much help, but come in – at least it gives me an excuse for another tea break. What would life be like without the joy of tea and coffee breaks? Unimaginable!'

Bridges was wearing a paint-stained, black artist's smock over bleached jeans and a white polo-necked jumper. In stature, she was petite, though not the least fragile, with quick, jerky movements, like a mechanical, battery-operated toy. Her age was tricky for Templeman to gauge. She had well-preserved, fair skin, and a piquant face – rather than a beautiful one – that hadn't been overexposed to the sun. Although her black, marble eyes were too large for the rest of her features, they didn't spoil the picture. Her raven hair was boyish short, with a severe fringe at the front. The absence of makeup produced an almost art-deco contrast between her dark hair and eyes and her porcelain cheeks. Templeman guessed her age at about forty, and he was wrong by only a couple of years – in her favour.

A white poodle snarled and snapped around Templeman's heels the moment he crossed the threshold.

'Don't be so silly, Teapot, he's friend not foe,' she admonished her pet dog affectionately. 'Whenever will you be able to tell the difference?' Then to Templeman, 'She's eleven years old and she could do with a pair of glasses or contact lenses! She's just as daft as when she was a playful puppy. My daughter, Gwendoline, named her Teapot. Unusual, don't you think?'

'Very unusual,' Templeman agreed.

Teapot, undeterred, was still hungry for Templeman's socks.

'Let's go into the kitchen. It's comfortable there. Not cosy, but comfortable. The lounge is a mess. Newspapers and magazines everywhere. David, my husband, will never put anything away. I'm currently making a stand, refusing to tidy up after him. It'll be a Custer's Last Stand, doomed to failure, because he's perfectly content to live in a piggery. He sells antiques. I think he'll have me and Teapot in his shop window one day. I shouldn't really talk about him behind his back, especially to a complete stranger, but no harm done and, anyhow, it's fun.'

The kitchen was spacious and equipped with all the latest gadgets. They sat at a round, pine table next to French windows that opened on to a patio and fenced lawn, an enclosure of shrubs, vibrant-coloured flowerbeds, and trees that provided plenty of shade on really hot days, such as this one. The tea came in bone-china cups. If Templeman had been able to examine the back-stamp, he would have known that the crockery had been manufactured by Spode in the Potteries.

'Please excuse the state I'm in,' beseeched Bridges, fingering her smock as she sat down opposite Templeman. 'Painting's my hobby – not painting and decorating, but art. I specialize in landscapes and still-life. I have a studio in the attic, but that's more cluttered than the lounge.' Her speech was free from a discernible dialect and as fast as a machine-gun, though far less penetrating.

'No apologies necessary. I'm the intruder. And although you don't think you can be of assistance, it seems that you must have been one of the last people to see Gloria Swift alive.'

Bridges' mood changed just as if Templeman had flicked a light switch, plunging them into darkness.

'That frightens me.'

'*Frightens* you?'

'Yes, the fact that my lack of observation may be helping Gloria's killer escape detection.'

'Take me through that last day, will you? I believe you were one of the two women to have lunch with Gloria Swift at The Mitre, as well as being with her at the Bodleian Library in the evening?'

'That's right. I'm a member of the Green Party. So was Gloria – and Phyllis Croft, the third person at that lunch. We'd meet once a month, usually for lunch, to talk politics most of the time.'

'Any special issues?'

'No, anything and everything; whatever was hot at that time. Usually it would be environment-based: you know, recycling rubbish strategy, what can be done to offset the harm of global warming, traffic congestion and pollution from vehicles.'

'The old chestnuts.'

'Ongoing concerns that have to be tackled if this planet is to be saved from self-destruct, we'd say,' she admonished him gently.

'How was Gloria at lunch?'

'Animated, as ever; a joy to be with. She had so much energy, mental as well as physical.'

'There was no mention of anything troubling her?'

'Such as? A lot was troubling her, especially the way the world was going down the drain.'

'I'm thinking more about personal threats?'

'I gave this a lot of consideration when questioned by the police.'

'And?'

'There was absolutely nothing. She was the same bubbly Gloria as ever. If she had feared in any way for her safety, she'd have gone straight to the police; I've no doubt about that. She wasn't the kind of person to tolerate any nonsense.'

'She was very outspoken, huh?'

'Oh boy, yes!'

'And something of a public figure?'

'Well, she was a successful author and her views received publicity, albeit mainly locally.'

'Didn't that attract hate-mail?'

'I suppose she got her fair share of that, though she didn't make a fuss about it. Everyone in the front line gets it these days – politicians, council officers, bank managers, doctors, paramedics, nurses and traffic wardens. Global warming seems to be raising all kinds of temperatures.'

'Did the three of you have pre-lunch drinks?'

'No, we went straight into the restaurant.'

'I believe you had a bottle of wine with the meal?'

'Between the three of us, yes.'

'How well did you know Gloria?'

'We were close, had been for ten years; maybe longer.'

'I understand she had a rather acrimonious divorce?'

'Aren't they all? I mean, isn't acrimony a constituent of most marital bust-ups?'

This wasn't the time for a debate, so Templeman didn't encourage one.

'At the time of her death, was there anyone special in her life?'

'Her children. They were very special to her.'

'Apart from her children?'

'I think it's safe to say that Malcolm had blunted her appetite for men. In any case, she was far too busy writing and so forth to juggle with lovers as well.'

'She never mentioned being pestered by anyone?'

'Never – and she would have said so, believe me. She wouldn't have been scared or intimidated, rest assured.'

'Did her ex-husband allow her to have their house willingly?'

'I don't know about *willingly*. That was all part of the divorce settlement, thrashed out by lawyers.'

'He wasn't trying to winkle her out?'

'Not at all. Any dispute over property and equity was history.'

'Nevertheless, the upshot of the murder is that her ex-husband is back in the house he'd been made to vacate.'

'Ironic, isn't it.'

'Did she have a drink problem?'

'In my view, yes, she did. The problem being that she never drank enough! Not for my taste, anyhow. Don't get me wrong, I'm not a lush, but I reckon to have a few glasses of plonk every day to smooth off the rough edges of the day around sundown. Gloria was a fair-weather, social drinker. Always wine. I never saw her have more than a couple of glasses.'

'Did she keep drink at home?'

'Only wine. Where's this leading, Mr Templeman? I fail to see what possible bearing this could have on her murder.'

'Please be patient for just a few more questions and it'll all become clear, I hope. After the lunch at The Mitre, you didn't have any contact with Gloria until you met that same evening at the Bodleian Library?'

'Correct. The poetry meeting was held in the Seldon End of the library.'

'Was that a long-standing engagement?'

'We'd both had it pencilled in our diaries for a couple of months.'

'And the poetry-reading evening had been well publicized in advance?'

'In the local press, yes. Priscilla Somerfield is quite a big name in the poetry world. She's also an editor with the publishing house that publishes Gloria's books.'

'Did you and Gloria know everyone at the Bodleian that evening?'

'Not *everyone*, gracious, no! I think we both knew a few, but that was all.'

'What was the mix?'

'I beg your pardon?'

'The ratio between men and women?'

'Seventy per cent women, I'd say, at a rough estimate.'

'Was Gloria on any medication, as far as you're aware?'

'No, she was the fittest woman for her age that I've ever met. I can't recall her ever being ill, not even with a cold or the flu.'

'Was there any indication that she might have been drinking perhaps at home – before arriving at the library?'

'Absolutely not!'

'No smell of alcohol on her breath?'

'No! Haven't I made that absolutely clear?'

'Indeed, but it's essential for that to be watertight. You see, in your statement to the police, you said that your last view of Gloria Swift was as she walked away from you with a *swaying* motion.'

Bridges ruminated at length, before replying, hesitantly, 'Yes, that's right.'

'Did she normally walk that way? You know, with an exaggerated gait?'

Now her face became pinched and highly focused in thought.

'No, she didn't.'

'You see, the fact that it left such an impression on you – perhaps only in your subconscious – that you included it in your statement, seems to me that it has some significance.'

Bridges didn't answer immediately. After taking her time to gather and arrange her thoughts, she said, weakly, 'I suppose you're right. I'd never considered it that way.'

'How pronounced was her *sway*?'

'Oh, considerable.'

'Like a limp?'

'No, I wouldn't describe it as a limp; more an unsteady, oscillating motion. A wobble, as if the pavement was potted and was giving her problems in the dark, even though the lighting was good.'

'She didn't have an injury, a sprained ankle or damaged hip, anything of that nature?'

'No, I hadn't noticed it before; not at lunch nor as we circulated in the Bodleian, just before the event began and as we all began to disperse.'

'How would you describe your friend?'

'Intelligent. Strong-willed. Outspoken. Honest. Sincere. She could be fun and frivolous, just as much as she could be intense. She relished telling people about the days when she used to swim in the nude at Parson's Pleasure, often at midnight in summer, after parties. I think she experienced a thrill, a sort of frisson, from shocking people. She was bursting with life, a torch for a lot of people, a symbol of something pure, like the Olympic flame, until the moment some madman mindlessly snuffed it out.'

'Did anyone at that poetry evening – I'm thinking now mainly of the men – seem to be paying her undue attention? Hanging on, that sort of thing?'

Bridges was shaking her head before Templeman had finished his last question.

Later that afternoon, Templeman dug out the statement the police had taken from Damian, Gloria Swift's teenage son. From the boy's account, it was evident that he had been questioned thoroughly about his mother's last call to him, allegedly made from outside the Bodleian Library. He told the police that it was 'just after 9.15' when she had phoned on her mobile. The veracity of this was confirmed by the network provider. The exact time of the call was recorded as 9.15; the duration under a minute. Damian had been adamant that there was nothing in his mother's voice, or in the substance of the conversation, to suggest that she was in danger. 'She sounded absolutely normal,' he said. 'Maybe a bit sleepy, but she'd had a long day. She was perfectly coherent and very happy, obviously elated, by the exhilarating evening. Anything artistic always gave her a buzz. She said she would catch the first available bus and she expected to be home before ten.'

The word 'elated' leapt out at Templeman and he made a note of it in his yellow pad.

Then it was time to switch on the TV for the *Six O'Clock News*.

'There has been a sensational development in the hunt for the Oxford serial killer, announced by the police today,' the newscaster began in breathless, tabloid-speak. He gave details of the latest missive from the killer, before the camera switched to Chief Constable Humphry Badger. The interview went:

'How seriously are you taking this threat?'

'Very.'

'You believe it is genuine and not a hoax – that it is from the person who has already murdered at least three women in Oxford since January?'

'There's always the possibility that it could be a hoax, but we cannot afford to take that chance.'

'So what are you doing about it?'

'Well, for a start, we're not panicking. And we don't want the women of Oxford panicking, either. What I am appealing for is common sense and sensible precautions. Don't make it easy for this evil and dangerous predator within our midst to keep his hideous promise.'

'Just what are you suggesting – that every woman in Oxford should bolt herself indoors for twenty-four hours?'

'That might not be such a bad idea, but people have to go to work, take children to school and collect them, for example. I'm not calling for a complete disruption and suspension of women's lives – not even for just twenty-four hours.'

'What *are* you calling for, then?'

'For reasonable precautions, as I've already stated.'

'And what are they?'

'I'm recommending that women shouldn't go out alone after dark, unless it's absolutely necessary and unavoidable.'

'Isn't that making a concession to this maniac?'

'*Maniac* is your word, by the way, not mine. But, yes, it is indulging him, but I'd rather that than have another death on our hands.'

'Some people are already accusing you of having blood on your hands, through incompetence.'

'Not personally, I hope.'

'There's immense public unease, a feeling that you're getting nowhere and, as a force, you're out of your depth.'

'Such criticism is grossly unfair, in my view, but I do empathize with the public's frustration.'

'That's all very well, but what progress *is* being made towards an arrest?'

'It would be unwise of me to go into the minutiae. Suffice it for me to say that we have some strong leads.'

'The killer has intimated that he has already singled out his next victim, I understand?'

'So the author of the anonymous letter claims.'

'Do you believe that?'

'It is entirely possible.'

'Considering the previous victims, is there any particular

type of woman whom you fear might be imperilled; his kind of target?'

'There is, but I'd rather not attach too much credence to that.'

'Why not?'

'Because it could lull other categories of women into a false sense of security.'

'Are you still keeping faith with the chief investigating officer, Detective Inspector Hardman?'

'He will continue in charge of the day-to-day operation for the foreseeable future.'

'If there is another victim in Oxford within the next few days, will you hold yourself personally responsible and do the honourable thing – resign?'

'No, I shall not run from my obligations. I shall not rest until this inhuman predator is safely behind bars. But let's not be negative. We have perhaps the chance to avert another tragedy, so I plead with the women of Oxford to spoil this devil's day.'

Not bad, Templeman said to himself quite impressed, as Badger disappeared from the screen and the newscaster moved fluently to the next item.

Within ten minutes, Hardman was on the phone, calling from a pub.

'Did you see it, Luke?'

'I did.'

'What you think? Make you puke?'

'He was wise not to mention the "J and H" sign-off. That's certainly something worth keeping to yourselves for the time being. He pressed all the right buttons. Good PR. Good TV, too. The media will have a carnival tomorrow. Public awareness will be at an all-time high. I don't see how it could have been improved. How did *you* rate it?'

'Slick. Smooth. Typical of the arsehole. But – and this is the bottom line – it won't save a life.'

Templeman sighed. 'Defeatism isn't going to help, Mike.'

'I'm no defeatist, just a realist. Our man says his next victim has already been chosen, but I don't believe him.'

Templeman listened without interrupting.

'Think about it, Luke, it's not possible. Even if he had drawn up a shortlist and then made a final selection from that, he couldn't be sure of carrying out his pledge on the publicized date. His target could be taken ill and not leave her home. She may even suddenly be hospitalized. A sudden change of routine or domestic emergency could take her out of the city, out of the country even, on that day. No, this is just drama, sick theatre. He will take whoever's available on the night and then pretend that was his intended victim all the time. No-one will be able to prove the contrary.'

'You could be right, Mike,' Templeman agreed reluctantly.

'I *know* I'm right.'

Templeman wasn't totally persuaded, but kept his own counsel.

'And I'm on the case for the *foreseeable future* – a real public display of confidence in me, eh? What a slime!'

Hardman's vitriol for his chief was a salve for his own spleen. Because the subject made him scratchy, he changed it.

'How did you get on with that Bridges woman?'

'Very well, thanks, though I didn't come away knowing anything more than when I went in.'

'The story of my life! Some more bad news for you. Badger wants you to liaise with our ace profiler.' He made 'ace' sound like the ultimate insult.

'That's not such a bad idea,' Templeman said agreeably.

'Come on, Luke, you know as well as I do that it's going to be a faffing waste of time, like spending an hour soaking in the bath while the dinner's cremated in the oven. All you'll get for your time and trouble is burnt offerings.'

Templeman laughed to be polite.

'I don't think you ever told me the name of your profiler.'

'Of course I didn't, because I want you to solve this case, not have your brain fried by such hocus-pocus. Her name's Helen Ridout. I don't know whether she's a doctor or a professor, but she has the highest possible qualifications in bullshit. If you don't hate her on sight, you'll go down in my estimation. It's hard to believe that she beat a hundred thousand other sperm into this world. I'll have her join you for breakfast tomorrow, which means your day will be blighted at birth.'

'Seven o'clock sharp. Early bird catches the worm – my catchphrase.'

'No catching necessary, the worm's coming to you!'

Tandy was waiting at home in Florida for Templeman's call.

After a few intimate exchanges, Templeman asked her about the Tammy Carter kidnapping case she was handling.

'Nancy got the call at four o'clock this morning, hitting her when the body's at its lowest ebb – smart psychology. The demand's for three million.'

Templeman whistled. 'Is she in that league?'

'Her husband is. He's one of the south's biggest property speculators. He's also bought his way into politics, bankrolling Democrat candidates.'

'But Nancy's divorcing him, right?'

'And planning to squeeze him dry in the process.'

'I assume you had her phone set up for taping all calls?'

'Naturally. I've followed the standard drill.'

'I'm sure you have. What was said?'

'It was a short call, as you'd expect. "Unless you are prepared to pay three million for your daughter's safe return, she'll die and you'll never see her again. You'll live with the anguish of never knowing what happened to her. Think about it."'

'Man or woman?'

'Man.'

'What about the accent? Southern, Midwest, Californian, New York, New England?'

'Possibly Cuban, maybe Mexican, according to Nancy.'

'Did she demand evidence that her daughter was still alive?'

'She asked for Tammy to be put on the line.'

'And?'

'He refused, saying, "Not now, perhaps later."'

'I don't like the sound of that.'

'Me neither, though I didn't say that to Nancy.'

'How did the call end?'

'Standard. She'll be called again, but she'd better start getting the money together because in the final flourish of negotiations there'll be a very strict and inflexible timetable. Naturally, there was a repeat warning about the "inevitable consequences" of going to the police. "You are being watched and monitored," he said.'

'You must continue to press her to go to the police. The odds are that her daughter's already dead.'

'I know, Luke, but she's still adamant and won't hear of police involvement. She's in denial.'

'Does she propose paying?'

'Absolutely. She's going to tackle Ronnie, her estranged husband, sometime today.'

'He may well take a very different line from her and want the police brought in and you'll be caught in the crossfire.'

'That's always a possibility.'

'In the meantime, what are you doing?'

'Talking to everyone who was at the barbecue.'

'Do the kidnappers know you've been hired to mediate?'

'Not yet. In view of the tone of this morning's call, she didn't think it advisable to introduce me into the equation so soon.'

'Any indication of what time the next call will come?'

'No, only that it'll be tomorrow.'

'Nancy must stick rigidly, however rough the emotional blackmail, to refusing to negotiate any further without being certain that Tammy is alive.'

'I'm tutoring her, don't worry.'

'Of course, I worry – about *you*.'

'Well, don't. Tell me about the latest excitement in Oxford.'

When Templeman had finished his account, Tandy said, 'Are you working on the assumption that there are two killers, a duo act?'

'Well, all the messages have concluded with the initials J and H.'

Spontaneously, Tandy said, 'Surely the most likely explanation is that J and H stands for Jekyll and Hyde. One man, two personalities.'

'My God, so they could!'

Now Templeman had yet another reason for a restless night.

Helen Ridout was a pleasant surprise for Templeman after Hardman's negative appraisal. She was blonde, the lucky side of forty, magnetic, though not the least self-preening, presentable and sunny, matching the weather. What's more, she was punctual and waiting for him at reception five minutes ahead of 7 a.m.

Her handshake was vice-locking, while her watchful eyes seemed to be hoovering up every speck of detail.

'DI Hardman advised me to be punctilious,' she said, a little mischievously, a teasing smile playing on her slightly puckered, violet lips.

'And so you are. Let's eat.'

'That's all I'm here for, a free breakfast,' she laughed readily.

'I believe you,' said Templeman, tuning into the tempo.

Even before the first caffeine intake of the day had stimulated their metabolisms, Ridout said testily, 'So what's your prejudiced opinion of profilers?'

'It depends on the profiler. I have an open mind.'

'Well, at least that's progress.'

'On what?'

'On the attitude of some of your peers.'

'Ah! But I'm here because I'm regarded as peerless.' There was a serious, unspoken message in his levity.

'Let's just say next February I won't be expecting a Valentine's Day card from Hardman.'

'But neither shall I!' said Templeman, deadpan, his eyes wandering to the profiler's hands.

'No husband, no fiancée, no need for one,' she laughed again, not nervously but radiating confidence as she held up and splayed her ringless fingers.

'You read my mind.'

'That's what I do, don't I? Perhaps at least you'll take me seriously now.'

'That was never in doubt. Tell me something about your track record. Give yourself a free plug, a kind of rebuttal to Hardman's trashing.'

'Well, although I was born over here, I was brought up in the States. My dad's an American, a retired airline pilot. I guess it was the influence of TV and the movies that shaped my career.'

'Such as *Quincy* and *The Silence of the Lambs*, Hannibal Lecter, et al?'

'That sort of fodder, yes; though by the time of *The Lambs*, I was already qualified. The job is erroneously portrayed as glamorous. It has its moments, but not many. Lay folk tend to have difficulty understanding the job title, Forensic Psychologist, which simply involves the analysis of information and making it acceptable for use in court. Over a period of time, I got degrees in forensic psychology, clinical psychology and the philosophy of psychology. My first real job was in a hospital environment, but I soon gravitated to a specialist, private practice.'

'In New York?'

'No, Chicago. I rented an apartment.'

'How did you come to the notice of the Thames Valley police?'

'Well, I'd done some profiling for the Chicago P.D. with moderate success. Now I have my own consultancy here. I don't need UK qualifications. I'm not treating patients or prescribing drugs. The consultant psychologist is a very different species from the psychiatrist, who has to be a qualified doctor. I'm not a doctor and I've never claimed to be one. A lot of my work comes from large companies that are worried about certain members of staff. Anyhow, about a year ago, I wrote to the Metropolitan police, offering my services when there was a serial rapist terrorizing Hampstead residents. I didn't hear anything until he'd struck again twice, almost killing his victim on the second of those occasions. By then, Scotland Yard detectives were afraid that he was about to escalate from serial rapist to serial murderer. Each attack was more violent than the previous one and he was edging towards homicide in inexorable increments. That's when they contacted me. They were already using another profiler, but by now they were ready to experiment with anyone; even the fairies, even me. To shorten a long story, there was an arrest six weeks later, before he raped again.'

'Was the breakthrough down to you?'

'I like to think I played a part. They had three suspects. I told them that, in my opinion, they could discount two of them and should concentrate on the third. That's what they did. A few weeks ago, the commissioner of the Met recommended me to the Thames Valley chief constable, when it became obvious that Hardman's team was failing to make headway. It was Badger himself who invited me aboard, much to Hardman's chagrin. Hardman has resented me ever since.'

'I'm not taking sides,' Templeman said levelly.

'Well, you should. There are only two sides to choose from – the killer's and the catchers'. If we're divided, the killer conquers. Now, what do you want to know?' she asked briskly, getting down to business, after the bacon.

'You've seen all the written notes and heard the voicemails, so what do you make of them? Are we hunting a classic psychopath?'

'The one thing I'm reasonably confident of is that the Oxford serial killer isn't a paranoid schizophrenic.'

'So what is our man, then, apart from clearly being nuts – a term that you'll no doubt balk at?'

'Nuts is OK by me. It's just as good an umbrella term as personality disorder, antisocial type, and has the merit of being far more commonly understood. I think you could well be looking for someone with a narcissistic personality disorder.'

'I'm sure you're going to interpret for me.'

'I'll give you the bullet points that go towards such a diagnosis: an excessive need for admiration, a pattern of grandiosity, an exaggerated sense of being special, preoccupied with fantasies of limitless self-importance and achievement, a feeling of entitlement, exploitative and manipulative without regard for others, and a belief that they're deserving of enduring love and that everyone else is ferociously envious of them.'

'Let's assume you're right about our predator having the disorder you've just outlined. Surely he's still a psychopath?'

'No, he's not. Someone with a narcissistic personality disorder will have considerably more humanity than a psychopath. That may sound absurd considering the heinous nature of his crimes, but that is to miss the point.'

'Which is?'

'He's likely to be much cleverer than a psychopath, making him potentially far more dangerous. He'll be less inclined to make serious, unforced mistakes and his actions will be finely tuned, planned, rehearsed and perfected, and almost certainly not spontaneous.'

'You mean he'll be carefully choosing a victim well in advance and doing his homework, fitting the situation we appear to be in now?'

'Yes, what we have is the likely scenario of someone with a narcissistic personality disorder.'

'When you say a person with this disorder is cleverer than your bog-standard psychopath, just how intelligent could he be? A university don, for example?'

'Oh, yes; there's no limit, no ceiling. And when I say he's more compassionate than a psychopath, I mean he might be a doctor, a nurse or a full-time carer. He will be loving and caring towards all those people – or animals – whom he decides are worthy of his compassion.'

'So he could appear to be leading a normal life in society?'

'It could seem that way to outsiders, yes.'

'But not to his family?'

'Depends. It could be that his odd behaviour is dismissed as a quirk of character, something like a distinguishing feature.'

'Might he be married?'

'Quite possibly, but his wife would have to be ultra-submissive, compliant, and prepared to indulge his whims. He'll demand constant praise and obedience, and will be continually denigrating and devaluing others, particularly anyone his wife holds dear to her and in high estimation, such as her mother, father, brothers and sisters.'

'And if he's a father?'

'Because he's a control freak, there'll be explosive friction in the household as the children get older. There'll always have to be a pay-back. He'll be spurred by a thirst for retribution for any little, piddling disagreement. No argument can be lost without revenge, which will be sadistic.'

'So there could be a history of abuse against his children?'

'Yes, but not necessarily physical. More likely he's mean-natured and cruel with derision. Any friendship will be fragile. He'll hold the law in contempt, believing that rules are made for others to comply with, but not himself. Katherine Ramsland, an eminent teacher of forensic psychology at DeSales University in the US, has described narcissism as the "beating heart of psychopathy".'

'So our man is unlikely to stand out in a crowd as raving mad?'

'Not *raving*; no hope of that or the police would have had him in their net by now.'

'Could he have reached this level of criminality without already having a criminal record? With sexual crimes, there's usually a history of escalation; that's what we're taught at police college.'

'And that would be right if this predator was a conventional psychopath. You'd be looking for someone who had been a serial truant as a schoolboy, indulged in petty theft as a teenager, experimented with drugs and solvents, failed all exams, was a pathological liar from the first word he ever uttered, overtly aggressive, in persistent violation of all social mores and norms, and dedicated to a parasitic lifestyle. Everything about him would be glib and artificial. He'd have no control over his emotions and he'd hop, like a frog, from one relationship to another.'

'We're not faced with someone who hears voices commanding him to kill, either for God or the devil?'

'Not at all; you can forget all that kind of stuff, which goes with paranoid schizophrenia. A word of caution: without a suspect to analyze, it's imperative to avoid being too dogmatic. It wouldn't surprise me at all if there wasn't some cross-pollination.'

Templeman wore his puzzlement openly.

'By that, I mean there might be an element of narcissistic and histrionic personality disorders unbalancing this killer,' Ridout explained.

'And what are the characteristics of a histrionic personality disorder?'

'The sufferer will tend to be theatrical in everything, with a totally unpredictable temperament, desperate for attention, shallow and shifting emotions, prepared to do literally anything to ensure he's the centre of gravity, around which the world revolves. He'll overplay his involvement in any situation, projecting himself as the hero in a crisis, even though he may well have been only on the periphery. He'll see intimacy in relationships that don't even exist. Hence, these people are very prone to becoming stalkers. They have also been known to go to exceptional lengths to make themselves noticed, even changing their physical appearance dramatically through weird disguise or cosmetic surgery.'

'Well, our man certainly craves attention, I'd say, but it's also equally obvious he intends to remain invisible as long as possible.'

'This ambivalence is probably torture to him. On one hand, he's star of the show. *His* show, of which he's leading man, director, producer, scriptwriter, choreographer and genius in charge of special effects. He has a worldwide audience. And yet, his name doesn't appear anywhere in lights. He's the star without a star billing. And that will chafe. It'll gnaw away at him as if he has rats in his head.'

'And make him less cautious?'

'Possibly. More likely, however, he'll vent his anger on his victims.'

'By becoming more sadistic?'

'Not necessarily. Perhaps he'll kill more frequently.'

'You don't see him running out of steam?'

'That sort of thing does happen, but I shouldn't pin your hopes on that in this case. I've an awful gut feeling that this one's going to run and run.'

'I hope you haven't told Hardman that.'

'No, but if I had, he wouldn't have been listening.'

'In most case studies of serial killers I've researched, the victims have been prostitutes, hitch-hikers, students or drug addicts; in a nutshell, the vulnerable.'

'You're right, that's the norm, Luke,' Ridout agreed tacitly.

'But here we have the absolute opposite – all powerful and influential women, including my own wife, Charley, dammit! Let's not forget.'

'I hadn't forgotten,' Ridout answered him solemnly.

'Don't you think it's crucial, pivotal?'

'I'm not disputing that whatsoever. It tells us a great deal about the motivation. Once again, however, I appeal to you to keep an open mind, but, yes, it's reasonable to surmise that he has a grudge against women of strong character.'

'Perhaps he had an overbearing mother?'

'That's a speculation too far, Luke. You see, it could be the success and achievements of the women, rather than their personality, that he resents.'

'Because he's been overlooked for promotion, been bypassed by fast-tracked women?'

'Or maybe he's merely upping the stakes for a sexual thrill. He could be someone whose juice comes from living on the edge. It's not enough for him to be killing these women, he has to flirt with extra danger of his own making, hence the notes, voice messages and the cat-and-mouse game he's conducting with you. His belief in his own superiority and immortality will mean that he's confident of being able to manage his calculated gambles without being outfoxed. It's not uncommon for the quarry to conduct a dialogue with his hunters. Son of Sam, David Berkowitz, wrote to newspapers and police officers. Berkowitz terrorized New York city for thirteen months, walking up to strangers in the street late at night, pulling a .44 revolver, and shooting them. His preferred modus operandi was gunning young couples as they canoodled in a car. A letter addressed to police captain Joseph Borrelli said, "I love to hunt, prowling the streets looking for fair game, tasty meat. The women of Queens are prettiest of all."'

'Did Son of Sam fit a profile?'

'As a paranoid schizophrenic, yes, he did. He was small and childlike, lived alone in one room, lit by a single naked bulb, and slept on a bare mattress. The walls were defaced with graffiti slogans, such as, "In this hole lives the wicked king", "Kill for my Master", and "I turn children into killers". His mother had tried to have him adopted when he was a baby and ever since boyhood he considered himself a reject. When captured, he was still a virgin. A sex-killer who had only ever shot through a gun.'

They both brooded a while, before Templeman said, 'I assume you've had access to Charley's file?'

'I have. Is that a problem?'

'Not with me. I'm glad. It helps us to communicate in shorthand. I'm sitting here trying to picture this killer as a family man, while simultaneously able to store a body indefinitely, cutting off a part of the anatomy and sending it through the post.'

'Perhaps he hasn't stored the body. Have you considered that?'

'But ...' Templeman started to protest before Ridout quickly interposed with her exposition.

'He could have amputated the finger shortly after committing the murder.'

'Keeping only the finger, you mean?'

'That's possibly more plausible, don't you think?'

'So why hasn't Charley's body been found? He hasn't tried to conceal his other victims.'

'The odds are that it's all part of his game plan, within the outré script of his macabre, self-satisfying theatrical production.'

'Does water play a part in his psyche?'

'Location is always a telling factor. Trouble is, the reason behind a particular spot chosen for the killing or dumping isn't usually apparent until after the case is closed.'

'We keep referring to the perpetrator in the singular, yet the initials J and H have appeared at the foot of each missive.'

'A red herring, I'd say.'

'You discount the insinuation that there's a killing partnership?'

'I don't *discount* anything, but such crimes are too rare to even consider without a firm lead.'

'What about J and H standing for Jekyll and Hyde?'

An amused smile passed swiftly over Ridout's unblemished, fair-skinned face.

'That's as good a guess as any, I'd say. In fact, I reckon you could be spot on, Sherlock!'

Templeman devoted much of the day to talking to repair workers in the boatyards along the canal and people he regarded loosely as 'river people'.

'Not the place it used to be,' lamented Dick Roach, who had been foreman in a repair yard beside the canal in Jericho for forty-odd years. 'Unrecognizable is Oxford from the city as I remembers it as a boy. The whole character of the place has changed since then.'

'In what way?' enquired Templeman, not really interested, just tapping along the conversation, lubricating the rapport and loosening the tongue of the old-timer, having introduced himself as a private detective, now based in Florida, but currently contracted to Thames Valley police. This was to be the template for all future interviews.

'Pace of life's what's changed most of all. Everyone in a mad rush, chasing their tails, going round in ever-increasing circles, making everyone else as dizzy and daft as themselves, getting nowhere.'

'That's the story of the world, not just of Oxford,' Templeman empathized, in the manner of a doorstep salesman, agreeing in order to make headway.

'New folks come in. Thousands of 'em from London. Overspill, they called 'em. Might as well have been immigrants for all they knew about life in the shires. Riff-raff's my name for 'em. Not right for Oxford. Done the tone of the place no flamin' good whatsoever.'

'The university hasn't altered all that much, surely?'

'Don't kid yourself. Used to be for the cream. Now anyone with half a brain and a glib tongue can get in.'

'I suppose vandalism is a growing problem?'

'A pain in the bum, it is – and not just because of the kids. Canal and river folk, like me and my family, are being pushed out by the pond-life. Know what I mean? The rabble.'

Templeman just nodded, avoiding committing himself but continuing to bond.

'Nothing's sacred. You can put ten padlocks on a shed-door and iron bars on the windows and the buggers will still find a way to break in – just to thieve a screwdriver or electric drill. Parasites!'

'How about the weirdos?' Templeman egged him on.

'More of 'em than the rest of us. They're taking over the world, believe me. Only the other morning, not yet seven o'clock, I caught a couple of students red-handed shagging on the slipway here. The lad was still wearing his bicycle clips and straw boater. The girl was in fancy dress, dolled up like a young Marlene Dietrich, smoking a fag in a long holder, puffing away while he pumped. Brazen as you like! Didn't bat an eyelid when I yelled at 'em. Carried on as if they were just rowing along the river. In out, in out!'

'That's the young for you.'

'Society's sediment, I say.'

'Terrible business about the woman's body found around here.' Templeman at last foreclosed on the preamble.

'Especially when it was someone so respectable. No young tart, like you'd expect. That's what I mean about this city going downhill. There's no respect any more; not for anything decent, anyhow.'

'Was she known around here?'

'What, Laura Fleming? Nah! But she was well known in the city. Highly regarded. A good, no-nonsense woman. Worked bloody hard as a councillor. Nothing too much trouble for her, from all accounts. Always one to fight the good fight. A friend of mine had a load of bother from his landlord and he went to

Councillor Fleming for help. Best thing he ever did, he says. She sorted it. No messing!'

'What kind of trouble was your friend having?'

'Victimization. The landlord wanted him out, even though the tenancy agreement had another ten months to run. He accused Bob – that's my mate – of being behind with his rent, but bank statements proved he'd paid regularly every month by direct debit. The truth was that the landlord wanted to sell up and scarper, because he was in debt all over. Councillor sorted it, though, bless her! What a way for such a good woman to go! That's what this world's doing: killing off every-thing decent in it.'

'Do you reckon he's from this neighbourhood, Jericho?'

'What, the barmpot who's snuffing out these women?'

'Yes.'

'Who can tell. Could be my next-door neighbour, for all I know. The loonies are in the woodwork everywhere. It's getting more and more difficult by the day to distinguish the sane from the loonies. In my opinion, for what it's worth, Laura Fleming and them others would still be alive if we'd never done away with hanging. Visions of the noose and the trapdoor had a sobering influence on a man, even a deranged one. It was a deterrent, even if the statistics said something different. Figures can be messed with to suit any argument.'

The canalside was no place for an Oxford Union-styled debate on the merits of capital punishment, so Templeman eschewed one.

'What's the word on the jungle drums?'

Roach's weather-coarsened face became even more crinkled as he cocked his head curiously.

'You mean about the murder?'

'Yes, there must be a few notions in circulation, certainly in the pubs.'

'No-one can make head nor tail of it, to be honest.'

'No talk of other funny goings on? No sightings of someone lurking around the canal after dark, harassing women?'

'There's always that going on, blimey! But those hanging

around at night are mostly the outdoor shaggers, dope-dealers and petty thieves. I don't think the councillor ended her life down here. I'd wager my mortgage that the canal was just used as burial water and she was done in elsewhere.'

'The killer was taking a chance, considering the night activity around here.'

'Yeah, he must have known his way around, I'll grant you that.'

'So you'd agree he has to be a local?'

'Got to be.'

They both nodded in agreement.

'I'll leave you to it, then,' said Templeman, bidding Roach farewell and moving on.

During the early afternoon, he initiated similar conversations with couples who lived in houseboats on the Thames, along the sleepy, meandering Oxford waterways. They collectively complained about the nuisance of hooligans and drunks, but no one had a contribution to make towards shedding light on the murders.

At 5 p.m., Templeman had an appointment at the *Oxford Mail* with its editor, Simon King. The chief constable had decided there was more to be gained by Templeman breaking cover than by continuing incognito, now that the killer appeared to be fully aware not only of Templeman's presence in Oxford but also of his movements. Publicity would retain the high profile of the investigation, give it impetus, and help perpetuate awareness among the public. The local newspaper could also be of invaluable service in another way. A deal had been struck. In return for a candid interview with Templeman, with no area of his life – professional and private – off-limits, he would be allowed access to the newspaper's computerized archives.

The *Oxford Mail*'s headquarters were a one-level, purpose-built building, open-plan throughout, on the featureless Osney Mead industrial estate. The interview, conducted by the crime correspondent, took place in the editor's glass-panelled office in the editorial section, towards the rear of the building.

The editor was present, though he took a passive role throughout. The reporter's questions were predictable: what had brought him back to Oxford after so many bad memories, was this part of a personal crusade to catch his wife's killer, had he a score to settle – if so, with whom, was he seeking to exorcize his own ghosts, why did he believe Charley had been abducted and murdered, what was her connection with the other victims and how had he reinvented himself in the USA? There were also questions about his own arrest and trial. Throughout, Templeman was as frank as possible, telling no lies, though occasionally truncating the truth. That over, it was then time for the other side of the bargain. He was taken to the office of another editorial executive, who was on holiday, given a five-minute crash course on how to surf the in-house archives on the computer system, and left to it.

'Take as long as you like,' said the editor. 'We run a twenty-four-hour operation here. All I ask is if you come across anything that gives you a lead, you'll tip us off.'

'Naturally,' said Templeman, with a polite chuckle, meaning the opposite, of course.

Templeman began by tapping out the names of Gloria Swift, Caroline Marsh and Laura Fleming, and then clicking on 'Search'. There were more than 800 hits. Templeman scrolled quickly, ignoring everything relating to their deaths and the police investigation. He was looking for stories about them while they were still alive. Stories about controversies in which they were embroiled.

Gloria Swift had been one of the earliest campaigners in Oxford for the banning of smoking in all public places. Eight years ago she had tipped a bottle of red wine over a burning cigarette in the hand of a woman in one of the city's most expensive restaurants. The doused diner, with her new white outfit ruined, retaliated by pulling Swift's hair, scratching her face and kicking her ankles. Both women – and their partners – had been ejected from the restaurant and blacklisted 'indefinitely'.

The story, appearing on the front page alongside her picture, quoted her saying: 'It was a very costly bottle of wine, but I don't begrudge one penny of it. The wine went on a good cause and at least I went to bed sober, if rather hungry.

'The smoke was killing my taste-buds, not to mention making my eyes water and irritating my throat, to such an extent that I was coughing all night.

'If my action helps to galvanize the anti-smoking band-wagon into robust rebellion, then the slight distress and embarrassment to others will have been worthwhile.

'As for being banned from the restaurant, we're spoilt for choice around here when it comes to smart eating joints.'

Krissy Edwards, the woman who had the wine poured over her, told the newspapers: 'It was such a shock. If my smoking was upsetting her so much, all she had to do was make a civil request to me. Instead of that, she marched over to our table like a hormone-induced virago and attacked me. As if that wasn't aggravation enough, her language was that of the barrack room. The air was blue, I can tell you.

'I was entertaining a business associate, hoping to clinch a lucrative contract. She blew everything for me. I intend to sue her for lost earnings, make no mistake.'

Templeman clicked on to a follow-up story, in which Swift said she was prepared to compensate for a new dress 'but damn all else'.

Asked if she would compensate for Edwards' 'hurt feelings and lost income', Swift had replied, 'Over my dead body!'

The last story on this theme appeared two days later, when the *Oxford Mail* referred to Edwards as an advertising consultant, whose clients included a tobacco manufacturer. The innuendo was that Edwards hadn't been a random, spon-taneous target and that Swift's action was premeditated; that she had gone to the restaurant knowing that Edwards would be there with the executive of a tobacco marketing company.

'Nonsense!' had been Swift's terse riposte. 'If it was planned, you don't think it would have been such a puny performance, do you? And wouldn't I have given you chaps a nudge and a wink so you could have had a snapper in the wings to capture the moment for posterity?'

That seemed to be the end of that particular conflict. It appeared that Edwards had not pursued a claim for damages, though the dispute might have been settled out of court. In that event, why hadn't Edwards boasted of her legal victory? Templeman pondered.

Swift had exploited every possible platform to vilify the tobacco industry and the political legislators for their diffidence in protecting the public from 'passive pollution'.

She had also been in conflict with the county council over what she saw as tardiness in promoting the recycling of household rubbish. On this issue, both she and Fleming, a city councillor, had been featured in the same articles, but not always as allies, surprisingly. Frequently, Swift had accused her kindred spirit of being 'too cerebral, abstract and theoretical' in her approach, instead of pushing for solutions and change with 'revolutionary zeal'. Swift had trumpeted, 'Female zealots are the lions of civilization.'

Swift had also made serious enemies within the anti-abortion movement, many of whom believed she was using her novels, aimed at adolescents, as propaganda, preaching promiscuity and a quick fix for unwanted pregnancies through her fictional characters. Her books, published around the world, had ignited extremist reaction in the USA, where one group of evangelical conservatives had branded her a 'human cockroach'. The *Oxford Mail* had quoted from the Kentucky-based organization's website that declared: 'You all know the recommended treatment for cockroach infestations. Stamping on them isn't sufficient because they are so thick-skinned and resilient. Nothing short of mass wipe-out will suffice. Surely somebody out there is prepared to do the world a favour? Make the sacrifice! Do a good turn for the human race! The future of civilization is far more important than the life of one cockroach.'

Templeman pressed the key for a print-out of that story.

Cigarette manufacturers had fortunes to lose from anti-smoking legislation, but Templeman doubted that these women, even collectively, would have been classified a high-priority menace by the world's tobacco barons. There were much bigger fish to be spiked in that particular global war.

Engrossed, Templeman continued trawling. Swift, Marsh and Fleming had all been vociferous in their opposition to foxhunting with hounds and were at the forefront of the campaign for a complete ban. They were 'proud' to be paid-up members of the League Against Cruel Sports and Marsh had bragged of her earlier 'swashbuckling adventures' as a sabo-teur, disrupting hunts and drawing hounds away from fleeing foxes by laying false scent-trails.

Many rural hunting communities, entrenched in medieval traditions and a long way intellectually from the centre of gravity of mainstream society, were known to sport a thuggish underbelly. Killing was a way of life for them and some failed to differentiate between vermin and people they classed as their enemy. One hunting enthusiast – name and address withheld – had written a letter to the newspaper, saying that Marsh, as a Londoner, 'wouldn't know the difference between a fox and a foal'. The author of the letter went on to suggest that Marsh and her 'loutish, misguided gang of urban grumps should stick to spoiling the fun of town and city dwellers and leave us gentle countyfolk to run our own affairs', finishing with, 'We know what is best for us. Meddling outsiders tend to be accident-prone. Be warned!'

Once again Templeman struck the 'Print' key. A pattern was emerging; nothing definite, but spidery crystallization was beginning to take shape. Nothing within the columns of newsprint would positively identify the serial killer, of that Templeman was certain, but it was quite possible that the reason for the slaughter was embedded in the victims' public lives.

Lastly, Templeman initiated a search for any story that had included his wife's name *before* her dramatic disappearance. He had no recollection of Charley having appeared in Oxford Crown Court prior to the one that led to her abduction and certain brutal death, but she had defended in regional centres all over England and it was highly possible that she had peddled her magus skills on behalf of some hapless wretch in Oxford.

This search resulted in several hits, relating to three cases. The first concerned businessman Jason Fletcher, who was charged with murdering his estranged wife, although no body had ever been found. Templeman was immediately startled by the similarity with his own trial, when he stood accused in Oxford, in that very same court, of murdering Charley.

Fletcher had moved in with his lover, while his wife, Sara, began divorce proceedings. Sara, a nurse, was employed at Oxford's Radcliffe Hospital in the intensive care unit. Fletcher and his mistress, whom he planned to marry after the divorce, rented a cottage several miles south along the Thames, in Pangbourne, although his haulage company had its head office in the city. On the day that Sara disappeared, Fletcher was in the Moroccan city of Marrakech, trying to drum up trade. This checked out and there was no possible way that he could have been in two countries at the material time, but an examination of his personal bank account revealed large cash withdrawals during the previous month. Hence the speculation that this cash was used to pay for the services of a contract killer. When cross-examined in court about these cash withdrawals, Fletcher claimed he had turned to gambling because his business was as much on the rocks as was his marriage. Certainly there was plenty of evidence that profits from his company had nosedived in the previous two years' trading. And staff in at least two casinos confirmed that Fletcher was a regular at the gaming tables and was considered a 'mug punter' – a big-time loser. The prosecution talked of 'shady underworld characters' on the fringe of Fletcher's life. Immigration records showed that a suspect hitman had flown into London Heathrow from Chicago two days prior to Sara Fletcher's murder and had departed the day after, though there was no tangible evidence to make a connection with Fletcher or Oxford.

'What we have here is guesswork,' Charley had submitted. 'The prosecution, bereft of a shred of hard evidence and without even a body – no victim, no crime – has embarked on a smear campaign, a smokescreen for their own failings.' It was an argument that swayed the jury.

The second case concerned the murder in Reading of a prostitute, Karina Karpov, an illegal immigrant from the Czech Republic. The trial had originally been listed for Reading Crown Court, but had been transferred to Oxford because the preceding case had overrun badly. Much of the evidence was accepted by both prosecution and defence counsel, such as the fact that Karpov had advertised her 'very personal service' under the 'Escorts' heading in various libertine magazines. The only contact number she gave was her mobile phone. Douglas Crump, an historian specializing in the emancipation of the working class, had an appointment with the prostitute for 9 p.m. on the day of the crime. He was given her address during the one phone call he made to her. Crump was also a town councillor, having won his seat on an Independent Workers' Revolution ticket. Karpov, who had been dressed only in her underwear when Crump arrived, explained that she charged one hundred pounds for 'half an hour of fun and frolics'. Crump balked at that, deeming it 'extortionate'. She replied that she was 'worth every penny' and that the 'service' she gave would leave him 'replete'. She further prophesied that, rather than feeling cheated, he would be 'frothing at the mouth, eager to pay for more'. This was all common ground between prosecution and defence.

Crump had paid in cash the amount stipulated. Before they had sex, Karpov, a bottle-blonde, had deposited the money in a wall-safe, concealed behind a painting of the Virgin Mary. 'I am a bad Catholic,' she told Crump, according to his version, while they had sexual intercourse, which included a variety of kinky routines, such as a spanking with a satin slipper after hanky panky in a mock confessional. 'I still go to Confession every Saturday evening,' she allegedly said, while dressing. 'I repent. I say my Hail Marys. When I promise to the parish priest that I will be good, I mean it – at the time. But the truth is I'm bad, to the core. I come home. The phone rings. The priest's words are still echoing in my ears. And I say to the caller, "Come on round. Yes, I'll do that for you, no problem – as long as you pay." All the time I'm fingering my rosary. I do the business, then start to work out how many Hail Marys that'll cost me next week. You pay, I pay. The books get balanced, see.'

After Karpov and Crump had finished on the bed, the councillor said he needed to use the bathroom. Crump was given directions and off he padded, semi-naked. It was from this point that the dispute began between prosecution and defence. Charley Templeman, representing Crump, contended that he returned from the bathroom quicker than Karpov had expected and he had caught her 'red-handed' rifling through the pockets of his clothes, which had been tossed haphazardly over a bedside armchair. Karpov, allegedly, had his wallet in her hands and was removing all the paper currency, amounting to £400.

Crump admitted losing his temper. 'Who wouldn't have in his position?' Charley had argued. 'He considered he had already been over-generous to this avaricious tart. And here she was greedily and grubbily grabbing more in the role of common thief. Was there no end to her immorality? Apparently not. When my enraged client demanded that she immediately return the money to his wallet and then to him, she laughed, threatening that if he made a fuss she would make a complaint to the police that he'd raped her. Charley said that Karpov had also shouted at him, "I bet you've got a couple of bedrooms full of kids at home and a little wife waiting. Do they know you're here? What if they were to find out, eh?" That was the moment my client decided he had no alternative but to retrieve his money by force.'

Karpov had died from head wounds. Crump insisted that this was the outcome of the prostitute hitting her head on the corner of a dressing table during the ensuing tussle. The prosecution, supported by medical experts, contended that the injuries were consistent with a blunt instrument having been used as a weapon, such as the heavy base of Karpov's bedside table-lamp, although there was neither blood nor human hair on it, when examined by Forensics. Karpov's skull had been damaged in three different areas, which couldn't have been caused by only one bump, said the pathologist. But Charley told the jury, 'My client is a family man. This was the first time he'd ever erred this way. He was under a great deal of stress at the time. He is not a violent man. He has been active in all kinds of peace movements and he is a loving father to three young children. Only two people really know for sure what happened that apocalyptic night and one of them, in this country illegally and making a living selling her flesh, is dead. My client swears that Karpov's death was a tragic accident. He admits to being angry, but he did not intend to harm her. He was merely trying to get back his money and wallet, which were being stolen. In the absence of any conclusive evidence to refute that Karina Karpov's death was an unfortunate accident, it would fly in the face of natural justice to convict my client and condemn his loving children to a fatherless future. I beseech you from the core of my conscience to give Douglas Crump the benefit of the considerable doubt.'

The jury, comprising ten men and two women, had taken less than three hours to reach its verdict. Crump walked.

This case had triggered a mini-furore among women's lobby groups. They criticized Charley for mounting a 'scurrilous' defence, playing on the victim's 'irrelevant' lifestyle, using it as a smokescreen to blind the jury. There was also the customary deluge of letters to the *Oxford Mail* about the 'inherent injustice inculcated in middle-class juries'. Charley had replied, pointing out that Crump was 'anything but middle class' and would have been 'as alien to the petty bourgeois' as the prostitute.

Templeman noted a number of names and addresses, without much confidence of them leading him anywhere other than up a dead end. Our man is far too astute to have left markers – stepping-stones – that could be followed this easily, Templeman reasoned with himself. However, he had far from wasted his time. An abstract link between the victims –

Charley included – was taking shape. The reason for their deaths, so obscure for so long, was now much clearer.

The third trial concerned the alleged rape of a teenage girl. Once again the accused was acquitted. This case was allotted much fewer column inches. The accuser couldn't be named, of course. Neither could anything be reported that in any way might lead to her identification.

Templeman believed he was near to having the killer's number, if not his name.

Templeman was late with his call home, to Tandy, who had plenty to relate. That morning, she had had a meeting with Ronnie Carter, father of kidnapped Tammy.

'He'll go along with whatever I deem necessary,' Tandy reported.

'Does that mean he's willing to put up the whole three mill?'

'He's devoted to his daughter. Besotted. He'll do anything. She's still his little girl. You know what dads are like. I expected him to insist on bringing in his lawyers and financiers, but he was opposed to that right away. He took Nancy's line, that the fewer who know what's going on, the better.'

'So he's content with keeping the cops out of it?'

'He's adamant, even more so than Nancy.'

'And he's happy enough with your role?'

'Hardly *happy*, but I have his cautious approval. There's a natural undercurrent of suspicion that I'm Nancy's woman. I think he'd have preferred a hand in choosing a negotiator. I get the distinct impression he'd have gone for someone with their name in lights – and an American. The fact that Nancy had already used me to dig the dirt on Ronnie for a lucrative divorce settlement makes me his natural enemy.'

'I'm missing you like hell already.' And then, 'Has proof been provided yet that Tammy's still alive?'

'No. The kidnappers are keeping up the tension, pushing Nancy to the brink. She's told them about me, the fact that she's engaged me as a go-between.'

'And?'

'They're not happy bunnies. She's been warned that Tammy's safe return could no longer be guaranteed.'

'How did she react to that?'

'She explained to them she couldn't hold up alone any longer, that she hadn't made any attempt to involve the police and was still ready to comply with demands, but only when satisfied that her daughter hadn't been harmed and that a formula for her safe return could be agreed. She was warned that she was in no position to start dictating. Then he hung up. I'm anticipating he'll call again this evening. From now on, I'll be fielding all calls. I'm moving in with Nancy within the next hour, so in future call me on my mobile.'

'This doesn't appear to be a political kidnapping nor a vendetta, but purely commercial, which should make it less complicated than some of the alternatives. If it's as one-dimensional as I hope, you have a chance.'

'Luke, darling, I think my chances are a damned sight better than yours. I'll nail my man. How about you?'

'You rule me out at your peril.'

Templeman had far more policing experience than his partner, but Tandy compensated with uncanny intuition. They complemented each other, though not always with compliments.

Next day:

Templeman was pleasantly surprised by the article about him in the *Oxford Mail*, which was flattering without being fulsome. It intelligently explored his own complex, almost Freudian, motives for returning to cloistered Oxford after so much grief for him within its fabled city walls. It ruthlessly examined his unique role in the desperate race against the clock, without belittling the efforts of Hardman and other Thames Valley detectives. Running to more than 2,000 words of staccato prose, the story had been sectioned into self-contained panels to liven the presentation. One of these panels was dedicated to the reinvention of himself in the USA with Tandy. He had, of course, omitted to make any mention to the reporter of his agency's latest assignment, currently being handled so sensitively by his partner. Most gratifying for him, however, was the recurring theme throughout the piece – that any woman in Oxford, whatever her age or social status – could be next on the hitlist. One woman in the city, unknown to her and all but one deranged man, had by now drawn the short straw, her name already pencilled in on a tombstone. *'Spoil His Day'* was the supplication of the headline emblazoned across the newspaper's front page.

Hardman phoned late morning to say that the chief constable was 'relatively content' with the *Oxford Mail*'s treatment of Templeman's contentious involvement. 'Translated, that means the old sod is over the moon!' said Hardman.

'Until the PR is rubbished by the appearance of the next body. Fool's paradise was made specifically with him in mind, if you ask me.'

For another five minutes they alluded tentatively to the countdown and the fast-approaching deadline.

'I haven't been home for two nights,' confessed Hardman, further admitting, 'I must be hell to live with these days.'

Templeman refrained from comment, simply asking, 'Where've you been shacking up?'

'You're not going to believe this. Last night I was out following up leads until around midnight. When I say *leads*, I mean chasing shadows – checking up on known sex offenders in the county who've been released from gaol in the past two years. I didn't expect a pay-off, so I wasn't disappointed, but it kept me occupied. Going through the motions can be therapeutic, but the effects of the therapy were short-lived. The night-demons were soon back, making merry, making mayhem inside my head. I took myself to a club, got stoned – my one achievement of the night – and ended up catching a couple of hours' turbulent sleep in my office. I haven't had a change of shirt, underwear or socks in three days. The smell of defeat follows me everywhere.'

'I believe you,' Templeman said, with a certain irony.

'The previous night, I got myself locked into an all-night poker game. At one point I was three hundred quid ahead. On a roll. I really thought my luck was changing.'

'And then?'

'You know how it is.'

'Tell me.'

'I lost it all – plus a full month's salary. Every time the champagne in my glass dipped below the Plimsoll line, there was a bunny-type girl at my shoulder, treating me to a free top-up.'

'An expensive freebie!'

'Breakfast was included.'

'Wow!'

'It's the waiting that's breaking me.'

'That's his game.'

'We're doing everything, you included, but it's not going to make a jot of difference. The body count is about to go up and every tinpot politician and armchair detective is going to be baying for my blood. We're going to be crucified as jackass failures.'

'Stop whipping yourself, Mike.'

'Everyone else is doing it. A masochist would at least get pleasure from it.' And then, 'What more can I do?'

'Nothing, Mike. Nothing.'

'If I believed in God, I'd pray for a miracle, but I don't fancy adding hypocrisy to my list of sins.'

'I'll say one for you.'

'Amen.'

Templeman delayed calling Tandy until a few minutes after midnight – seven in the evening in Florida – so that Tandy had the cut and thrust of almost a full working day to recount.

The kidnappers had made contact three times, starting with a pre-dawn call, 'hitting us at our lowest ebb'.

'He swore at me, said I'd better learn to button my lip if I didn't want to screw up and that I hadn't anything to bargain with.'

'To which you replied?'

'That I held the ace of trumps – the fate of the money.'

'OK, Miss Moneybags, what then?'

'He told me not to move from the phone all day and to await instructions.'

'What time did call number two come?'

'Noon.'

'Same voice, same caller?'

'Without a doubt.'

'With instructions?'

'Sort of. There has to be just one drop, all the cash in used notes. Standard drill.'

'How long have you been given?'

'Twenty-four hours.'

'Ridiculous!'

'I used the word "absurd": it's shorter and more succinct.'

'I'm glad your sense of humour's holding up.'

'Just a front; self-protection.'

'What was his reply to your *absurd* comment?'

'"Do it or the girl gets it." I said that it would be impossible for my client to pull together that sort of ransom, in cash, with such short notice.'

'I like the *my client* line; very detached and professional.'

'I thought so, too.'

'What about the method and location of the two-way handover?'

'Those directions will follow, with details of where and when. That's how the second call ended. I fielded the third call less than an hour ago. He wanted to know what headway was being made harvesting the money. I said, "No headway." I also said that there could be no further dialogue over a deal without proof that they had something live with which to trade. Seconds later, a young woman's voice came on crying, "Please, please, do as he says. I know he'll kill me if you don't. He has a knife to my throat." I asked her what the time was, but he came back on the line, saying I'd heard enough.'

'So the voice was a recording?'

'That's my guess.'

'Did you make that accusation?'

'I said I wasn't prepared to accept what I'd heard as evidence of Tammy's well-being. I demanded I be allowed to put questions to her.'

'And he refused?'

'He became agitated and aggressive again; all bluster and bluff.'

'Maybe they're holed up in a different time-zone location, which would have been revealed if Tammy had answered your question. Perhaps he suspected you of being devious.'

Tandy wasn't persuaded.

'We keep referring to *kidnappers* and *they*, but so far everything points to a solo operation,' Templeman moved on.

'That's my assessment, too.'

'How did the third call end?'

'With his saying that Tammy's mother would regret my delaying tactics.'

'Nothing else?'

'No. Down came the guillotine. Symbolic castration.'

'No time-fix for another call?'

'Nothing. Left in limbo. Keeping the tension taut, as you'd say.'

'Did you play Tammy's message to Nancy?'

'Yes. It was her daughter's voice, all right.'

'How did she take it?'

'Hysterically. She's pleading with me to settle. "Just get it over with and let me have my baby back," she keeps sobbing. It's hard – on us both.'

'That's exactly why anyone emotionally involved should always be kept out of the frontline in these delicate negotiations.'

'I pointed out to her she was smart enough to recognize that very fact at the outset, the reason why she turned to me, and now it was crucial that she kept her nerve.'

'Have you given Ronnie, Tammy's dad, an update?'

'Within the last few minutes, yes.'

'Is he still on board?'

'He's as ragged as Nancy and is also pushing for a quick-fix solution. I explained, as patiently as possible, that it doesn't work that way, if you want to avoid being ripped off and to give the hostage the best possible chance of survival.'

'Did he buy into that'?'

'As best a father could, in the circumstances.'

'This is too big for one person to handle.'

'You've got your hands full in Oxford. You can't walk away from that, not after giving your word. There are more lives at stake there than here. This job is strictly business. Oxford is personal; it's all about you, your destruction, your resurrection and absolution, and settling the score over the unsolved mystery of Charley, plus the cat-and-mouse killer's determination to draw you into the ultimate mind-game. Like it or not, you're pivotal to the killer's nemesis.'

Templeman went to sleep that night feeling like a body in a murky river, weighed down by a cement weight. Sinking. Drowning. Depressed by the daunting knowledge that, without an eleventh-hour reprieve, the unknown next victim would be waking in the morning to her last full day among the living – a script for the worst of nightmares.

The nocturnal nightmares, however, didn't compare with those of the morning.

Templeman was called to reception just as he was leaving the restaurant after a late breakfast. A small package, wrapped in brown paper and bearing the previous day's Oxford date-stamp, had been delivered for him in the morning mail. His name and the address of the hotel had been written in capital letters with a ballpoint pen.

As he mounted the staircase, two steps at a time, to his room, he was overcome by an oppressive foreboding. Cold with fear, he entered his room with his pulse fluttering in his neck and temples, and a nervous tick developing in one eye. A sweaty suffusion, like an autumn dew, had spread in seconds to every surface of his goose-pimpled flesh. His heart was beating to the frenetic rhythm of panic. Instinctively, he knew what awaited him, yet denial was irresistible as a temporary salve and hiding place.

Professionalism quickly took over. He knew better than to tear off the wrapping paper, so he proceeded methodically and with care. Beneath the brown paper was a slim, jeweller's cardboard box, no doubt originally the resting place of a neck-lace or bracelet. The lid hadn't been sealed and came off easily. Inside was a ring. A gold wedding ring. Charley's ring – no question about that, because it was still around her finger.

CHAPTER 10

The wedding ring was passed to Forensics after being removed from the severed finger by a Home Office patholo- gist, using facilities at the Radcliffe Hospital. Inside the ring an inscription, so small that it was legible only under a micro- scope, read: *From Here To Eternity. Saw the film, loved every minute of it, but not as much as I love you!*

A note – once again a printout from a computer or word processor – had been neatly folded beneath the finger, its tone a mocking allusion to the sentiment of the inscription: *How breathtaking the brevity of eternity! How feckless the female species, especially the so-called existentialists! By midnight tomorrow, there will be one less cockroach in the world. Vermin, beware!* The 'J and H' sign-off was repeated. Forensic detectives lifted finger- prints from the ring, but they all belonged to Charley.

There were no surprises from pathology. The finger had been amputated, after death, with a clean, clinical chop, prob- ably with something like a butcher's or surgeon's implement. Echoes of Jack the Ripper, thought Templeman. Like the previous hacked-off finger, it had been preserved in cold storage and had thawed while in the postal system.

The profiler, Helen Ridout, was summoned to a mid-after- noon meeting with Hardman and Templeman in Oxford's central police station, sandwiched between Christ Church College and Folly Bridge.

'You *have* to be there,' Hardman told Templeman, in a beseeching supplication rather than a bullish order, as they snatched a beer and ploughman's lunch in The Head of the

River pub, alongside the Folly Bridge pontoon. 'I daren't be alone with that woman. She gives me the creeps. They all do.'

'*All?*'

'Those profilers. All that mumbo jumbo! The new breed of arty-farty chief constables love the drivel, of course. They call it a part of cerebral policing. I call it crap.'

'I've met worse,' said Templeman, erring on the side of diplomacy, straddling the fence and diluting his candid opinion of Ridout, which would have been, I think she has a lot going for her. Give her a break. She's OK.

The meeting took place in one of the compact conference rooms. The three of them spread themselves at the round table, writing pads and drinking glasses in front of them. A lonely jug of water, positioned like a flower vase in the centre of the table, deputized as the room's only ornament. Sparsity was the theme, especially when it came to the agenda.

'We're having this meeting at the request of the chief constable,' Hardman began. Hardly coded at all was the real message: *Let's play the game just to pacify old Badger and get it over with as quickly as possible, so we can return to grown-up detective work with those who have already mastered joined-up writing.*

Not once did Hardman allow his eyes to engage Ridout's. His hostility hung in the air like a miasmic smog over downtown Los Angeles. 'I take it we're all familiar with the contents of the latest wish-you-were-here despatch from Mr Genocide?' He glanced at Templeman as he spoke, though really addressing Ridout.

Neither Templeman nor the profiler answered; there was no need. The question was rhetorical and merely a formula for making a start.

'What, if anything, can we learn from it?' Hardman continued, pained.

It was a collective appeal, though, in reality, only one person was expected to reply at this stage, and she performed on cue.

'The latest communication confirms that *he* is of at least average intelligence and has had a reasonable education. There is the use of alliteration – "breathtaking the brevity" and "feckless the female" – that demonstrates a certain appreciation of our language. "Existentialists" isn't a word you'd expect to see in a communiqué of this description. It's showy; bizarre exhibitionism, really. *He's* attracted to strong words, which go with his actions: cockroach, vermin, beware. He also displays a sense of drama: "By midnight tomorrow, there will be one less cockroach in the world." He's fussy – yes, that's something that leaps out, to my mind – and he's even particular about punctuation. Probably a perfectionist, precise and punctilious. *He's* angry, very much so, but it's suppressed for much of the time, until suddenly exploding. It erupts in his messages, then when he kills. Yet there's no compulsion to murder.'

'So he can control that anger?' Templeman ventured, ending the monologue.

Hardman, continuing to thrum the table impatiently with his nicotine-stained fingers, cocked his head inquisitively towards Templeman, still assiduously avoiding eye contact with Ridout.

'That's certainly a peculiar feature of this case,' Ridout agreed. 'His killing doesn't appear to be choreographed by a biological impulse.'

'What the fuck does that mean?' Hardman, unlike the serial killer, had difficulty controlling himself.

'He plans ahead, he's clinical about his crimes, spontaneity plays no part, thus reducing to a minimum the chance of a mistake, and there's logic to it all,' Ridout answered equably.

'*Logic!*' Hardman exploded, his bloodshot eyes popping from their frayed sockets and spume seeping out of the corners of his empurpled mouth.

'It all makes sense to *him*,' Ridout explained, her tolerance intact. 'In his own addled mind, his victims deserve to die. Their sins have put them beyond redemption. The *sins* are what millions of other people probably regard as virtues.'

'So he's a religious nut – in your *esteemed* view?' Hardman couldn't bring himself to be polite, not even for just a few minutes and in his own interest.

'Not necessarily; very unlikely, in fact, as I've already explained to Luke.'

'How do you figure out that, then?'

Hardman was working hard at being difficult.

'He's judging women by his own morality, his own distorted code. He *is* God. These women have transgressed his commandments, *sins* for which there can be no forgiveness. But he's not acting as self-appointed executioner for the god of any of the world's traditional religions. He's his own god, without disciples; a secret, unyielding deity, known only to himself.'

Hardman was tired of this talkie-talkie hogwash, as he thought of it.

'Who is this psycho, then?' Hardman now confronted Ridout with goose-necked aggression.

'I can't tell you that; that's not the job of a profiler.'

'Exactly!' Hardman boomed, banging a fist on the desk. 'What's the point of all this clap-trap if it's purely academic and doesn't help us get any nearer the bastard? In fact, if anything, it hinders us because we've just squandered more precious minutes. Thanks!'

'My analysis of the latest note should assist in identifying the type of person who *isn't* the serial killer,' Ridout defended herself.

'Bloody marvellous! My job's to catch the killer and here we are listening to a so-called expert who has the ability to give us an insight into everyone who didn't do it! Are you being paid for this?'

Templeman decided the time was ripe to break up this fracas.

'The killer read the inscription I had engraved on Charley's wedding ring. This means he removed the ring, used some kind of magnifying glass to read what was on the inside, and then put it back on her finger. No fingerprints of his on the ring, so he was being meticulously careful yet again. He was wearing gloves, suggesting foresight and forward planning, rather than impromptu behaviour. Charley's fingerprints haven't been wiped off, so he wasn't worried that he might be leaving any trace of himself on the ring.' And then to Ridout, 'Wouldn't you say that this latest communication is brimful of antipathy towards strong, independent women?'

'Categorically, yes.'

'So we've narrowed down the number of suspects to about ten million!' Hardman seethed. 'Great detective work! Which one of us is going to collect the commendation?'

Kicking back his chair petulantly, Hardman leapt to his feet and headed for the door, addressing his next remarks to Templeman. 'I think we both have more important things to do than sit around a table playing the game of guess-and-seek.'

Just before slamming the door behind him, he said to Ridout, while his eyes darted elsewhere, 'When you have the name, address, phone number and e-mail address for our serial killer, please call me. Until then …' He somehow managed to impose self-censorship just in time. The glass panels vibrated on his departure, as if Oxford had just been hit by a mini-earthquake.

'See what I mean?' complained Ridout, alluding to her professional incompatibility with Hardman.

'I saw … and heard,' Templeman said flatly. 'How about a coffee?'

'No, thanks, but offer me a triple gin and tonic, and the answer's yes, yes, yes.'

It was only after they had parted, following a couple of stiff drinks in the Randolph, that the word "cockroach" from the note, assumed a significance far greater than a mere casual insult. Templeman was reminded of his trawl through the archives at the *Oxford Mail* and the website of the Kentucky-based, extremist evangelical group that had denounced Gloria Swift as a 'human cockroach'.

Cockroach! Coincidence or a clue?

Templeman vowed to find out – if possible, before the deadline.

Tandy was running on high octane in rarefied air. In the clouds. Flying. Animated. Irrepressible. 'She's alive, Luke!' she effused. 'We've got something to play for. A live show! How about that?'

'You're sure?' Templeman said, doubtfully, not wanting to dampen her spirits.

'OK, let me fill you in. It got to 4 p.m. and still no call,' she trilled. 'I was beginning to fear the worst. I really thought I'd blown it. Nancy was in a state, I can tell you, popping valium like feeding crumbs to ducks and washing them down with vodka, turning into a schizo – comatozed for an hour, then waking in an aggressive rage. Ronnie was calling every half-hour, becoming increasingly agitated with each negative bulletin. Then, just after 4.30, the call came that we'd been waiting for since dawn. A young woman said, "This is Tammy and I'm just calling to let my mom know I'm being treated OK, but this won't last much longer. You must help me. You must get mom to follow instructions to the letter." At that point, the phone was taken from her and the guy came on, saying, "Satisfied?"'

'But you weren't?'

'Course not. I said that Tammy's little speech could have been prerecorded and that I had to be allowed to ask her one question. He said, "OK, just one," and Tammy came back on the line.'

'What was your question?'

'I simply asked her to tell me what date Christmas Day would be this year.'

'Nice one.'

'I thought so, too. It wasn't something anyone could have anticipated and had prerecorded, ready to play with the punch of a button, which could have been the case if I'd asked for the current date, day or time.'

'What was her reaction?'

'Kind of spaced out.'

'Natural, in other words.'

'Yeah. After a sort of nervous giggle, she said something like, "December 25th, of course!" as if I was the one in need of help.'

'Then she was taken off air, right?'

'Brusquely, I'd say. I heard her crying as she was bundled away from the phone, as part of the special effects, I guess. The guy told me that there would be no further opportunity to speak with Tammy until the exchange. I was determined to stay in control as far as possible and said there'd be no deal without verification just prior to the handover of the cash that Tammy hadn't been harmed.'

'How did that go down?'

'Same as every other condition I've ever tried to impose. He swore at me and reiterated that I was in no position to make demands. I just took it on the chin and prepared to beef it out. All the money has to be in hundred-dollar bills.'

'Can you come up with that?'

'Ronnie says no prob.'

'What about the timetable and location?'

'He'd say no more than that from tomorrow I should be ready to be on the move.'

'How the hell are you going to cope without back-up?'

'It's not as if we'll be angling for an arrest. I'm not setting a trap, hoping to lure him into the net. I have only one objective – to get Tammy reunited, unharmed, with her family. After that, who knows.'

'When will you be in possession of the moolah?'

'Ronnie's promised to have it to us before midnight. He'll be coming round with one of his minders.'

'Was Nancy with you when you spoke to her daughter?'

'No. I've insisted she be in another room at all times during negotiations. If she'd been there, she'd have been uncontrollable. I can remain disciplined because I don't have a loved one to lose.'

'I hope you're prepared for a twist in the tail; hopefully, not a scorpion's tail.'

'I know there'll be hiccups and a catch; at least one catch. Yes, I realize it won't go as smoothly as it sounds.'

'The odds are still stacked against a happy ending. The kidnapper won't believe that the police will be kept out of this for ever. Tammy will be able to ID him. Alive, she'll be too big an ongoing danger. And I'll also be amazed if he's prepared to gamble on her parents' continued silence – plus yours. He'll suspect that the Feds are already part of the circus.'

'You reckon I'm heading towards a double-cross, eh?'

'You can bet on it.'

Tandy began the descent from her high.

They were both jumpy about their respective countdowns and this night's transatlantic catch-up call ended without the usual endearments.

Morning came too soon for Templeman. His wake-up alarm seemed to be sounding just as he was slipping into the best bit of his sleep.

Around the same time, Rita Cardew was taking her black labrador, Bruiser, for its routine early-morning walk around the tree-lined roads of north Oxford. Halfway along Linton Road, not far from Wolfson College and the sleepy River Cherwell, she heard her name being called from behind. She stopped, turned, then smiled, while Bruiser cocked a leg businesslike against a tree.

'You're out early, George.'

'Best time of the day. Especially in summer. I always jog before breakfast. Nothing too strenuous, mind you. Just enough to get the lungs pumping and the circulation flowing.

Ten minutes outward bound, ten minutes back. Sets me up for the day.'

'I hardly recognized you in a tracksuit.'

'You don't think I'm the athletic type, eh?' He was breathing laboriously, his face red and sweaty.

'I didn't mean that at all,' said Mrs Cardew apologetically. 'It's just that I've never seen you before like this, all sporty. You look like a boxer out training for a fight.'

'I'm flattered, Rita. Will you and Henry be at the Ashomolean this evening for the preview of the new addition to the Raphael collection?'

'I'll be there, but Henry's got to motor up to Birmingham on business and expects to be staying there overnight.'

'See you this evening, then, Rita.'

'Yes. Take care. Don't do yourself an injury!'

After giving the air one flamboyant punch, startling Bruiser, the jogger trotted off, quickly fading into the leafy distance, leaving Rita Cardew muttering to her dog, 'What an obsessive!'

A few minutes after 11 a.m., Carla North had descended the stone steps of the town hall into St Aldate's, when she collided with a man apparently hurrying down the hill in the direction of Folly Bridge.

'Fancy bumping into *you* like this!' she exclaimed chirpily.

'You could say you swept me off my feet – quite literally,' the man joked. 'What have you been up to in that den of iniquity? More lobbying of the parasites? More hell-raising?'

'No politicking this time. Just booking the hall for a public meeting.'

'Oh, no, not another call to arms to the blue-stocking brigade of Oxford?'

'National Sexual Harassment Awareness Week is coming up shortly and I'm taking part in its launch, kicking off with a public meeting. You should come along, George, you might learn something. Men are victims these days as well as women.'

'You never change, Carla.'

'And what's that supposed to mean?'

'Always the woman with a cause.'

'Always a *good* cause.'

'And always with the last word.'

'I don't believe you're the chauvinist you'd have me take you for.'

'That could be a big mistake, Carla. Fatal, even.'

They parted laughing.

George, with a copy of that day's *Oxford Mail* tucked under an arm, continued down St Aldate's, beyond Christ Church College and the police station and law courts (on the opposite side) to The Head of the River pub, where he ordered a coffee rather than an alcoholic drink. This was a day for staying sober and clear-headed.

Business at this ever-popular riverside watering hole wasn't yet brisk. The lunchtime trade wouldn't start in earnest for another hour, so he had a choice of tables under parasols on the patio. He chose a spot next to the water's edge, put his feet on the low parapet and idly followed with his eyes the pleasure boats starting their downstream trips from the landing-stage across the Thames. Further down, a couple of college eights were just taking to the water from their respective boathouses. It was the perfect day for people-watching. Not a cloud in sight. The sun was burning its way towards its meridian. A southerly breeze was moderating the temperature and a comfortably warm day was forecast.

After a few minutes of sipping his coffee and soaking up the soporific scene, he turned his attention to the newspaper. Almost the entire front page was consumed by the heading, *D-Day*! In this instance, D stood for death, of course. A faint smile began creeping across his sardonic face as he read on. The story turned inside to pages two and three. The background to the previous murders was repeated on pages four and five. There were warnings to all women from the police. Quotes from Templeman and Hardman expanded his smile. 'No one should underestimate the danger posed by this maniac,' said

Templeman. 'He started by killing my wife, for an obscure reason known only to him. He happily allowed me to take the blame for that crime. Since then, he has pitilessly sent three more talented women to their graves. He has vowed to add to that terrible toll today. For God's sake, make him fail. Frustrate him. The police are making progress, but unless he makes a rare mistake today, he's unlikely to be caught before the deadline. If I were an Oxford woman, I'd lock my doors, stay at home and cancel today. What's twenty-four hours in the context of a lifetime?'

But you're not a woman, Templeman. Therefore you don't think like one. You're wasting your powers of reasoning. They don't deserve your protection. What's more, they'll resent your advice as well as ignore it.

Hardman's quotes pushed the smile into a chortle. 'I can't say we're any nearer catching him than when he first killed, but we're closing in. All we need is a little more time, just one stroke of luck.'

How can they be closing in if they're no nearer than they were more than two years ago? What a prat! It's a contradiction. The man's a buffoon. At least Templeman is rational.

He stayed at The Head of the River until a little after noon, when the pub began filling quickly with lunchtime tipplers. He made his way purposefully back up to the High Street, past University College, the Examination Schools, until arriving at the Botanic Garden, just before Magdalen Bridge. Now he loitered awhile, checking his wristwatch repeatedly, as if waiting for someone who was late for a rendezvous. He lit a cigarette and drew on it heavily, as if sucking venom from a snake-bite. He was still outside the Botanic Garden as Professor Pamela Easton emerged through the golden stone gateway. She was preoccupied, bearing a faraway expression and not seeing further than her mind's eye.

'Hello, Professor.'

Startled out of her reverie, Professor Easton looked up just before crashing into the man blocking her path.

'Oh, hello, George. There's no need to be so formal. Surely

we've known one another long enough for us to be on first-name terms?'

'Blame my professional training. It makes me rather stuffy, I'm afraid. How's Champ?'

'Oh, much better, thanks. I really was worried about him, but he's definitely on the mend.'

'Glad to hear it. Will you be going to the Ashmolean tonight?'

'I wouldn't miss it for anything. We discussed the invitation last week, didn't we?'

'We did indeed. Will Edward be coming, too?'

'Afraid not. Too busy; as always. Won't be leaving the office until gone eight.'

'Well, I'd better be getting along, Pamela. See you later.'

'I'm looking forward to it.'

Lemmings. Helpless, hopeless lemmings. Pushing and shoving to be first to the abyss. Heedless of warning upon warning, they keep coming, offering themselves unwittingly as sacrifices at the altar of human arrogance and stupidity. Always the martyr! So let's give them an epitaph. Let them have their big day. So consumed by themselves. Bloated with self-importance. Judgment Day. Which one shall wear the crown of thorns? Who is most deserving? Which one has the ugliest mind? Too late to review the situation. The decision has been made. Done and dusted. Ashes to ashes. Dust to dust. Those spared today can pay their dues at a future date.

Three apparently accidental meetings within six hours. Each one, in reality, engineered with clockwork precision, an artifice to confirm that the shortlisted trio were keeping to the schedules he had garnered from inside sources without arousing suspicion. Homework was the key. Homework, homework and then more homework.

Rita Cardew, Carla North and Pamela Easton had much in common. Cardew was a zoologist who lectured at Merton College. Her husband, Henry, was chief executive of a stockbroker firm, with offices in Oxford, London and Birmingham.

Cardew, aged thirty-eight, was twelve years younger than her husband. They didn't have children and Rita was proud to project herself as a 'career woman'. She was renowned world-wide for her academic papers and media articles to justify the proposition that the female was the dominant gender of the human species. She had caused much controversy – not to mention outrage – with her contention that man would be redundant as soon as scientists had perfected laboratory reproduction. She saw the day when chemical sperm was mass-produced by drug companies and the role of men would decline to the point where they were nothing more than pet eunuchs, treated like cats and dogs within the family – if they were lucky! Anyone less attractive would probably have been dismissed as an eccentric, but Cardew was blessed with that potent combination of brains and beauty.

Carla North had been championing women's causes ever since she was asked at her first job interview how soon it would be before she was pregnant and was applying for maternity leave. A solicitor by profession, she specialized in industrial law. Most of her clients tended to be women, because of her politics, and the majority of her working time was spent in industrial tribunals or preparing for them. She wasn't married, but had a partner – another woman, Christine Lockyer. The two women had first met at a women's refuge, to which Lockyer had fled after taking one beating too many from her husband. The police had sent for North, who was now approaching her fortieth birthday. Her temperament matched her fiery red hair, but the pain she had witnessed over the years was reflected in her eyes. She always seemed to be shrouded in a mist of melancholy.

At the ripening age of forty-three, Professor Pamela Easton was one of the country's leading botanists, but her reputation in the cerebral city of Oxford went way beyond her specialist subject. Since her student days at Keele University in Staffordshire, she had been a vociferous feminist, the bane of every male bastion. Although she had been living with Edward Lombard, an advertising executive, for almost fifteen years, there had been numerous other men in her life in that period. 'Our free spirit outlook strengthens our relationship,' she was on record as saying. 'If Edward spends a night away from home, I never ask him where he's been and with whom. And if I'm the one who stays out all night unexpectedly, then Edward is equally unfazed. Next day, we pick up the thread of our relationship without recrimination. To be trapped in an unyielding, airtight relationship is my idea of the most frightening form of claustrophobia.'

Professor Easton was childless, but she confessed to two abortions while at university and another two within the first five years of setting up home with Edward. Described variously as a 'velvet virago' and a 'beguiling viper', she concealed her intensity behind a mask of self-effacing urbanity.

Three doughty women in the prime of life. All with so much to live for. Yet, in under twelve hours, there would be only two. Which one would be gone? Only one person knew and he wasn't telling. Such a deadly secret could never be shared. Well, not until *he* was ready. Not until *he* was prepared for full recognition; his place in history. To retire undefeated. Invincible. Peerless among predators. To have won the criminal contest of the century. To have defeated Templeman. The challenge had him salivating.

The beast of the night, so benign by day, waited for sundown, when he reigned supreme.

On the stroke of one o'clock, Templeman made a call from his temporary office – his hotel room – to Joe Parmitter, an FBI agent in Washington who had become almost a friend since Templeman had migrated to America. Templeman had helped Parmitter out a couple of times with freelance surveillance and the FBI agent had said, 'I owe you.' Twice.

In Washington it was 8 a.m. and Templeman, in his mind's eye, could see the heavyweight black officer shedding his jacket at his purely functional, metallic desk, yawning and stretching expansively, then padding to the temperamental drinks machine in the corridor just outside his office to coax out a sweet black coffee. Back at his desk, like a tanker that has just docked, he would loosen the knot of his sober, dark-blue tie, adjust the gold-studded cufflinks in his freshly laundered white shirt and appraise his day's horrendous workload. The incoming-call light would flash mutely on the console just to his right on the tidy desk. He would swear under his breath as he took the polystyrene cup from his lips, muttering something to himself like, 'How is it that someone somewhere always knows the moment I clock in?'

And then, politely into the phone, 'Good morning, Agent Parmitter speaking.'

'Hi, Joe.'

'Who's that?' Parmitter was momentarily thrown by the English accent, but he had coupled the voice with face before Templeman had a chance to identify himself. 'It's Luke, right?'

'Got it in one, but no prize, I'm afraid. Too easy.'

'Well, what can I do for the early bird?'

'Nothing early about this bird where I am.'

'And where might that be? Don't tell me you're cruising the calypso seas and you just called to make me jealous.'

'No. Oxford, England, where it's currently 1 p.m. Half the day gone already.'

'Well, well, I *am* honoured. You paying for this call?'

'No, but if I was I'd still have made it.'

'OK, so I'm excessively honoured.' Parmitter's voice was baritone-deep and rich. 'What's the favour you're touting for?'

'I didn't know mind-reading was included in your catalogue of talents.'

'I wasn't born yesterday, that's all. I got the smell, man. I can smell favour requests way off, down phones and across oceans.'

'OK, I'll get straight to the point.'

'I doubt whether I'll hear a better idea all day.'

'There's a zealous anti-abortion organization, based in Kansas, calling itself God's Revolutionaries for the Unborn. It has a website, but what it preaches doesn't seem very godlike.'

'You mean its disciples advocate nuking, garrotting, castrating or plunging in acid baths anyone who doesn't agree with them?'

'Something like that. But you're wondering what has this to do with Oxford, England?'

'Now who's the mind-reader?'

Templeman side-stepped the diversion. 'There's a serial killer on the loose here.'

'Only one! Lucky old Oxford! Must be paradise. But what's your angle?'

Templeman treated him to a succinct synopsis, majoring on his role as a consultant and excluding the personal downside that had sucked him into the macabre vortex, blown up by the cyclone of murders.

'And you have reason to believe these Kansas freaks are in some way involved?'

'It's a long shot, but there's not much else so far.'

'Sounds to me like you're pretty desperate.'

'Desperately desperate, I'd say!'

'You're not really suggesting that someone from Kansas is commuting to the UK to prune the female population of Oxford? Even for these freaky times, that's pretty far-fetched.'

'No, you're right, that *is* too far-fetched. It's just that there could be a connection. There's a possibility – put it no stronger than that that the perp has been influenced by the website.'

'And for that to have happened, he'd probably be a regular visitor to the site.'

'Exactly.'

'And you want me to try to find out if someone from the Oxford area, England, has been among the hits?'

'I couldn't have put it better myself. Any chance?'

'How soon?'

'Within the next five hours.'

Parmitter manufactured a derisive guffaw. 'Listen, man, we have enough of our own top-priority serial investigations to pursue without going global, never mind promoting them to the top of the pile.'

Templeman resorted to emotional blackmail. 'You could be helping to save a life. The perp has sworn to strike again tonight. One thing we've learned to our cost is that he's a man of his word. It's no hype to say we're into the final hours of a race against the clock. You could make the breakthrough. You could make the difference—'

'Don't tell me, the difference between life and death,' Parmitter interrupted. 'Oh, shit, Luke! You reckon that mawkish crap's going to cut ice with me? What you think I am, some greenhorn sucker?'

'I'm not thinking any of that, Joe. I'm approaching you as a friend and a fellow professional – and one who owes me. Twice.'

Templeman knew exactly where to find the pressure points.

'Oh, shit!' Parmitter repeated himself.

'Well?'

The FBI agent was nibbling at the bait.

'I'm not going to make any promises.'

'That's good enough for me.'

'Don't get excited. No promises, I said.'

'None expected.'

A contrived sigh. Laboured breathing. Amateur dramatics. A melodramatic production. Templeman could picture Parmitter's big frame expanding and contracting like the lungs of ambivalence, giving oxygen to a decision, then taking it away. The tapping of Parmitter's pen on his desk resonated 3,000 miles away like a monotonous beating metronome; a heartbeat that kept alive Templeman's hopes.

'Give me a number, so I can get back to you … if necessary.'

'You'll be rewarded in heaven, Joe.'

'Is that a promise *you* can keep?'

'No promises.'

'None expected!'

Their reversal of dialogue made for a comradely adieu.

Hardman started his working day with a 6 a.m. briefing in the main conference room at Oxford's central police station. After that, he made a statement over the phone to the *Oxford Mail*, before doing the rounds of television and radio studios for 'live' interviews. While he was making his media appeals, his team were out on the streets, reminding women via loud-speakers on their vehicles to be extra vigilant and wary this day, especially after sunset.

By two o'clock, he was overdue for an alcoholic top-up.

'What you doing?' he said, without preamble, when Templeman picked up.

'Waiting for a call.'

'You just got it.'

'Long distance; transatlantic, in fact.'

'There are more pressing matters today than watering the flower of your life.'

Templeman decided to leave him out of this particular loop. So he said, 'Such as?'

'Such as meeting me in the Lamb and Flag. It's a two-minute walk from the Randolph, in St Giles. I'm just pulling up outside the pub this very minute. I recommend a pint of Spitfire brew. It's firewater, take my word for it. I'll get you one in; make a man of you.' It was a fait accompli. Hardman ended the call before Templeman had a chance to demur.

Templeman was amazed by the change in the detective inspector. Templeman fully expected Hardman to be the shipwreck *before* the storm. Instead, he was the most composed he'd been since Templeman's return to Oxford. Not only had his charcoal suit been pressed, it looked as if it might even have been dry-cleaned. He also wore an unblemished white shirt and black shoes that really appeared to have been polished. His plain blue tie was so dark that indoors anyone would have assumed it was funereal black. He could very easily have been mistaken for an undertaker, seizing the chance for a quick pint and a pie between burnings or burials. That was it, Templeman suddenly realized, as he threaded his way to the bar: Hardman was dressed for death, paying his last respects to the unknown in advance, a down-payment on the grieving to come. He had even done something with his thinning hair to reduce its freedom. But he could not do anything about the dead eyes and ravaged face, of course. However, the improvement was sufficient to make an instant impact on Templeman.

Before Templeman could reach the bar, the detective was heading – with two pints of ale – for a table, so Templeman fell in behind him, making a little, shuffling procession.

'Ah! You're here!' exclaimed Hardman, as Templeman claimed one of the pints, before it even landed on the table. 'Good timing. Cheers!'

Hardman drank half of his drink before sitting. He smacked his lips, rolled his eyes in ecstasy, and wiped the spume from his mouth, knowing that very quickly he would be feeling the benefit of his medicine.

'Well, I'm resigned to my fate,' Hardman said at last, with a world-weary shrug, as soon as they were settled, as if he was the one facing the executioner. 'There's nothing more that can be done now today. What will be will be. All we can do is brace ourselves and wait.' He paused and almost finished his pint before Templeman had started. 'My, that was good! Heady nectar!'

'Good health, good luck,' Templeman said, out of meaningless habit, before wetting his beak. Then, 'You seem remarkably collected, considering.'

'No point being anything else,' Hardman said philosophically. 'I intend spending the rest of the day reviewing the evidence of the old cases. Just keeping the investigation ticking over. How about you? Anything to report? Has the fresh pair of eagle eyes spotted something everyone else has missed?'

'I'm not sure.'

A flame of hope suddenly flickered in the detective's eyes and burned into his cheeks. 'You're on to something,' he said eagerly, as if a last-minute lifeline had been thrown to a drowning man. 'I know you are. It's written all over your face. I can read you as easily as a book for four-year-olds.'

'I might have something, I might not.'

'Come on, Luke, don't *mess* with me. Let's have it. Share.'

'I'd rather not.'

'For God's sake, man, time's running out.'

'Mike, if I'm on to something, it won't come in time to change the course of today's events. It's nothing more than a line of inquiry. Already you'll have had hundreds of those. I'm just throwing a dart at a board and waiting to see what number, if any, comes up. Maybe no number at all. Maybe I'm way off target. No score.'

'You can't whet my appetite, then snatch the chalice from my lips.'

'All in good time, Mike.'

'No better time than the present.'

'You realize this could be a tasteless wind-up,' said Templeman, changing the subject.

'What? The perp's published intentions?'

'Yes. The IRA loved to frustrate the British security forces.

Giving false bomb warnings was their party trick. They'd do it half a dozen times. Town centres would be sealed off. Streets would be evacuated. Bomb squads and their sniffer dogs would take over. And they would find nothing. Not even a briefcase filled with stale sandwiches. But the seventh time, when the troops were saying, "Here we go again, another day wasted," and residents and shopkeepers were loathe to leave their premises once more, would be no bluff Bang! And goodbye.'

'This guy doesn't bluff.'

'You don't know that.'

'*I* know.'

'This is the first time he's given advance notice. In the previous cases, the communication has come afterwards.'

'Nevertheless, *I know*. He wouldn't put his *reputation* on the line without being sure of being able to deliver. He'll deliver, you see. We'll have a body by morning. And get this, as dreadful as it might sound, I hope we do. I'm ready for it; fully prepared.'

Templeman flinched and frowned, in that order. 'I shouldn't let anyone else hear you say that.'

'I'm not *that* daft, Luke. I knew you'd understand, though.'

Templeman wasn't sure that he did, so he waited for the explanation.

'The waiting's been the worst part of it, fraying the nerves, driving me to drink.' He emptied the last drops in his glass, as if to underline his point. 'Now life in the waiting room is almost over – hopefully for the last time. Another body might well give us the quantum leap we need. To anyone not in the trade, this would appear callous, but another corpse could be the answer to our prayers. Deliverance! Sooner or later, he has to blunder.'

'Jack the Ripper didn't.'

'Jack the Ripper would have been caught after his first if the police in those days had been blessed with a tenth of the science at our disposal.'

Kidology had become Hardman's palliative for tension and

stress, and Templeman saw nothing to be gained by rubbishing that therapeutic brainwashing.

'If the next victim is the last because, for some reason, her body proves to be a footprint, leading to the door of dénouement, then it won't be such a squandered life as the others. It'll have some meaning.'

Templeman allowed the detective's flawed homily to go unchallenged. 'What's Badger up to?'

'Spinning, as if trapped in a washing machine, while I'm doing everything possible to keep out of his way. How about another Spitfire for short-term relief? Cheaper than a massage.'

'Count me out, but I'll get you one.'

With the refill in place, Hardman tried once more to elicit an insight into Templeman's new line of inquiries.

'Is it possible, just possible, no matter how remote a possibility, that you might turn over a stone today and find a gem of a clue underneath?'

'Of course it's possible. And if I do, you'll be the first to hear about it.' With that, Templeman drank up and made an excuse to leave.

The one man with all the answers was in no hurry. Daylight still had at least another three hours to run. He had returned to Magdalen Bridge to idle in the soporific serenity: punts making slow and silent progress beneath him, powered by young men in college blazers and white flannels, mastering a long pole to generate power. Reclining nubile women in summer frocks. Silent seduction. Coded looks and almost indiscernible body movements, but as decipherable to the recipient as a nod or a twitch to an auctioneer during bidding. Picnic hampers. Wine on water, sipped from crystal glasses with stems as long and thin as drinking-straws. Expensive chocolates nibbled daintily. Cheap condoms protruding from back trouser-pockets. Weeping willows bent in respectful genuflection to the next generation of the country's protagonists. The sound of a cricket ball being hit somewhere beyond the fringe of trees. The perfume of affluence far stronger than nature's summer scent. This was mid-summer's bliss at its best.

And the man with all the answers dropped a coin from the bridge into the muddy-brown water and imagined he was peering into the fountain in Rome's St Peter's Square. The font of the future. He remembered watching one Christmas Day an old movie on TV, *Three Coins in the Fountain*. The eponymous song rang in his ears: *Three coins in the fountain, which one will the fountain bless?* The coins in the movie had been thrown in by three young women. And to the same tune, he put the words of his own corrupted version: *Which one will the fountain curse?* Adding: *I know, but does the fountain?*

The incoming transatlantic call to Templeman, at a few minutes after 3 p.m. that afternoon wasn't the one he'd been hoping for, though it was most welcome.

'I'm calling you because I'll be out of touch for most of the rest of the day,' Tandy began in a torrent. 'I've a tight timetable to keep; that's why I'm talking so fast. I want you to be aware of what's happening, just in case it ends in tears all round.'

Templeman tensed up.

'These are my instructions: I drive from Naples to Miami International Airport, where I leave my car in the long-stay parking lot. A return ticket to San Francisco is being held for me, in my name, at the United Airlines sales counter. The caller said I'm booked on the three o'clock flight.'

Templeman instinctively checked his wristwatch and made the time conversion. 'That gives you just under three hours,' he said.

'It's a two-hour drive, as you know, without a hold-up, which means I must get cracking within the next five minutes. I have the money in a briefcase, as instructed. Apparently, I have a pre-designated seat, 22C. I have to board the flight as early as possible, placing the briefcase in the overhead locker. Just before the plane is about to leave the gate, I've to complain of feeling ill and insist I'm taken off the flight. It's standard procedure, anyhow. No airline wants to take the risk of a medical emergency in the sky when it can be avoided. Having to make unscheduled landings is not only very costly, it also results in disgruntled passengers, especially if it means that connections and important business meetings are missed. The flight will be delayed only a few minutes because I won't have any luggage to be located in the hold and removed.'

'So you vacate the aircraft, probably in a wheelchair, leaving behind the briefcase?'

'So it would seem.'

'What then?'

'Tammy will be left for collection in the foyer of the Sheraton Riverside Hotel, just outside the airport.'

'I know it. Let's run through this again because it doesn't stack up. It's full of holes. Certainly it blows away our theory that there's only one kidnapper. There must be at least two. One of them will be on the aircraft, presumably in a seat from which he or she has a clear view of you; maybe in the seat next to you even. Once you're taken off the plane, the kidnapper on board has to have a means, without arousing suspicion, of checking the contents of the briefcase to verify that all the money's there.'

'I'm only guessing now, but the plan must be that he texts his accomplice or accomplices to confirm that the ransom has been paid. He'll also probably have a text ready to shoot off should cops board the plane at Miami, before take-off, to impound the briefcase. If that happened, Tammy wouldn't be released at the hotel. She'd be driven away and disposed of, that's the intimation.'

'Even so, it's still all wrong. The flight from Miami to San Francisco takes almost six hours; tons of time for the Feds to be out in force to meet the aircraft on its touchdown on the west coast. Once you've got Tammy back safely, what reason have they to believe the cops wouldn't be called in?'

'I reckon that's all accounted for.'

'What do you mean?'

'I think that's included in the equation, that I'll be thinking exactly what you've just said, that we'll have almost six hours in which to arrange for the briefcase and its carrier to be bagged as the passengers disembark at San Francisco.'

'But what we see as the big flaw isn't really there at all, like a conjuring trick, an illusion?'

'That's how I figure it.'

'At least this gives us the chance to do our public duty, without endangering Tammy's life.'

'No, Luke. The police must be kept completely in the dark, at least until I have Tammy safe and sound.'

'I have no quarrel with that. The moment you have her, call me. You need say only two words – 'Got her!' I know just the man to tip off after that; someone who would then owe me such a big favour that he might even come up trumps for me.'

'For *you*?'

'Well, for the Thames Valley police, for those hunting the Oxford serial killer, which, yes, includes me. Very much me. For me, this is as personal as it gets, don't forget.'

'Close to your heart, huh?'

'I didn't say that.'

'Good. Now I must go.'

Rita Cardew, resplendent in a white lightweight summer trouser-suit, caught a bus in the Banbury Road for the city centre. Ten minutes later, at 7.18 p.m., she was trotting across St Giles, with St John's College behind her. The traffic was still coming in pulses and she had to dodge cars as she headed deliberately for Beaumont Street and the grandiose Ashmolean Museum. Just as she reached the wide steps of the museum, she spotted Professor Pamela Easton approaching hurriedly on foot from the opposite end of Beaumont Street, so she waited to allow them to go in together.

'Hello, Pamela. I'm glad you could make it. It's always nice to have an ally.'

Easton returned the greeting with equal cordiality. She was also wearing a trouser-suit, though hers was a pale pink. Neither of them had bothered with makeup and their hair had a left-alone, natural look to it. Both wore patterned platform shoes. Easton had decorated herself with accessories crafted by North American Indians, while Cardew ostentatiously displayed a necklace and bracelets of bulky amethysts.

'I hope there's a good turnout,' remarked Cardew.

'Well, we'll soon find out,' said Easton.

A few seconds later they were inside Britain's oldest museum, famous not only for its Raphael drawings but also the masterpieces of Michelangelo and Turner, plus the richest collection of Greek pottery and Egyptian artefacts from 200,000 BC to AD 640.

Simultaneously, Carla North was hosting in Ruskin College

a 'Know Your Rights' workshop for women employees. Ruskin College was just around the corner, in Walton Street, from the Ashmolean. She, too, would have liked to have been among the lucky levees in the historic museum, but the preview clashed with her weekly commitment at Ruskin.

Cardew and Easton left the Ashmolean together at a little after 9.30, with Cardew commenting, 'I didn't see George, did you?'

'George?'

'George Carey.'

'No, now you come to mention it, I don't think he could have been there.'

'Strange. Only this morning he assured me he would be attending.'

'I had a similar conversation with him, also today,' said Easton, then suggesting, 'Maybe he was called to an emergency.'

'More than likely,' Cardew agreed.

Then they went their separate ways into the airless night, with summer, even after dark, still strutting its stuff.

It would be another half an hour before Carla North finished her workshop session, less than a quarter of a mile away, and also set off for her home on foot.

Hardman stayed in his office all night, while Templeman reclined, fully clothed, on his bed, channel-hopping by courtesy of the remote, faraway thoughts pushing local issues to the back-burner. Just before ten o'clock he received the two-word call from Tandy: 'Got her!'

'I don't believe it!' he exclaimed, truly astonished, disbelief still dominant.

'Got her!' Tandy echoed, obviously euphoric, then killed the call.

Parmitter began to protest the moment he recognized Templeman's Anglo voice on the line. 'Harassing me isn't going to help your cause,' he began irritably, before Templeman had got beyond, 'Me again, Joe …

'No harassment, Joe, I'm doing a favour in advance of the

one I just *know* you'll be doing for me very soon. I suggest you have a pack of your west coast hounds meet the 3 p.m. United Airlines flight from Miami to San Francisco. I haven't the flight number, nor the exact time of arrival, but that's information you can find out for yourself in a matter of seconds your end.'

'And why, may I ask, should I be showing an interest in that particular flight?'

Templeman told him, as synoptically as possible.

When he had finished his explanation, there was a hiatus of about three adrenaline-driven heartbeats before Parmitter said challengingly, 'Where you get all this garbage from while sitting on your lazy butt in another goddamn country?'

'That's irrelevant.'

'Hell it is!'

'Do you want a headline-screaming federal bust or don't you?'

'Sure I do, just as long as I can justify the operation to those who control the quality of my work-life and my monthly pay-cheque.'

'Call my partner. Say you're responding to my whisper in your ear. She has the chapter and verse, though don't expect more than a précis. She's wary about talking to strange men. Strangers she can handle, but strange men spook her.'

'Very funny,' said Parmitter, not amused.

'Listen, that flight isn't even halfway to San Francisco, so you have plenty of time to assess the strength of what I'm telling you and to rustle up a suitable reception party with all the balloons and poppers.'

'Leave it with me,' Parmitter said professionally.

'You won't forget the little research job on my behalf, will you?'

'I've already farmed it out. Leave everything with me. Now buzz off!'

Templeman could sense suppressed frisson, even across the ocean.

Christine Lockyer reported Carla North missing a little after 8 a.m.

This was roughly an hour after a woman's fully clothed body had been plucked from the canal in Jericho.

Lockyer's prompt action led to an early identification of the dead woman. Hardman didn't wait for the pathologist's report before adding the name Carla North to the serial killer's roll of wanton conquests, although he stopped short of going public on that score.

Templeman was called at 9.50.

'He's delivered,' Hardman said starkly. 'Body in the canal at Jericho. We already have a positive ID. Carla North. Well known in the city – even to me. One of those old-style women's libbers. All mouth and trousers. A solicitor by profession – wouldn't you know it! A pain in the bum to employers all over the county. No more, though.'

'What's the narrative so far?' said Templeman, crossing his hotel room in loping strides to a chair by the window, his mobile pressed tightly against his right ear.

'She was at Ruskin College yesterday evening until about ten o'clock. The time is only an estimate at the present. Close, though.'

'What was she doing there so late?'

'She ran a weekly workshop, lecturing women about their legal rights in employment. How to harass their paymasters. There won't be many tears shed in the boardrooms of this city, trust me. She had a reputation for being an agitator, stirring up unrest, always fanning the flames of mutiny on the work-deck. She was as unpopular with women bosses as with men.'

'How old?'

'Thirty-nine.'

'Young for a dragon,' Templeman observed dryly.

'Dragons are defined by a state of mind and the fire from their mouths, not by age.'

Not the moment for semantics, so, 'How come you've been able to estimate her time of departure from Ruskin so quickly?'

'Because she had a weekly clockwork routine. The workshop began at 7.30, finishing at 9.30. She'd leave her house in Jericho, which she shared with her lover – another stroppy woman – at 7.15. Although the workshop packed up at 9.30, it would be another half-hour, approximately, before she got away from the college. There'd always be one or two toady prats wanting to speak with her privately at the end, apparently. She also had everything to put away and tidy up. Of course we haven't yet got around to talking with any of the sad cases who attended last night's stir-up, but assuming nothing occurred to change her usual timetable, we can presuppose that her clock stopped after ten.'

Templeman ignored the detective's prejudices. 'Was she reported missing by her soul-mate?'

'Yes, but not until around eight this morning.'

'Why the delay?'

'No delay, really. Quite the opposite, in fact. Christine Lockyer, the lover, likes her vino. After North went out, Lockyer settled down with a bottle of red plonk to listen to music. Classical, of course. Nothing short of Beethoven or Bach. Net result? She slept as heavily as if in a coma until about seven this morning. On the settee. In her day clothes. With her head full of hammering woodpeckers, she tottered upstairs this morning in search of painkillers and also to take her beloved a mug of coffee. She found one, but not the other. Their bed hadn't been slept in. Not even by Goldilocks. She looked in the spare bedroom: still no North. She checked her mobile to see if a text had been sent to her. No joy. Neither had a message been left on the answer-machine. She hasn't said this, but I guess her first reaction was to suspect that her true love had been playing away from home.'

'So she gave it almost an hour's consideration before notifying the police.'

'Natural enough,' Hardman opined.

'Who found the body?'

'A dog-walker. What would become of the world without dog-walkers, the eyes of the universe."

'Man or woman?'

'Woman. It was floating against the canal bank, beside the western towpath. Probably where she was dropped in. The canal's like a duck pond; no tide, no current. And that's as much as I know for now. You're as wise as I am.'

'Has the body been moved yet?'

'Coroner's officers have taken it to the Radcliffe. Post mortem's scheduled for noon. Scene-of-crime team has taken over at the canal. Mind you, I doubt whether that's the real scene of the crime. Like the others, she'll have been snuffed out elsewhere.'

'You'll get him this time.'

'Don't patronize me, Luke. What earthly justification have you for saying that? I'm not a child, so don't treat me as if I need humouring.'

'I mean what I say; you'll nail him. There's no doubt now about the category from which he selects his victims. He has a murderous hang-up about dominant women. Not just powerful women. They're achievers, high-flyers, women at the cutting edge of change and reform. Controversial women in the spotlight. Trail-blazers. Ball-breakers.'

'Could be me, then. Could be ninety per cent of the male population.'

'There's a vast difference between the urge to prick a balloon and to strangle it,' said Templeman. 'Something else.'

'Better be good.'

'Our man had to be familiar with Carla North's lifestyle and her itinerary. Take that one logical step further and it's reasonable to suppose that he was privy to the itineraries of the other victims. Which means ...'

'He moves in their social and professional circles,' Hardman completed Templeman's analysis.

'Which dramatically reduces the field of runners. This time is the last time. I mean it, Mike.'

'Let's hope your optimism is well founded. In the meantime, have you anything to report on the follow-up to your hunch you mentioned yesterday?'

'Not yet.'

'Has anyone told you how infuriating you can be, Luke?'

'Frequently. Keep me posted.'

'As it happens, I promise.'

'Ciao for now.'

Templeman felt helpless. He *was* helpless. There was nothing – absolutely nothing – he could do without input from others. It was too early at 5 a.m. Washington time to call Parmitter. Same time in Florida, so calling Tandy was also ruled out, even though he was itching for news about the outcome of her saga.

Seeking a distraction, he turned on the TV. Scheduled programmes on all channels had been interrupted with newsflashes about the macabre discovery in Oxford. Councillor Hugh Grimshaw, the leader of the city council, was pontificating in front of the cameras, acting, badly, as if on the Hollywood set of a basement-budget movie.

'This is becoming intolerable,' he was saying in a contrived orotund To-Be-Or-Not-To-Be Shakespearean voice. 'This cannot be allowed to go on. I will not allow it to go on. Enough is enough. This is Oxford, for heaven's sake! The mother of academia. The centre of intellectual gravity. The meeting place for the world's mighty young minds. Oxford, reduced to a dog-end Detroit by one mindless moron with the intellectual capacity of a maggot, yet capable, it would seem, of running rings around our beleaguered police force. I shall be asking searching questions today. Big questions.'

'Of whom?' asked the pushy woman reporter, who was using her mike like a boxer's leading fist, jabbing away at the councillor's pendulous face.

'The police,' Grimshaw answered vaguely.

'You mean the chief constable?'

'No less.'

'Will you be accusing him of incompetence?'

'Not personal incompetence, no.'

'Collective?'

'What I shall be saying is that the public has lost faith in the police in this particular matter. Rightly or wrongly, the investigation appears to most people to be botched. Bungled. Lacklustre.'

'That would imply you are critical of Detective Inspector Hardman's handling of the strategy.'

'What *strategy*? There doesn't appear to be any strategy; that's the point. That's the bottom line.'

'Will you be calling for Hardman to be replaced?'

'That is something for me to discuss in private with the chief constable. It would be wholly inappropriate to air the minutiae of these concerns in public, pre-empting official discussions.'

'Thank you, Councillor.'

'My pleasure.'

Everything about Grimshaw's posturing and pained insincerity had been vote-grabbing. As he was faded out, the cameras outside the county's police headquarters projected on screen pictures of Chief Constable Humphry Badger, who was posing in his most absurd, sculpted pugnacious stance.

'You've just heard what the leader of Oxford City Council has had to say,' said the TV reporter, this one male and just as goose-necked aggressive.

'I have and I share his worries,' replied Badger, using agreement as a tactical ploy to dilute the poison.

'Does that mean you're dissatisfied with the lead officer's performance?'

'I'm dissatisfied with the lack of progress, another death, and the absence of an arrest.'

'What action will you be taking?'

'Whatever's necessary.'

'Which is?'

'First there has to be an overall appraisal, a rigorous assessment. All will be revealed in the passage of time.'

'But isn't *time* the very luxury you don't have?'

Badger, like a cornered sly fox, searched shiftily for a verbal bolthole. 'Remedies will be swift,' he assured, hamming it up for the cameras; another amateur Thespian.

'Will Luke Templeman be continuing as a consultant on the case?'

'Everything will be reviewed.'

Templeman turned up the volume and looked hard for lies from the feckless face on screen.

'Mr Templeman's appointment was an unusual one, to say the least,' said the reporter, hoping to open yet another can of worms.

'Very.' Badger had got his job in no small part to his commitment to economy, even with words.

'It was at your instigation, I believe.'

'Let's just say I approved it, in principle.'

Ah! The scorpion's tale.

'Have you any regrets?'

'About Mr Templeman's appointment?'

This was hard work.

'Yes.'

'None whatsoever.'

'What *exactly* has he achieved since he arrived?'

'I cannot possibly go into those kind of operational details.'

'Has he been value for money; *public* money?'

'That's something we shall be able to judge only retrospectively. Don't forget, Mr Templeman has been involved for only a relatively short period of time. This is the first killing since his recruitment.'

'There have now been five murders of high-profile women.'

Badger winced at the unpalatable reminder.

'Starting with Templeman's own wife,' the reporter continued remorselessly.

'Correct.' Badger's face went blank as he braced himself for a question that was being disguised until released with maximum top spin.

'A lot of people are asking whether it was wise to bring in someone with such emotional entanglement. Not only was his wife the first victim, he was charged with her murder – and convicted by a jury. He went to prison, wrongfully condemned. There must be a lot of bile and corrosive bitterness trapped inside him.'

'Which might be just the fuel to drive him the extra mile. Of course it's been a gamble, but the situation demanded something unorthodox.'

'But is the gamble paying off?'

'Clearly not in the short-term, but, as I've already stressed, it's early days as regards Templeman's participation.'

Interpret that as meaning I'm into the final hours of my probation, Templeman warned himself.

Hardman, as usual, had been kept away from the cameras, even at the canal, where the body had been hauled from the water and where now the forensic team combed for clues.

Templeman's compulsive viewing was interrupted by the person still uppermost in his thoughts – Tandy.

'I was going to call *you*, but I didn't want to rob you of catch-up sleep,' said Templeman, relief in his voice.

'Me sleeping! No such luck. No sleep. No bed, even. Doing your public duty wasn't one of your better ideas, after all – as I feared. Well, not from my end – the receiving end. To say it backfired is an understatement on a grand scale, like describing the Blitz as party pyrotechnics.' She was prickly, with her mood choreographed by her spleen.

'Tell me about it,' Templeman requested gloomily.

She sighed a tired, exasperated sigh. 'Everything appeared to be going to plan. I got to the airport in plenty of time for the three o'clock United Airlines flight to San Francisco. My ticket was ready for collection at the United Airlines sales desk. I had the money. I boarded as early as poss. I followed instructions to the letter, placing the briefcase in the overhead locker. The aircraft filled up. There was all the usual pre-flight activity. The doors had just closed when I made my move, going to a flight attendant, clutching my chest, complaining of pain and feeling unwell. She immediately fetched the cabin-crew leader, who, in turn, informed the captain via the internal phone system. He made an instant decision that I should be evacuated from the aircraft before we departed the gate. The door was reopened. I was questioned about my baggage. I said I had none, which made everyone happy because any delay would be minimal. Ground staff turned up with a wheelchair and I was rolled off the plane. Easy peasy.'

'Where were you taken?'

'They were going to send for an ambulance, have me whisked off to hospital.'

'Which you couldn't allow to happen.'

'Precisely. So I enacted one of those miraculous biblical recoveries. I didn't just arise and walk, I leapt from the wheel-chair, saying thanks to one and all, explaining I was feeling much better – fine, in fact – and took off, leaving my carers stunned. I retrieved my car from the parking lot and drove to the Sheraton Riverside – and there was Tammy, in a daze, walking around the antrim in circles, looking wretchedly lost, like an abandoned waif.'

'How did you recognize her?'

'Her mother had given me a portrait photo of Tammy, but it was superfluous. She stood out like the proverbial sore thumb. Tangled hair. Unwashed. Bags under her eyes that would have incurred an excess charge if she was catching a plane. Tear-stained cheeks. Chewed-away fingernails. There was no missing or mistaking her, believe me. I ran to her. She was shaking. At first she recoiled from me, afraid that I might be going to harm her. I told her she was safe, that I was the woman she'd spoken to on the phone, and that I was going to take her home. Then I called Nancy with the triumphant news. She was hysterical again, this time with joy. I handed my mobile to Tammy so she could say a few words to her mum. She broke up, too. I was embarrassed in the unwitting role of voyeur. Later, during the drive along Alligator Alley, we stopped for a burger and Coke – the two things she'd missed most. That was when she told me she'd been kept blindfolded the whole time, from the moment she was snatched to her release at the airport hotel.'

'She has no idea where she was kept?'

'None whatsoever.'

'What was the MO of her release?'

'Driven blindfolded in the back of a car, hands tied behind her. When the car stopped outside the hotel, her bonds were cut and she was pushed out.'

'Still with the blindfold on?'

'Yes. She was able to pull it off easily enough once her hands had been freed.'

'Did she get a good look at the car?'

'No, Luke, she'd been blindfolded for all those days. It was a hundred degrees Fahrenheit in the shade. Except there wasn't any shade. She was as blind as if the blindfold was still on when her eyes were mugged by the dazzling sunshine.'

'Were there witnesses to this?'

'I didn't ask her any of those questions. We were being paid solely to get her back safely, if at all possible. I did the business. You didn't believe it could be done. Neither did I, in truth. But I beat all the odds and I expected big celebrations, but I hadn't calculated the effect on the family of your double-cross.'

'*Double-cross*?'

'Doing your damned public duty. Being the honourable gent. Calling your Washington buddy. Trying to keep all wheels oiled. What a boomerang!'

'Go on, hit me with it,' Templeman said, miserably.

'You gave Parmitter my mobile number, right?'

'Nothing wrong with that, surely? I gave you advance warning. You raised no objection then.'

'OK, OK, no recriminations. Too late for that "if only" negative stuff. I was nearing Alligator Alley when he called me. I pulled over. He was demanding to know what the hell was going on, though his actual language was ten times stronger than that. The more I told him, so the more he raged.'

'Why?"

'*Why*! Are you serious? He was raging because the kidnap hadn't been reported at the outset. We were guilty of concealing a federal crime, he screamed. We would have been accessories to homicide if Tammy had ended up dead. He reckoned he could drum up around a hundred crimes for us to be indicted with; each one carrying a sentence that would keep us out of circulation for ever. I thought he was going to have a fit.'

'I take it you explained the terms of engagement.'

'He wasn't listening to reason. In his book, I wasn't doing him a favour, I was making a confession. To everything I said, he kept repeating, "Irresponsible! Reckless meddlers!" Over and over. After I'd given him everything, he cursed and hung up on me.'

'Surely he changed his tune after his troops boarded the flight in San Francisco? Don't tell me they fluffed it?'

'Worse.'

'*Worse*?'

'No briefcase. No money. No-one to arrest. Cuckoo flown the nest.'

'But ... how?'

'I'll tell you how. The cabin crew were questioned at the airport in San Francisco. It transpired that seconds after I'd been wheeled off the plane, a man approached a flight attendant, saying he was a doctor, called to check over Simone Tandy, 'the medical emergency', and that, although she had no luggage in the hold, she'd left a briefcase in the locker above her C22 seat. The flight attendant assumed he had just boarded the plane as part of the ground-staff team. He'd come from the right direction. And, bear in mind, the cabin crew were focused on losing as little time as possible and getting the flight on its way. So she just stood there while he took the briefcase from the locker and walked off the plane, with a friendly wave and a "Have a nice day!"'

'But he hadn't just stepped on the aircraft, he'd been there all the time, as a passenger, watching and waiting for the moment: one of the kidnappers.'

'That's how it looks.'

'And he just strolled off with the ransom.'

'A gift! So simple. So uncomplicated. All the usual problems of the handover neatly avoided. He just vanished into the ether. Even worse was to follow.'

'Do I want to hear this?'

'No, but you're my captive audience, so you're going to have to. Tammy had been reunited with her mother only a couple of hours when the cops descended on their home like the cavalry charging over the hill. Nancy, of course, was outraged and flatly denied everything. Tammy followed her mother's lying lead. Nancy told them I must have invented the whole "fairy story" for publicity purposes, to drum up business.'

'That kind of advertisement we can do without.'

'Luckily – I think! – Ronnie, Nancy's estranged husband, readily admitted he'd put up the money for his daughter's release. Now Nancy is threatening to renege on the remainder of the fee she owes us, on the grounds of breach of faith, breaking the terms of the contract.'

'Surely keeping the lid on it applied only until Tammy was found – either dead or alive?'

'That's my argument. However, in the meantime, I've pleased no-one. I've made lifelong enemies of not only those I hindered, but also those I helped. *Especially* those I helped! And to you, my darling, I might well say, another fine mess you've got us into, Stanley!'

'Was Nancy's upfront payment to you paid by cheque?'

'Yes. And it's been cleared. Why?'

'Because it's proof of her hiring your services.'

'I already made that point.'

'And?'

'She's claiming that I was engaged to dig more dirt on her husband for the divorce.'

'Where are you now?'

'Home. I just got in. I've been up all night answering questions. That's not true. I've been up all night being *interrogated*. Everything but the thumbscrew and Chinese water torture. I've been cautioned not to leave town. The rumpus isn't over by a long way, I fear. The Feds won't settle for anything less than their pound of flesh. And we're the meat. Dead meat if they have their way. The past few hours have been ghastly. The future is going to be ugly.'

This wasn't the moment for Templeman to update Tandy on the latest grisly development in Oxford. He was holding the receiver of his bedside phone with one hand while squeezing the sinus region above his eyes and nose with the thumb and two fingers of his other hand, seeking inspiration and clarity, his thoughts as mixed up as the ingredients in a cocktail-shaker.

'Something's wrong about this whole blasted thing,' he murmured, finally, his confusion less cloudy.

'You're not kidding!' Tandy wasn't yet on his wavelength.

'Have you spoken with Ronnie?'

'I called him from the Riverside. My first call was to Nancy.'

'What was his reaction?'

'Same as Nancy's. I imagined him doing cartwheels.'

'Did he ask to speak with Tammy?'

'Of course.'

'Did you hear any of that conversation?'

'Only what Tammy was saying, plus the occasional word from her father, such as, 'Oh, princess, my little princess!' And she was sobbing, 'Daddy! Daddy! I'm all right. It's all over. I just want to put it all behind me, to get back to normal.' I felt heady, sort of intoxicated, as if at last I'd achieved something really worthwhile in my life. Now ...' Her voice trailed away as emotion rose as a lump in her throat and watered her eyes.

A rogue thought wouldn't leave Templeman alone.

'Have the cops a make on the guy who marched off with the briefcase?'

'If they have, they won't be confiding in me. I do know, however, they're running a check on the passenger list.'

'That won't get them anywhere. *He'll* have paid cash for his ticket, using a bogus name and address.'

'More productive will be the CCTV footage,' Tandy said. 'They'll be going through every inch of film of everyone who checked in for that flight and boarded at the gate. They'll also have *him* on film sneaking off the plane with the briefcase.'

'I can understand Parmitter's reaction, but not Nancy's. She's got her daughter back. The kidnappers have the money, so they're happy. They're not going to come after her now for talking, exposing themselves and multiplying the chance of capture. So what's she carping about?'

'You're seeing it logically, Luke. As a cop.'

'Ex-cop.'

'Same thing. She's a mother who's just emerged from the darkest tunnel known to parents and she's neither seeing clearly nor thinking straight. Human nature being what it is, she's probably not too disappointed that the kidnappers got away with the loot.'

'Because the money came from the man she despises and is divorcing?'

'Exactly.'

'That's flawed, too.'

'Why, Luke?'

'Because at least half of his is likely to end up as hers in the divorce settlement. No one, especially a modern, materialistic American woman, is going to merrily wave goodbye to one and a half million dollars. No, I tell you, something is way off kilter.'

The debate wouldn't have concluded there if it hadn't been for the red message light, beside the phone's cradle, catching his eye as it began blinking.

After telling Tandy how much he was missing her, he promised to call her back after he'd 'mulled over things' and had 'something constructive' to propose.

Then to the message. And a voice that was hauntingly familiar.

'One less cockroach in the world to worry about, thanks to me. How long do I have to wait for a medal? A winner's medal!'

'Just had a call from our mutual friend,' announced Templeman, initiating the conversation with Hardman teasingly.

'*Friend*?' Hardman was in no mood for oblique repartee.

'We seek him here, we seek him there, we seek him everywhere, but instead he finds us, only to disappear into thin air.'

'Are you pissed or just a rubbish poet?' Hardman said fractiously. 'Who are we talking about, for God's sake?'

'Our man, of course! He just can't keep out of touch as he continues desperately to solicit our approval.'

Hardman's breathing shortened into a smoker's wheeze. 'Did you get to speak with him this time?'

'No. Just another mocking voice message.'

'What's the arsehole saying now?'

'Just that he's rid us of another cockroach and he wonders how much longer he has to wait for a medal.'

'*Hell*! What a fruit! Definitely the same voice?'

'Stake my life on it.'

'That might be asked for yet! I'll have someone come round right away to speak with the management again, so we can add the latest bullshit to our vintage collection.'

'Perhaps you should consider having the public serenaded with this one on air – TV and radio,' Templeman advocated robustly. 'There's a plausible chance someone would recognize the voice.'

'Of course it makes sense. I'd do it without hesitation. Dickhead Badger's the obstacle.'

'What's his objection?'

'Afraid of losing face.'

'How?'

'By looking a piss-pot when the nation hears Clever Clogs ridiculing us and calling to say, "Hey, look, I'm over here!" As you said a few seconds ago, *he* finds *us* but we haven't a clue how to catch *him*. Badger won't listen to me. I'd be wasting my breath. He's had a voice expert working on the previous recordings with negative results.'

'How *negative*?'

'No detectable regional accent or dialect of any kind. No speech impediment or peculiar identifying feature. That's negative to Badger. He's limited by his rhino brain.'

'Might he listen to me?'

'Possibly,' Hardman conceded grudgingly. 'Trouble is, currently he's too busy courting the media and his local political cronies to give the likes of you house-room.'

'E-mail him for me, saying I want words. Say I'm threatening to pull out.'

'You *are* bluffing?'

'Yes, but he won't know that. From the X-rated conversation I've just had with Simone, I have every reason to be on the next plane to Miami.'

'Trouble at the ranch, eh?'

'The ranch is burning – metaphorically, of course!'

'Nothing ever changes, which leads me neatly to the subject of that loopy profiler, Helen Ridout. Badger's keen on my having another seance with her, but I'm going to pass. I recall your saying you got along hokey-cokey with the daft bat – I won't hold it against you, promise! – so I've taken the liberty of kicking her butt your way once more. She's probably already making your doorstep untidy.'

For once, Hardman was right about something.

Ridout was waiting for Templeman in the hotel lounge on the ground floor. She'd ordered a pot of coffee for two, on Templeman's suggestion when she contacted him from reception.

After a warm handshake, they sank into the armchairs with the relaxed body language of old friends. The profiler was wearing a smart, sky-blue suit, the skirt barely knee-length. Her blonde hair had recently been cropped short and combed forwards with a straight fringe, angelic choirboy-style. Her glossy tights encased long, chorus-girl legs, crossed near her ample thigh. A dangling stiletto heel, like a dagger poised to damage, glinted menacingly in the dusty shafts of shimmering sunlight.

'*That* man's impossible!' she fumed, nostrils flaring and her luminous eyes radiating more amusement than genuine anger. The target of her exasperation was identified without being named.

'He's under a lot of pressure,' said Templeman in mitigation for Hardman.

'So he should be!'

'Everyone's on his back.'

'All the more reason why he should welcome help.'

'He's an old-fashioned copper. He'll never change.'

'Then he should be swapped for a new generation model. A role model, preferably.'

'You're a hard woman.' Templeman's tone and smile indicated he meant the opposite.

'This case is going to crack *him* long before he cracks *it*.' She spoke with her mouth almost brushing her cup, as if there was something sensual between them, like a teasing kiss and the hot breath of intimacy. Ridout's rouge imprint was stamped on the rim of the porcelain china like a scarlet ensign, contrasting starkly with her waxen complexion, like blood against the backdrop of a corpse's hue. Almost Gothic.

'Perhaps not.'

Ridout put down her cup slowly and rested her resolute chin on her clenched right hand, her pivotal elbow playing a key supporting role, with the wing of her chair serving as a fulcrum. She eyeballed him searchingly. 'What have you got? I'm hooked. All ears.'

'Don't get too excited,' he warned her.

'*Any* excitement will do.'

Templeman massaged his chin thoughtfully. 'I can't help but feel that this killing is a defining moment and we're poised on the threshold, almost *there.*'

Ridout's intrigue blossomed. 'I haven't sensed any such optimism elsewhere. In fact, pessimism rules. Hardman's future is in freefall. The chief constable seems to be relying on the power of prayer with the conviction of a non-believer. To be honest, he's more into pagan rites; crossing fingers and toes, just in case the gospel has been nothing more than gossip. The politicians' witch-hunt is hotting up by the hour, though they can't seem to agree on which witch should be hunted. As for the frontline beavers, I've seldom encountered such a dispirited bunch. And here you are purring like a fat cat with all the cream, whiskers still wet. What justification do you have for such confidence?'

'There's no doubt in my mind now that our serial killer moves in the same circle as his victims.'

Ridout was sceptical. 'Hating a certain type of person isn't necessarily synonymous with being a part of that fraternity.'

But Templeman was unshakeable. 'Our man had to be privy to the victims' schedules, especially in the case of Carla North.'

'Surely he could have been stalking her in the shadows over a period of time, piecing together her lifestyle and regular, repeat weekly activities?' Ridout argued.

'Not possible, in my view, without arousing suspicion. Maybe in the build-up to the previous murders, but not this one. This time he gave advance notice of intent. The date was pre-fixed. The city was put on red alert. Badger flooded the streets with officers, uniformed and plainclothes. Women were warned to be neurotic about safety. In that climate of fear, our man couldn't afford to stand out. In fact, I reckon he gave due notice of the killing to come for the very reason that he knew he wouldn't be transparent. He was confident of remaining the invisible man.'

Ridout took her cup between her lips with two hands as if taking communion wine at the altar-rail, seeking divine inspiration.

'If you're right, that really does reduce the field.'

'Add to that the fact that we have recordings of the killer's voice.'

'Which someone ought to be able to put a name to immediately.'

'And it's almost all over.'

'So, why the manic depression overhanging HQ?' Ridout asked.

'For a start, Badger's blocking the thematic move of broadcasting at least one of the voicemails.'

'On what grounds?'

'Probably because it's Hardman's idea.'

'Well, a year at a charm school for the detective inspector wouldn't be amiss, I must say.'

'Personality clashes in teamwork are the allies of the enemy. They're as destructive as they are disruptive.'

'I agree, Mr Preacher Man. Trouble is, your sermon's directed at the wrong congregation. I'm here talking with you because just the sight of me gives Hardman the shakes. I'm his leper.'

'And I was thinking you were here because you enjoyed my company.'

'There's that, too. Nothing wrong with mixing business with pleasure, is there?'

'Nothing at all,' Templeman said neutrally. 'In fact, I recommend it.'

'Then do as you preach. Keep mixing!'

Templeman read no more into the invitation than harmless banter. To have done otherwise would have led him to dangerous ground. So he steadied himself and ignored his testosterone, pressing on with the business in hand. 'What have you gleaned on the grapevine this morning?'

'Which one?'

'Any. You've just come from team HQ. You must have heard something.'

'Such as?'

Suddenly mountain-climbing was an easier option than this

uphill struggle.

'Anyone see anything? Have they got anything?'

Ridout wasn't being deliberately obtuse. 'From the measly titbits to come my way, I'd say they're doing as well as in all the previous cases. In other words, they have zilch. Carla North left Ruskin College alone and wasn't seen until this morning. But I agree with you, if the killer *does* come from her social or professional circle, and the police have his voiceprint, then this should be his nemesis.'

Templeman flipped a mental coin, which came down in favour of his taking Ridout into his confidence. Then he related to her the line of inquiry he had been softly, softly and secretly pursuing about the possible link between the posting of the word 'cockroach' on the Kansas-based website and its use twice in communications from the Oxford killer.

'A bit tenuous, don't you think?' said Ridout, still evaluating, frowning.

'The biggest mistakes always appear that way. That's why they're made in the first place. The offender doesn't give it a thought, doesn't believe for one moment that anyone could possibly make the connection, because it's so minuscule, so far removed. As you said, it's so tenuous, yet could be so focal. What sway have you with Badger?'

'More than with Hardman.'

'If we present a united front to Badger in pushing for him to go public with the voice, he might be persuaded.'

'I'm game. Anything to put one over on the Birdbrain of Britain.'

As they shook hands on it, they both pumped flesh a little longer than was necessary and their fingers lingered together as if reluctant to part. The smoke signals from Ridout's eyes seemed to Templeman to spell out an invitation that threatened to compromise him, so he refrained from revealing that the message had been received and deciphered, let alone that he was mulling it over.

Leaning across the table with predatory stealth, Ridout said in a stage-whisper, 'My problem with those two men, Badger and Hardman, is that one wants to screw me, while the other wants only to fight. I can stop one having his way, but unfortunately not the other.'

'I assume it's the fighter you can't do anything about.'

'You can *assume* all you like!'

Frost travels at the speed of sound when it comes in conversation, even across oceans and continents.

The frost in John Rickson's voice was ice-cold.

'I'm a colleague of Joe Parmitter,' he began, a little too formally for Templeman's liking. 'He's rather busy right now. Too busy to talk with you.' That message was clear enough. 'He's attending to some other rather urgent matter, which you might know something about ...' He allowed his Bostonian voice to trail away, so that the full meaning of what he was saying had time to be digested.

'I understand,' said Templeman, impervious to the poorly disguised insults.

'I'm sure you do,' Rickson continued, his tone laced with sarcasm. 'However ...' *However* was about to have a whole new connotation bestowed upon it. 'Agent Parmitter has some information he feels should be relayed to you without delay. It's my understanding you requested assistance from the Bureau.'

Templeman allowed Rickson to tell it his way and in his own tempo. After all, it was the Bureau's bill that was burning.

'Agent Parmitter passed this *non-urgent* inquiry on to me, so it's not so inappropriate that I should be reporting to you. We know quite a lot about the operators of the website in which you have an interest. *Suffice* it for me to say that we have somebody on the inside and much of the information we hold on file in that connection is strictly classified. What I can reveal is that a number of its followers are suspected of involvement in a series of serious urban guerrilla crimes against abortion clinics, their staff, and entertainment venues specializing in explicit sex shows. Our investigations over here are ongoing and emphatically covert.'

Templeman fiddled and yawned over the histrionics.

'However ...'

How many more howevers?

'Agent Parmitter believes we can be of limited assistance without jeopardizing our own interests. Consequently, I was able to get something for you from our agents working this one in the field, especially from our inside man.'

'I'm obliged.' Templeman thought he'd better say something, make some noise to demonstrate that he was still there, still alive and still awake, even if only just.

Rickson took a couple of seconds to refocus, as if he'd temporarily lost his place in a recital.

'I'm sure, in view of your background, you're aware of *some* of our methods. Naturally, I'm not at liberty to divulge how we came by what I'm about to impart to you.'

'Of course not.' Templeman knew his part as if there was a script. Clap, nod and swoon according to the crib sheet.

'What I *can* tell you ...'

At last!

'... there have been quite a number of hits on that website from an Oxford, England subscriber. Some months ago he was accessing it almost daily.'

Now Templeman's antennae was suddenly receiving on full power.

'Do you have an ID for him?'

'Only an e-mail address.'

Gimme! Gimme! Gimme! Templeman was beseeching to himself and salivating. 'That could be gold-dust.'

'OK, well, let me see ... here we are: G.Carey@vetsurgery. co.uk.'

Templeman read it back to Rickson, who confirmed dourly, 'Correct.'

'Thanks for all your help. Please pass on my gratitude to Joe.'

Stretched pause, then, 'I think Agent Parmitter will have something to say to you personally very shortly.'

'Message received and understood.'

Rickson was gone.

Templeman found a local phone directory in a desk-drawer beneath the TV. He thumbed through the pages until he came to the Cs. 'Carey,' he muttered impatiently to himself as he ran a finger up and down the columns of names. 'G. Carey, where are you?'

There were several, in fact, but George Carey, veterinary surgeon, of The Beeches, Linton Road, Oxford was one that immediately leapt from the page of small print. This was an obvious match with the e-mail address of G.Carey@vetsurgery.co.uk.

'Bingo!'

Hardman was talking with the pathologist surgeon at the Radcliffe Hospital when he answered his mobile, recognizing the Randolph Hotel's number on the screen of his handset.

'Mike, I've a name for you to run through the system,' Templeman began as equably as possible in the circumstances.

'Hold on,' said the detective, as he dug deeply for his note-book and then a flick-top ballpoint pen from inside his crumpled jacket-pocket. 'OK, shoot.'

'George Carey, a vet of Linton Road,' Hardman spoke aloud as he wrote. 'What's the pitch?'

'Dunno. Could be the jackpot. Could be sweet fanny. I need to know nothing more at this stage than what, if anything, is known about him. What's his history? No rushing in, Mike. No police presence. No stormtroopers. Intelligence is what I'm after.'

'Intelligence isn't what we're renowned for, according to Badger and all the other armchair critics,' said Hardman, with self-deprecation. Then, 'Come on, Luke, give me a steer. You can't just drop a name into the pond and not expect ripples of excitement.'

'Now's not the time.'

'When is?'

'Later. Incidentally, did you e-mail the chief?'

'Which chief? Our place is crawling with 'em. Not many Indians, though.'

'Badger. About having the voice recording broadcast.'

'Forgot. Sorry. Something came up. Had to drop everything to scramble over here.'

'Where's *here*?'

'The Radcliffe. Post mortem's done and dusted. Just.'

'And?'

'No surprises. Nothing new. Same as before. In every detail. Struck from behind, then strangled. No rape. No clothing removed, as far as one can tell. Carbon-copy crime of all the others. Gets dead boring, doesn't it? Ha! Ha!' Hardman sought refuge in gallows humour.

'OK, leave Badger to me.'

'The pleasure's all mine. Best of luck.'

'In the meantime, I strongly suggest you make George Carey a high priority.'

'How can I possibly do that without knowing the score?'

'Because you need it. Because, as you've admitted yourself, you don't have anything else. But above everything, you need a break and this could just possibly be it.'

'Put like that, how can I resist?' Hardman said quickly, never one for spurning a lifeline.

Templeman first negotiated with the chief constable's PA, Ruth Crabtree, whose nature was as sour as her name signalled. Nevertheless, she did agree to petition Badger on Templeman's behalf, revealing, 'I've already had a similar request from Ms Ridout. You do appreciate that the chief constable has an overflowing diary already, don't you?'

'Busy with the urgent business we wish to discuss with him, no doubt,' Templeman argued clinically.

'Yes, well, I'll see what I can do. No promises for today, though.'

Ten minutes later, a somewhat mellowed Crabtree was

trilling to Templeman that he and the profiler would be 'granted an audience' with the pope of the police, Humphry Badger, at five o'clock 'prompt' that same afternoon.

'Don't be late,' she said, swiftly reverting to type. 'Mr Badger has a tight schedule. He's doing another live TV interview at six in his office. Cameras and lights will have to be erected by 5.45, latest. Then there'll be the makeup lady wanting a piece of him. Such a performance!'

'The price of fame!' said Templeman, tongue in cheek.

Templeman and Ridout rendezvoused at county police headquarters just before five and were ushered almost immediately into Badger's plush sanctum, which was furnished as a chief executive's office.

'So we have a deputation!' Badger greeted them with excessive pomp, rubbing his hands, playing to his audience, in particular to Ridout. He peeled off his jacket, with the same eagerness that he might well put on a condom, and slung it showily over the back of his soft-leather swivel chair. Sinking into the comforts of power, he used his thumbs to expand his red elastic trouser-braces. His naturally florid face was even more flushed than normal, enhanced by the star treatment from the national media. He was luxuriating in the convenient position of being able to keep himself above and beyond the day-to-day operation of investigations, unloading failure on his subordinates and reserving the accolades, whenever chanced upon, for himself. In that respect, he was no different from most bosses.

'We share a certain view and we considered it essential that we made it known to you, without delay,' said Templeman, taking the lead.

Badger glanced from Templeman to Ridout. 'A lobby group of two, eh? Not exactly an army of opinion.'

'It's quality not quantity that counts, something you know better than most, I'm sure,' said Ridout, transmitting a smile that was designed to melt resistance. 'We have reason to believe that the serial killer has run out of luck and that Carla

North can be made the last of his victims. She is the catalyst for his exposure.'

'Indeed! Now that *is* interesting! You're talking my language. But how come the so-called chief investigating officer hasn't said anything about this to me?' He couldn't bring himself to mention Hardman by name. 'How can you two be so hopeful when I'm engulfed by such a suffocating miasma of hopelessness?' Turning back to Templeman, he added, 'I assume you are equally upbeat?'

'That's why we're here together.'

'Does Hardman know about this dove-tailed representation to me?' He grimaced as if he'd just taken in a mouthful of poison; an allergic reaction to a man who brought him out in a rash of hostility.

'I told him of my intention,' said Templeman.

The chief constable snorted. 'Did you happen to see me on TV this morning?' This question was for Templeman.

'I saw it all.' Self-control prevented him from saying, 'Warts and all.' Instead, he said, 'A polished performance, if you don't mind my saying so.' Templeman was prepared to creep as much as anyone in pursuit of his objective.

Badger, a sucker for flattery, had no difficulty believing anything he wanted to hear, hence his overt smugness. 'Sorry you were brought into it. Hope it didn't cause too much embarrassment? I couldn't duck the question. That would only have made matters worse.'

'No embarrassment.'

'Good. I meant what I said in that interview. You're not implicated in any of the highlighted cock-ups. I'm glad to have you on board. Without my backing, you wouldn't be here. It could never have happened in the first place. I've been praying you'd make a difference.' Badger wasn't noted for his reliance on spiritual intervention. Mischievously, he then said, 'I hope you're here to leak secrets.' His ferrety eyes darted to and fro between his visitors.

'First a request,' said Ridout, her redolence seeming to have a hypnotic effect on her *prey*.

'Anything within reason,' Badger declared magnanimously. 'Anything to get a result.'

Ridout made an impassioned plea for one of the voicemails – or a composite assembled from them all, to be released to TV and radio for playing, especially on the Thames Valley regional network.

Templeman weighed in with his support, arguing for a composite, sensing that this would most appeal to the chief. 'That way you could achieve the goal of voice identification without bringing ridicule on your force.' Avoiding mockery was the key, Templeman and Ridout both knew.

For almost a whole minute Badger regressed into sullen reverie. When he did surface, it was to say, in spaced-out speech, 'Ever since the Yorkshire Ripper debacle, the top brass in every police force in the land has been running scared of tape-recordings from self-proclaimed maniacal murderers. Know what I mean?'

The visitors knew *exactly* what he meant.

West Yorkshire police were duped by a hoax tape during Peter Sutcliffe's killing spree over many years. Deputy Chief Constable George Oldfield received the tape in the morning mail. Posted in the north-east – Sunderland, to be precise – it ran for three minutes and sixteen seconds and went as follows:

'I'm Jack. I see you are having no luck catching me. I have the greatest respect for you, George, but lord you are no nearer catching me now than four years ago when I started. I reckon your boys are letting you down, George. They can't be much good, can they? The only time they came close to catching me was a few months back in Chapeltown, when I was disturbed. Even then it was a uniformed copper, not a detective. I warned you in March that I'd strike again. Sorry it wasn't Bradford. I did promise you that, but I couldn't get there. I'm not sure when I'll strike again, but it will definitely be some time this year. Maybe September, October, or even sooner if I get the chance. I'm not sure where. Maybe Manchester; I like it there. There's plenty of THEM knocking about. They never learn, do they, George? I bet you've warned them. But they never listen. At the rate

I'm going, I shall be in the book of records. I think it's eleven up to now, isn't it? Well, I'll keep on going for quite a while yet. I can't see myself being nicked just yet. Even if you do get near, I'll probably top myself first. Well, it's been nice chatting to you, George.

'Yours, Jack the Ripper. No good looking for fingerprints, you should know by now it's as clean as a whistle. See you soon. Bye. Hope you like the catchy tune at the end.'

The tape had concluded with amateurish singing from the ballad 'Thank You For Being A Friend'.

'The "I'm Jack" destroyed Oldfield,' said Badger, his mood hardening. 'It killed him, as surely as if he'd put a gun in his mouth and pulled the trigger. He loaded all his eggs in one basket, the bloody old fool. He was obsessed by it. No matter how many warnings he got from experts concerned that he was dangerously blinding himself to the possibility that the tape was fraudulent, he wouldn't entertain doubt, because he'd allowed himself to become caught up in a personal duel. Consequently, he rubbished any investigative work that pointed to a suspect without a Wearside accent. This bigotry not only led to his downfall, but also cost lives. The *real* Yorkshire Ripper went on killing, notching up a total of thirteen victims, even though he'd been a long-time suspect with juniors on the team, but Oldfield wouldn't give Sutcliffe serious consideration, just because his accent was *wrong*.' Badger was hunched forward, bear-like, over his desk, hands clenched into white-knuckle fists. 'I've no intention of being made to look an idiot, the way that Oldfield was. Taunting confessional tapes have been anathema to men and women in my position ever since the Yorkshire Ripper debacle. It tarnished the reputation of West Yorkshire police for years afterwards. No one's going to make a laughing stock of me that way. No, sir!'

'I fully appreciate your wariness,' said Templeman, wisely eschewing head-on conflict. Sycophantic diplomacy was his best bet. 'But ...'

'I'd have wagered my wife's life on there being a "but" or a "however".' Badger managed a chortle, slapping his portly belly, playing the avuncular card.

Ridout squirmed while fixing her face with a mask of defer-ence.

'I want to confide in you about a development that I think will convince you we should give it a shot,' said Templeman. Always share a secret if you want to speed up bonding. After synoptically outlining his liaison with the FBI over the Kansas organization and its possible relevance to the Oxford murders, he added confidentially, 'I haven't even entrusted this infor-mation with DI Hardman.'

'Very wise,' said Badger derisively, warming to the conspir-atorial overtures. 'He'd only screw it up for you this end. How about you, Helen?'

'I've already talked it through with Helen,' Templeman answered for her, in case she was unsure what response he expected from her.

'And?'

'We're united on this,' Ridout replied, as affably as possible. 'I believe, like Luke, that the potential gain more than compen-sates for any possible loss.'

'I'm confident that a composite tape could be released that would fulfil all purposes, without compromising your integrity or that of your force,' Templeman opined.

'Hmm.' Badger threaded the fingers of both hands as he cogitated agonizingly. 'You can hear the first question from the media, can't you?' he said, at last. This was hurting. 'Some cutey will say, "Excuse me, but were you trained by George Oldfield by any chance?"' The chief constable was most comfortable when answering his own questions.

'I suggest you pre-empt that,' said Ridout.

'How?'

'By introducing the Yorkshire Ripper "I'm Jack" tape your-self, before taking questions. You can begin by stressing that lessons have been learned since the disgrace of Oldfield; that you're sceptical over the authenticity of the electronic evidence you have, but you must test it, and that's exactly what you're doing. Not to do so would be to leave yourself wide open to charges of irresponsibility. Oldfield's over-reliance on the "I'm Jack" tape resulted in more murders that may well have been prevented. You should be careful not to allow a similar outcome due to *under*-reliance, I suggest.'

Templeman knew instantly that Ridout had just delivered the winning blow.

Badger made a show of holding out, but that's all it was. Ham acting.

'You realize we'll probably be getting "I did it, I'm your man, catch-me-if-you-can" tapes from all over the country,' Badger grumbled. 'There are more copycats out there than alleycats.'

'Of course that's the downside,' said Templeman, knowing there was no need for further pressure.

'Oh well!' Badger said extravagantly, throwing up his arms and making theatre out of his apparent capitulation. 'I've been wary of taking this action, but I've been converted by the quality of your argument. I like doing business with cerebral coppers.' That compliment was for Templeman. 'Boneheads give me the jitters.' That broadside was for the absent Hardman. 'I'll have our technical wizards work on it right away. We'll have something ready for release in the morning. I suppose I should inform DI Hardman of my decision, in the form of a fait accompli.'

'Fingers crossed,' said Templeman, as a way of saying thanks.

'I'll be crossing more than that.' And then, 'We haven't had a chance to chat since you came on the payroll.' He was addressing Templeman again, of course, although his expression was that of someone posturing in front of a bathroom mirror. 'Lots of mistakes were made in the past that impacted badly on you. There's no way of making amends fully, but rest assured you wouldn't be here now if I wasn't certain beyond all doubt that you were horribly wronged. Such things happen. It's an imperfect world, you know that. The important thing is to live in the present and for the future, and not the past.'

Badger's homespun philosophy and homilies were legendary for their banality.

'This country lost a fine police officer through an unfortunate chain of circumstantial red herrings. From what I've heard from your ex-superiors in the Met, you were peerless, in a class of your own, without being a maverick, and that takes some doing. There's no room for loners in my force, but you managed to combine individual flair with teamplay. That kind of testimony carries clout with me. Hence my willingness to give ground. If you bag this bastard for me, I shall be eternally grateful. There'll be much kudos.'

Especially for you! Templeman and Ridout both thought simultaneously.

'*We'll* do our best,' said Templeman, emphasizing the collective effort, befitting of a team player.

Audience with the pope was over.

'We're in business,' Templeman enthused to Ridout when they were out of the lion's den. 'But the way he trashed Hardman was out of order.'

'Speak for yourself!'

Templeman almost invited Ridout to dinner at the Randolph, but decided against it, though only just. It was a close call, but this was no time for tempting emotional complications. Dinner was one thing. But a tasty dessert was something else.

There were no means of keeping a news blackout on the Naples kidnapping drama and no excuse for trying to do so, now that Tammy Carter had been rescued unharmed and was reunited with her family.

United Airlines' cabin crew and San Francisco airport personnel had chirped like canaries to the media. The FBI had been more forthcoming than usual, doing everything possible to embarrass and compromise the PI agency run by Templeman and Tandy, with Agent Parmitter giving interviews ad nauseam.

'It's a disgrace,' he told a press conference. 'These guys will have their work cut out to keep their PI licences.' *These guys* translated into Tandy and Templeman.

'Tammy Carter is alive today by pure chance. Luck. What those guys did was irresponsible beyond belief. Criminal, I'd say. They're culpable and I'm going to see they're hung out to dry. By playing at detectives, they've allowed a bunch of amateur crooks to milk millions from a family not thinking straight because of the black-hole trauma into which they'd been plunged. We have more than enough home-grown cowboys without having any imported from Europe.

'One of the partners of this PI agency in question has been imprisoned for homicide in the UK, convicted of slaying his own wife who was divorcing him. That's the quality of these so-called Good Samaritans.' No mention, of course, that the conviction had been quashed and Templeman was back with the police, albeit only as a consultant, in the very city where he had stood trial – the best testimony possible that his good name had been fully restored.

In this electronic age, all news travels fast. Bad news, however, travels the fastest of all because it is good news to editors. What appeared on American TV was flashed on to British screens with a time-lag of only minutes. Headlines in the evening newspapers of New York and Washington were the headlines of the following morning's nationals in the UK. No corner of the globe escaped the prying eye of the press any more. Hence echoes of the uproar over the kidnapping shambles were quickly reverberating around Oxford.

Badger wasn't the first to demand to know 'what the hell' was going on; a knee-jerk reaction to crack-of-dawn calls from the Home Office in London and a few of the more pugnacious local politicians. Then there were the locusts from the media who had been swarming around his home and county head-quarters ever since the first news reports had leapfrogged the Atlantic the previous evening. Quite a few reporters and photographers from the London national newspapers had booked rooms at the Randolph and spent half the night banging on Templeman's door and slipping pieces of paper under his door with requests for 'just a few minutes' of his time in the cause of 'fairness', so that he could give his 'side of the story'. *Yeah, yeah, yeah.* Other journalists, finding the Randolph fully booked, camped on the pavement outside. TV crews set up their cameras and arc lights at the hotel entrance, just in case Templeman should show his face. Uniformed police officers did their best to keep the peace and break up minor scuffles among rival hacks.

Templeman, needless to say, didn't sleep; yet again. Neither did he speak to any of the journalists, despite their pushy persistence. Badger's breathless call came at around 7 a.m.

'This is *all* we need!' he grumbled, meaning the opposite, of course.

'Bad timing, I agree,' Templeman said, contrite. No point being bullish when shorn of your horns.

'What's your involvement?'

'None. I'm here. Simone's there. She's in charge of the shop, running the show. It was her call.' He wasn't dumping on his partner, simply telling it the way it was. More importantly, he was giving Badger what he wanted to hear, in order to be able to embark on damage limitation.

'It doesn't look good.' Window-dressing was everything to Badger. 'It's one banana skin after another.'

'Simone's operation has nothing to do with anything here,' Templeman protested.

'Wrong. It has *everything* to do with you. And you're *here*.'

'I don't have to be,' Templeman said petulantly. 'That's *your* call.'

That was enough to bring Badger quickly off the boil. 'I didn't think you were a runner.'

'I'm not. Never have been. Never will be.'

'Me neither, so don't be so pathetic. We'll brazen this out, together. Leave the vultures to me.'

'My pleasure.'

'Now … what we discussed and agreed yesterday: our electronic technicians have cobbled together a composite. It's good quality. It meets our requirements, without putting ourselves in the pillory. Several copies have been made. They're going to be distributed to our regional TV and radio networks, with a statement, from our press office. I expect I'll have to do the rounds of TV and radio stations throughout the day. Everyone wants a bit of you when you're in my position.'

'It must be hell,' Templeman said wryly.

'It comes with the territory,' said Badger, too vain to recognize the jibe. 'Don't forget, no statements to those newshounds. You may be their fox, but they're the ones with all the vulpine instincts. Say one word to them and they'll have your tail for a trophy.'

'I'll bear that in mind.'

'Short shrift is the answer. Being dumb is sometimes smart.'

'I'll remember that,' said Templeman, with no such intention.

'You could do worse. A lot worse.'

The ending of their conversation was an improvement on the beginning.

Hardman was next in line for a piece of Templeman's ear. 'I'm grateful,' he almost chuckled.

'I'm glad I've made someone happy.'

'A rabid dog can have its teeth only in one leg at a time. While Badger's biting you, he can't give me the runaround.'

'Your turn will come.'

'I've had my turn every flaming minute of the last six months. Incidentally, I hear you and that crackpot profiler managed to get your way over the voice recording.'

'*Our* way, Mike. It's what you wanted, too.'

'That won't be the official version.'

'That's life.'

'Having to eat shit every day never did anyone any good.'

Another depressing conversation.

By midday, the composite voice tape was being played on every TV and radio news programme nationwide. Rita Cardew heard it at home on her radio, when it was the lead item on the noon news. She listened again an hour later and again at two o'clock – just to reinforce her suspicions. During the afternoon, she tried several times to contact Pamela Easton, but she wasn't answering her mobile, so Cardew sent a text: *Must talk with u soonest about a mutual acquaintance. Very urgent.*

Easton was lecturing that afternoon in London and had her mobile switched on 'discreet' mode. It wasn't until she was settled on the Oxford-bound train at London's Paddington station that she checked for text and voicemail messages. Intrigued by Rita Cardew's teasing text, Easton phoned her friend as the train gathered speed through the dreary western suburbs of the capital.

'Rita! It's Pam. I've been lecturing most of the day, in London, and I've only just read your text. Who is the mutual acquaintance? And what's the urgency? You've got me wetting myself with anticipation!'

Cardew hesitated. 'Where are you now?'

'On the train, heading home. Why? What's the matter, Rita? You sound agitated, not at all your normal self.'

'Have you seen any TV or heard any radio news programmes since lunchtime?'

'No. What's this all about, Rita? What's going on? What's happened?'

'When you get indoors, Pam, listen to the next news bulletin on one of the local radio stations.'

'Why? What for? You're not making any sense.' Easton was becoming exasperated, but the carriage was crowded and other passengers were beginning to give her odd looks. Inhibition began to kick in.

'The police have issued a voice-recording of the man they believe could be the serial killer.'

'So?'

'Just listen to it, then call me.'

Three hours later, Easton called her friend from her home in Oxford.

'Rita, I heard The Voice just a few minutes ago on the radio.'

'And?'

'Are we thinking the same man?'

'Well, if it isn't George Carey, it's certainly his soundalike.'

'I can't believe it!'

'Remember how strange we thought it was that he was absent from the Ashmolean preview, when he'd told us both that very same day he'd definitely be there?'

'And that was the night of the murder, when Carla was just around the corner from the museum,' said Easton, not that either of them needed reminding. It was more a case of under-lining the fact. 'We shouldn't rush to conclusions, though. Anything could have turned up at the last minute. A vet's life is very much the same as a doctor's – always being called out at godforsaken hours. A pet hamster caught in a mousetrap; something like that.'

'What are we going to do?'

'There's only one thing *to do*.'

'But what if we're wrong?'

'Then no harm done.'

'It seems so sneaky to go behind his back, making accusations.'

'We won't be making accusations. We'll just be giving a name, saying the voice sounds rather like his. That's all.'

'Which one of us is going to be Judas?'

'How about sharing the betrayal?'

'Yes, I'd feel happier with that.'

'Let's not delay, then. Other lives may depend on it. Let's do it.'

And they did.

Templeman resisted an urge to hotfoot it to Linton Road to snoop. He would have liked to loiter around The Beeches, photographing it from all angles with his eyes, filing the prints in his memory, but it would have been a mistake, of course. He couldn't take the chance of being seen. George Carey, if he was the killer, knew what Templeman looked like and would probably recognize him even in the dark, especially if Templeman was caught nosing around furtively.

After the broadcast of the composite voicemail, the killer was bound to be extra vigilant if, like Cinderella's slipper, it was an accurate fit. So Templeman suppressed his instinct, forcing upon himself a fortress mentality. He locked himself in his room and fed and drank from room service. When not indulging in food or drink, he lay restlessly on his bed with a paperback novel as a companion, reading the same pages over and over again, without retaining a single sentence in his overloaded head. The TV talked to him in a whisper from a corner, but the characters were wasting their breath; he didn't hear a word. He was somewhere else; in a veterinary surgery, surrounded by surgical instruments and facilities for dissecting. Probably cold-storage equipment for preserving animal tissue and deep-freezing human parts, too, if so desired. Parts of Charley. Charley's fingers. God only knew what else!

Everything was coming together. With nothing more to go on than the flimsy evidence – if indeed it qualified for that – of the FBI, he knew with visceral certainty that George Carey was their man. Now time was of the essence. The tempo couldn't be allowed to slacken. They had to strike while everything was hot. Like seafaring folk of old, cops knew the importance of catching the tide. And right down to the size of his feet, Templeman was still a cop in spirit.

Rita Cardew and Pamela Easton arrived together in a shared taxi at the Thames Valley police station near Folly Bridge.

A civilian employee, on night duty at reception, talked with them briefly before speaking on the internal phone with Detective Constable Dave Lowen, one of the murder-squad team in the pool. 'There are two ladies here who think they can put a name to the voice we put out on the networks,' said the civilian receptionist, unable to keep excitement from his voice.

After just a couple of minutes downstairs with the women, DC Lowen *invited* them to follow him to the detectives' main, open-plan operations room, where he plied them with coffee from a machine while he set about locating Hardman.

Hardman, no more than a hundred yards away in The Head of the River pub, answered his mobile with a grunt.

'I have two women here,' said Lowen.

'Lucky you, but greedy, wouldn't you say?'

Lowen ignored the barbed wit at his expense. 'They say they recognize the voice that we had broadcast.'

'What are they like?'

'They're right beside me now.' That told Hardman that Lowen would have to be circumspect with his answers and that Hardman would have to do most of the talking.

'You know what I'm really asking, don't you?'

'I think so.'

'Are they nutters?'

'Not at all.'

'Vindictive?'

'I wouldn't know that, but very doubtful, I'd say.'

'Respectable?'

'Backbone of the community.'

'I'm on my way. I'll be with you in five. Don't you dare let them out of your sight.'

'You can rely on me.'

That was the kind of bold boast on which Hardman had learned, from bitter experience, to pin zero faith.

Hardman led the women and DC Lowen into his office, where, after a few perfunctory social preliminaries, he played the composite tape three times before saying tensely, 'Right, now are you still one hundred per cent?'

'Absolutely,' said the women, in unison.

'OK, so who is it?'

Hardman was really fired up when Easton gave him George Carey's name. This was the same name that had come from Templeman. Instinctively, he knew he was in business.

Looking from one to the other, as if following a tennis match rally, he asked them collectively, 'What can you tell me about this man?'

'Well, he's a very good vet,' said Rita Cardew. 'I've a black labrador, Bruiser, and George has nursed him through a couple of potentially life-threatening conditions when we feared we might lose him.'

Hardman smiled patronizingly. 'I was thinking more of anything you could tell me about his character, habits, lifestyle?'

'Everyone speaks highly of him,' said Easton. 'He's a caring man, most certainly when it comes to animals. You must understand that we're here, basically, to prevent you squandering valuable time by going after the wrong man.'

'We've both known him a long time,' Cardew elaborated. 'I live in the same road. We're neighbours. Not next-door neighbours, but on the same block, so to speak. He's never been anything but neighbourly and professional towards me.' 'Neighbourly' and 'professional' seemed rather like a contradiction, so she enlarged. 'Whenever I've been to see him about Bruiser, he's been a consummate professional. But if we've met on the social circuit, then we've chatted like friends. Oxford may be a city, but it's also a village, especially when it comes to the academic and professional fraternities. He always asks after Bruiser. My husband likes him, too, and *he's* a pretty shrewd judge of character. Mind you, they don't have much to do with one another, mainly because Henry regards George as something of a loner.'

'Is he married?'

'No, he's a confirmed bachelor. I once asked him why he'd never married and he said because the idea had never occurred to him, just the way he'd never considered having a sex-change operation. He preferred staying the way he was. I rather liked that.'

Unimpressed, Hardman sniffed as he scribbled notes. 'He works from home, right?'

Cardew handed over to Easton, as if they were in a relay team. 'He lives above his veterinary practice, which is on the ground floor. There are three storeys. You know the size of properties in that area. He has two doors for living quarters, plus an attic and basement. More than adequate for a single man, I'd say.'

'What about staff? Does he have employees? A vet partner?'

'He has a woman helper,' said the professor. 'A young woman. No older than twenty or twenty-one. Wouldn't you say so, Rita?' She looked to her friend for agreement.

Cardew gave a couple of affirmative nods.

'She acts as receptionist and assistant, like an animal nurse, or whatever they call them,' Easton continued. 'I don't know her name, do you, Rita?' Cardew shook her head.

'Does she live in?'

'Oh, no,' said Cardew. 'I often see her cycling to work around 7.30. He starts his surgery at eight. Six days a week. It's a long working day for them. His evening surgery doesn't usually finish until eight. Mind you, if he has a social engagement he'll knock his evening surgery on the head. During the day he makes house-calls to farms, examining livestock.'

All Creatures Great and Small, popped into Hardman's head as he asked of them both, 'When did you last see Mr Carey?'

Cardew related how she had 'bumped' into him early in the morning on the day of the latest murder, when she had been walking Bruiser and Carey had been jogging.

Easton told of meeting him outside the Botanic Garden 'around lunchtime' on the same day, when he'd enquired after Champ, her dog.

Both women recalled 'clearly' that Carey had made the point that he would be seeing them that evening at the Ashmolean Museum.

'But he never showed?'

'He was not there,' Easton said emphatically.

'You're certain of that?'

'He wasn't there, take it from me,' Cardew endorsed her friend's unyielding answer.

'Did that surprise you?'

'Well, it didn't alarm us, if that's what you mean,' Easton answered for them both. 'I suppose it's fair to say we wondered why he hadn't put in an appearance, but only because he'd been so adamant that he'd be there.'

'That's why we mentioned his absence to one another as we left the museum,' explained Cardew. 'We assumed some emergency had come up. Vets are like doctors, aren't they? Always getting called out at unearthly hours.'

Hardman had stopped taking notes. 'Was there anything unusual about him, his behaviour, the last time you spoke to him?'

'Not at all,' said Cardew spontaneously. 'He was the same George I've always known. In any case, when someone's jogging, it's hardly the time for much of a chat.'

Hardman turned to Easton.

'He was relaxed. There was a bit of inconsequential banter between us. So inconsequential that I can't recall a word of it. He certainly didn't look like a man with murder on his mind, if that's what you're getting at?'

'One last thing: has he ever said anything that might make you think he holds a grudge against your gender?'

The women eyeballed each other. A telepathic message between them gave Easton the right to answer first.

'Do you know, I couldn't tell you anything about George Carey's real opinion on a single subject. I've had numerous conversations with him, but he's never revealed his own hand on any issue. I'd never really given that thought before. He's a very private person, I'd say, who builds a protective wall around him. He has a certain gift for getting others to open up, but he doesn't reciprocate. In that respect, he's like a lot of journalists I've met. Good at poking into other people's affairs, but not allowing anyone over their own threshold.'

'I agree with all that,' concurred Cardew, as soon as Easton had finished. 'I haven't a clue what he stands for, either, except I do know he abhors cruelty to animals, but you'd expect that, wouldn't you, what with his being a vet? How stupid of me! You'd expect it from any decent human being, wouldn't you? And *we* have no reason to suspect him of being anything other than *decent*, save, of course, that *voice*.'

Hardman was through with them. 'I'm obliged to you both. I want you to carry on as normal. If you should meet Mr Carey, I ask that you don't say anything to him to give him any idea that you might have been to the police or were contemplating doing so. People quickly notice any change of attitude towards them. Our inquiries will be discreet. If he's in the clear, that will be the end of the matter and no harm done. You've done the right thing and you can sleep with a clear conscience.'

Neither woman was comforted, but they exited the police station feeling they had fulfilled their public obligation with the least possible treachery.

Badger was pontificating at the bar of his Freemasons' lodge when his pager bleeped.

'Not another body already?' quipped one of his tipsy masonic brothers as Badger, cursing, struggled to read the message. It had been an initiation ceremony for another police officer, a uniformed inspector whom Badger had proposed as a candidate for his own lodge. After the ceremony, they had dined in style, with Badger proposing the toast to the initiate. True to character, he had used the platform more to promote himself than the newcomer to the brotherhood. Now he scowled as he identified the perpetrator of this inconvenience.

'Sure to be another cock-up,' he prophesied irascibly as he parked his large brandy on the bar, adding to his drinking pals, 'See no thieving bugger gets his mitts on my nectar.'

There was amusement all round as Badger waddled unsteadily from the bar to call Hardman from the privacy of a phone-booth downstairs.

'What is it *now*, man?'

Hardman, with a slight slur of his own, though considerably less distinctive than the chief constable's, outlined developments.

'How much reliance can you put on those tarts?'

'They're not tarts, sir. They're intelligent, professional women. Very level-headed.'

Badger was about to retort, *More than can be said of the officer who interviewed them,* but decided it would only be counterproductive, though that would not normally have deterred him.

'Let's pull him in,' Badger decreed decisively. A cocktail of gin, red wine, port and brandy in his blood had emboldened him.

'I'll want a search warrant.'

'Of course you do. Knock up one of our tame magistrates. You know the drill as well as I do.'

'I'll have everything set up for 6 a.m.'

'Make it five. It gets light early these mornings. He could be an early bird. You need to hit him before his metabolism's on the move. Always drag them in at their lowest ebb. You should know that by now.'

'Five it is, then, sir.' Hardman was doing his utmost to retain civility.

'Make sure you field the A-team.'

'Leave it to me.'

That was an entreaty too far. 'Have you tipped off Templeman?'

'Not yet.'

'Do so. Now. I don't want any more cock-ups. Understood?'

Hardman understood only too well.

Badger returned to his closely-guarded brandy as if he were Winston Churchill, having just sanctioned the D-Day landings, a bumptious bounce to his step that had been missing for several months.

When briefed on the phone late that night, Templeman said, 'Count me in on this one, Mike. I want to be with you when you go in.'

Hardman knew exactly what he meant.

'Will you be able to sneak out of the hotel without being spotted by the press-squatters? If you're seen, they'll follow you like lemmings. The last thing we want is the media blowing this for us. If that happens, I can kiss goodbye to my balls.'

'I can sneak out via a fire exit,' Templeman said confidently. 'At that time of the morning, the hacks will have only the main entrance covered. Most of them will be sleeping off hangovers.'

Hardman felt his own tender skull in a gesture of sympathy.

'Let's rendezvous outside St John's College in St Giles at 4.30.'

'I'll be there.'

'Set your alarm. If you're not there, too bad. I go.'

'Don't worry, I'm too wound up for sleep.'

'Don't get too excited. We could be in for an anti-climax.'

Somehow that was something neither of them really believed.

More bitter-sweet news came for Templeman at 1 a.m. with a call from Tandy in Florida.

The young man captured on CCTV leaving the San Francisco-bound aircraft at Miami with the briefcase full of ransom money had been identified as José Sanchez, none other than the Mexican boyfriend of Tammy Carter. The alleged kidnapping had been an inside job from beginning to end, aided and abetted by Tammy's mother, Nancy.

Faced with the incontrovertible footage evidence, Tammy had broken down and made a full confession.

The ruse had been to rip off Tammy's father before he had the chance to salt away a large proportion of his ill-gotten fortune and fritter away the rest on his new, avaricious mistress. Tammy had planned to use the ransom money to buy a luxury home on the west coast, possibly in Malibu, where she hoped to live happily ever after with her handsome boyfriend, who was gifted in the bedroom but had little flair for anything that required hard work without coitus as the pay-off. Nancy had endorsed the scam as a means of reaping revenge against her philandering, estranged husband. She had denied any knowledge of the swindle until confronted with her daughter's taped confession.

The arrangement was for José to hole up in the beachside Hawaiian motel in Lantana, a small residential community just south of Palm Beach on the eastern shoreline of Florida, the opposite side of the peninsula state from Naples. He would wait there until the police had finished debriefing Tammy and then she would join him to begin their financially insulated life together, free of the economic struggles most young couples had to overcome.

The cops raided the motel in Lantana, but – no surprises – José wasn't there. The cuckoo hadn't flown the nest; he'd never been in it. Gone with the wind – and the money. Winning Tammy's love had been a mere stepping stone towards a pot of gold for himself, not to be shared.

'They used me as their sucker,' Tandy told Templeman, tearful with anger. 'I was taken in. Now it's so obvious why Nancy insisted on the police being kept out of it. She and Tammy must have guessed that the police, especially the FBI, wouldn't be so gullible. I was the perfect patsy.'

'This is negative introspection, darling. Self-flagellation achieves nothing, except unnecessary added pain. You acted in good faith. You followed your client's instructions. There is also the consolation that Tammy was never in danger.'

'But you hinted that it didn't smell right.'

'Only after you were too far down the road to turn back.'

'Down the road on which they were taking me for a ride.

Parmitter's insufferable now. Like he's the first man on earth to give birth.'

'At least he's happy now. Far better a smug FBI agent than an angry, spiteful one.'

'At my expense.'

'No, at the Carters' expense. They even have to pay you – us. There's no way now they can duck that debt. Every way they try to wriggle, they lose. They're the proverbial cornered rats. With that thought, you should sleep like a baby.' The sun was setting in Florida.

'Most babies cry in the night.'

'Not *my baby.*'

He didn't have the heart to reveal how helpful to him Parmitter's office had been in the last few hours and that by dawn the Oxford serial killer and brutal slayer of Templeman's own wife would almost certainly be in hand-cuffs.

The first cracks in the night sky were appearing as twenty uniformed officers stealthily surrounded the house. Hardman waited tensely until they were all in place before sticking up both thumbs, the signal for the knock-up to begin. One officer kept a finger pressed on the bell-button, while others thumped with fists on the sturdy front door and downstairs windows.

'Wakey! Wakey!' Hardman shouted through cupped hands, his head tilted back at the angle of a plane taking off, his eyes scanning upstairs windows for any sign of human life. 'This is your wake-up call, Mr Carey. Shake a leg! Rise and shine!' Hardman couldn't remember when he'd last enjoyed himself so much. These were the magic moments of his work that compensated for all the bureaucratic monotony and crap from the Badgers of his world.

Lights popped on all around in the road, but the suspect's house remained ominously in darkness.

'It's the police, Mr Carey. Open up or we'll have to bust our way in,' Hardman threatened, now using a hailer.

A uniformed inspector repeated the warning at the rear, in case Carey's bedroom was at the back of the house.

The only response was an empty silence from within.

Hardman, his feet crunching on the gravel driveway, returned to his car, where Templeman was waiting in the front passenger seat, the door open.

'We're going in,' he said, which was Templeman's invitation to join the party.

Just before the raid began, Hardman reassured the

shoulder-charging bulldozers, 'There's no need for nerves. This guy targets defenceless women, not armed men.'

The front door caved in only after half a dozen beefy rams with bone, muscle and gristle, by which time a group of neighbours, still in their nightwear, had gathered like ghouls for a hanging outside Carey's home-cum-surgery.

Within five minutes of forcing an entry, it was established that Carey wasn't at home. His bedroom was located on the top floor. The bed hadn't been slept in.

Templeman was immediately struck by the neatness and cleanliness of the living quarters, considering that this was the domestic sanctuary of a man living alone. There wasn't an item out of place throughout the entire property. No Plimsoll-line stain around the inside of the bath. All shaving gear, including aftershave and soothing balm, was stacked tidily in the bathroom cabinet, along with non-prescription headache tablets and an extra-strong mouthwash. A solitary toothbrush rested in a spotlessly clean glass beside the cold-water tap of the wash-basin. The bristles were dry, indicating that the toothbrush hadn't been used for several hours. There wasn't even a sign of overhanging toothpaste around the cap on the tube. A bone-dry face-flannel was hung over the side of the bath. All towels had been folded and put away in the airing cupboard.

Books beside the bed gave little away about the reader, except that he had a catholic taste in literature. There were three contemporary crime novels, a biography of the American world chess champion Bobby Fischer, a history of the Kennedy dynasty, an anthropology of Victorian England, with special emphasis on vice in London during that period, and a couple of specialist books on animal husbandry.

The wardrobe was filled to capacity with suits, many of which appeared to have been worn hardly at all, and at least twelve shirts, all neatly pressed. An even greater number of ties hung from a rail. Six pairs of highly polished shoes were lined up regimentally at the bottom of the wardrobe.

Templeman was intrigued by the absence throughout the house of a single photograph: no portrait of a mother, father, brother or sister, no family group, no nostalgic alma mater or alumni snapshots. To Templeman, Carey's home was an emotional icebox. Two rooms had been prepared as spare bedrooms, but clearly weren't in current use.

The main living room was elegantly furnished, but lacked a lived-in feel: there was nothing to suggest that anyone spent much time in it or relaxed here while unwinding after a hard day's work. The kitchen resembled a clinic where one might go for a blood test rather than a coffee and a fry-up. A smaller room on the first floor at the back was obviously Carey's study. It was equipped with a computer, printer, grey metallic desk and matching cabinets, all of which were locked.

'We'll have this little lot opened and searched,' said Hardman, tapping the cabinets. 'I'll also have one of our IT aces hack into this thing.' The *thing* was the computer. Hardman was only semi-computer literate and, therefore, true to Luddite tradition, was disparaging about all things driven by modern technology.

Templeman and Hardman then climbed together into the attic, which was used as a storeroom and was crammed with old furniture. Years of dust had accumulated, making upturned chairs and tables look as if covered in dandruff as the gilded shafts of dawn sunshine, filtered through a skylight, gave the long-settled dirt a white and silvery glitter.

From the attic, they descended, via the wide, spiral staircase in the main part of the house, to the surgery waiting room at one side of the front door. It was a bog-standard waiting room: chairs around the walls, magazines (all at least two years old) on a low table in the centre, and a horseshoe-shaped reception desk nearest the entrance from the hall. One flick of a wall switch immediately flooded the room with harsh, tubed lighting. The treatment room was across the hall, on the opposite side of the front door, where there was an operating table, medicine cabinet and luminescent, spotlight lamps to assist with surgical procedures. Instruments, including scalpels, had been kept overnight in a sterilizer. One long white coat was hooked to a peg on the door.

The door to the basement was situated off the downstairs hall, under the stairs.

'Locked,' Hardman grumbled, twisting the brass handle.

'I noticed a set of keys hanging on the wall at reception,' said Templeman.

'Worth a try.'

They tested all of the thirteen keys on the ring, but not one of them unlocked the door to the basement.

'I'll fetch a couple of the heavies,' said Hardman, hurrying off in search of the two biggest gorillas among the uniformed bunch.

A few minutes later, the basement door, splintered and unhinged, was clattering down stone steps into the dark, cavernous interior.

'There must be a light switch,' said Hardman, feeling the damp wall to his right, just over the threshold. 'Got it.'

Sickly yellow light from a single naked bulb gave them enough illumination to safely descend the twelve uneven steps to a concrete floor. The plunge in temperature from the rest of the house made both men shudder, as if stepping under a cold shower after a day sunbathing in a heatwave.

The single bulb at the top of the stairs was insufficient to throw much light on anything beyond the steps.

'There must be another switch,' said Hardman, groping his way to the wall. 'Here we are.'

Tubed lighting flickered to life uncertainly, then pinged into full fluorescent bloom.

'That's better,' said Templeman, as his eyes acclimatized.

Dominating the room was a surgical slab, which Templeman assumed must be an old operating table that had been replaced upstairs in the surgery by a newer one. As they shuffled closer, they could see that it was heavily blood-stained.

'Animal blood or human, that's the billion-dollar question,' said Hardman, mirroring the teaser that Templeman had already begun to agonize over.

Around the walls were cardboard boxes, most of them

empty. Labels, still stuck to their sides, showed they had been deliveries from surgical supply companies and manufacturers of drugs and medicines for animals. Medicine bottles, some empty and others semi-used, lined a shelf along one wall, which was completely covered in beaded dampness, resembling a suffusion of body-sweat. On the floor, next to the slab, was a container of embalming fluid.

'I wouldn't have thought there was much demand around these parts for embalming cats and dogs,' Hardman observed dryly. 'In the United States, maybe, but Oxford? Never. Not even my dear old long-gone granny would have dreamed of having her Tibs mothballed in a glass display case next to her false teeth in a jar.'

On top of one of the boxes lay a twenty-pack of cigarettes. Hardman picked up the filter tips, peered inside, saw that five were missing – presumably smoked – and put back the pack where he'd found it.

Templeman looked at the embalming fluid and then the cigarette packet, the spark of a thought making a connection and progressing from flicker to raging forest fire in a split-second. He took out one of the cigarettes and sniffed it.

'One mystery solved,' Templeman said conclusively, passing the cigarette to Hardman. 'Smell it.'

'What is it?' Hardman enquired, mystified, pulling a face as he removed the cigarette from under his nose.

'Fry.'

'What?'

'A cigarette laced with embalming fluid is known as Fry in America. When smoked, it makes the smoker giddy and disorientated. It can cause unconsciousness and even death in extreme cases. The pong of petrol or surgical spirit is the give-away. The first recorded case of its use in the UK was in 2004. Now we know why Gloria Swift was swaying as she walked away from the Bodleian Library shortly before being murdered. Remember Fiona Bridges' statement?'

'You're right, it fits, Luke.'

'Carey must have been at the Bodleian that evening,'

Templeman speculated. 'He must have also known that Swift was a smoker.'

'He got chatting to her during the meeting ...'

'Probably at the end,' Templeman cut in.

'He offered her a fag, like the generous, sociable gent he purported to be, to all and sundry.'

'Then followed her, knowing that within a few minutes she'd be groggy,' Templeman continued with the extrapolation. 'In the States, Fry is a common date-rape weapon.'

'He probably had his car parked nearby and it would have been easy for him to steer her to it, offering her a lift home. Do we know what sort of car he drives?'

Templeman shook his head.

'We'd better find out – quickly,' said Hardman, talking more to himself than to Templeman. Then, 'Did you notice the garage?'

'Yes, it's detached from the house. The drive forks just before the frontage. The right fork leads to the brick garage, under an archway of branches.'

'Was it locked?'

'I don't know about it being locked, but the metal door was down: it looked as if it could be remote-controlled.'

'I'll have someone check it out in a minute,' Hardman said, making a mental note, simultaneously kicking a box that appeared to have been opened and re-sealed with sticking tape.

'Let's see what we have here,' Hardman muttered, as if beginning a running commentary, breaking into the cardboard box with his bare hands, with the eager expectation of a down-and-out stumbling across a Fortnum and Mason picnic hamper. 'One charcoal woman's trouser-suit,' he said, in the manner of reciting an inventory into a Dictaphone, as he extracted items of clothing one by one. 'A white, silk woman's blouse. One pair of black tights. Black briefs. Black bra. One pair of black, flat women's shoes. Size five.'

'Charley's size,' said Templeman, putting out a hand. 'Let me see.' As he examined the shoes, he said, 'Charley had a pair just like these, I'm sure of it. A black trouser-suit, too. Black and white was the uniform of her job. You know, as a barrister; formal and austere. Hard-nosed.'

'Yes, I know,' Hardman said, helplessly.

Templeman bullied himself into keeping focused, despite the mounting emotion. 'Plenty to keep Forensics busy,' he said, bleakly.

'Plenty for everybody.'

The last feature of the basement to be inspected was a white upright freezer that hummed and vibrated gently in a far, cobwebbed corner.

'Now let's see what ice cream he licked while dissecting,' said Hardman, pulling open the freezer door. 'Forgive my bad taste,' he added quickly, the pun unintentional, as he realized the implication in respect of Charley Templeman.

The freezer was bare except for two items: a jar containing a pickled human female hand with two fingers missing and a handwritten note on a sheet of lined paper. The note was pinned under the jar and read:

Sorry I missed you, but, as always, you're at least one step behind. Please try harder in future. Think about the game plan, then you just might anticipate my next move, though I doubt it very much. Imagine we're playing chess. Think of the moves so far. Try to fathom how I might be seeking checkmate. Contemplate the kind of sacrifice I might be prepared to make if it presented me with the ultimate prize.
As ever, J and H.

CHAPTER 21

Yvonne Church arrived on her bicycle for work at George Carey's veterinary practice punctually at eight o'clock, only to find the premises and grounds swarming with police officers, who had secured the murder scene. By that time, Forensics were there in full force, taking away everything that might harbour clues. An on-call police doctor had already performed his perfunctory duty. Coroner's office agents, the state's authorized body-snatchers, hovered in the background, awaiting their cue. Digging in the grounds would begin within the next hour as part of the grim search for Charley Templeman's body.

'What's going on? What's happened? Where's Mr Carey? Is he all right? Has something happened to him?' Miss Church, bewildered and panicky, was ushered indoors by a po-faced constable to the waiting room, where Hardman and Templeman were debating an action plan with senior officers.

The young woman's hands were shaking and her normally rose-pink face was bloodless as Hardman peeled away from the others, shadowed by Templeman, to greet her.

'You *are*?' Hardman asked, endeavouring to manufacture a smile, though producing something more predatory.

'Yvonne Church. I work ... for Mr Carey. Where is he?'

'That's what we want to know. It's what I was hoping *you'd* be able to tell us.'

'*Me!*' She was shaking all over now, as if in shock. Her eyes, large pools of aquamarine inquisitiveness, jumped between the two men. 'Who smashed the front door? Has there been a burglary? Has Mr Carey been injured?'

'Nothing like that, but Mr Carey appears to be missing.'

'*Missing*?'

'Well, he's not here and we're looking for him,' said Hardman, a cigarette dangling between his fingers at his side.

Yvonne's eyes clicked on a 'No Smoking' notice hanging on the wall, but even she, in her confusion, recognized that this was not the occasion for the enforcement of petty house rules.

'Mr Carey lives here. He's always in the surgery, preparing for the day, by 7.30, half an hour before me. Or even earlier. This is unheard of.'

'Take my word for it, Miss Church, he's not here.'

Yvonne was wearing jodhpurs and russet riding boots, giving the impression that she might have already groomed a horse or pony and had been for a pre-work gallop. Her hair was long and blonde, trailing over her square shoulders, and her friendly face was oval, not defined by bone-lines. Everything about her screamed outdoor girl. Although not fat, it was easy to believe that she wasn't one for diets and rigid healthy-eating regimes.

'I don't understand what's going on.'

'We need to talk urgently with your boss,' said Hardman, firmly.

'What about?'

'We're hoping he can help us with our inquiries … into a serious crime.'

'A *crime*! I really can't get my head around this and I can't fathom, for the life of me, why Mr Carey isn't here now.'

'Let's try to be methodical about this, Miss Church. When did you last see him?'

'Yesterday afternoon. About three o'clock. He said I could go early. Very early!'

'Why was that?'

'He said he was having to cancel evening surgery.'

'Was that unusual?'

'Very, especially without prior notice. Unheard of, in fact.

He's so very conscientious. If he's going to cancel a surgery because of a prior special business or social engagement, he plans well ahead and there'll be a notice displayed in the surgery, giving plenty of advance warning.'

'So you were surprised yesterday?'

'Yes, but pleasantly.'

'Did you ask for an explanation?'

'No, but *he* offered one, saying something unexpected had come up.'

'But he didn't elaborate?'

'No.'

'And you didn't press him?'

'Of course not. I just work for him. If he wants to shut up shop early, that's his affair.'

'You obviously enjoy your work,' said Templeman, smoothly taking over the questioning, sensing some friction creeping in between the young woman and Hardman, who had the bedside manner of a hungry wolf.

'I love it.'

'How long have you been employed by Mr Carey?'

'Oh, getting on for two years now.'

'Straight from uni?'

'No, I went on to a farm from school, missing out university. I always wanted to work with animals. When I saw this job advertised, I applied. It was nearer home than the farm and I also liked the idea of helping to cure sick and rescued animals.'

'You still live with your parents?'

'No, not any more. I share a small flat with my boyfriend.'

'Have you noticed any change in Mr Carey in recent months?'

Yvonne screwed up her face in a gesture of non-comprehension. 'I'm not sure I follow.'

'What's he like normally?'

'Very nice, polite, compassionate, but demanding.'

'Not bad-tempered, usually?'

'Never.'

'Not even of late'?'

'No, as I said, not ever.'

'How about appearing preoccupied, as if worried, with a lot on his mind?'

'No, if anything, he's seemed more jaunty and easy-going than ever just lately.'

'We know Mr Carey has been living here alone, but has he ever been married? Is there a wife, ex-wife or ex-partner anywhere?'

'Not to my knowledge, though that's pretty limited in that respect. He's never alluded to anything like that. But even if he was separated or divorced, it's not something he'd ever discuss with me. We never talk about anything personal.'

'*Never*? Isn't that strange in itself?'

'Well, when I say *never* I mean nothing at length, nothing in depth, nothing too serious.'

'Give me an example of something he *has* talked about lately, other than work.

Yvonne giggled nervously. 'That's as hard as saying, "Tell me your favourite joke." It's impossible to think of one, let alone your funniest, when put on the spot like that. He might mention something that's in the papers or on TV, something topical and in the news.'

'Such as?' Templeman persisted, like a beachcomber religiously prizing open every oyster-shell he could find in the hope of uncovering one pearl.

Yvonne scratched her head, symbolically shaking her brain, but the fall-out was minimal.

'He often makes a comment about the troubles in the Middle East and the horrible things that went on in Iraq, for example. I never take much notice. I think he may have a few little hang-ups, but don't tell him I said that or I might be looking for a new job.'

'What sort of *hang-ups*?'

She retreated into reverie again, before saying, 'He might chunter on about the Americans and how they could learn a thing or two from the Arabs. He's never said anything in support of anyone like Saddam Hussein, but once or twice he's remarked that at least the Arabs know how to treat their women.'

'What do you suppose he means by that?'

'I dread to think because my education taught me that women traditionally have been regarded as second-class citizens in Arab states. They are respected and to an extent revered in some ways, though, so he could have been thinking along those lines.'

'But you never tackled him on it?'

'It's none of my business and I don't really care what he thinks, to be honest, as long as I'm happy in my work and my pay is paid punctually.'

'So that's the extent of his *hang-ups*?'

More thought, then, 'He'll sometimes have a dig after a woman has left the surgery, saying, "What a bitch! And I'm not referring to her dog!" There's one woman in particular he takes exception to, but I must admit she is a bit mouthy. One of those bossy sort. Mr Carey reckons she must be a teacher or professional muck-raker. That's what he calls those in lobby groups.'

'What's her name?'

'I think it's Grantham. No idea what her first name is. Here, she's just Mrs Grantham. And "the witch" and "bitch" when she's gone.'

Templeman smiled appreciatively. 'You say he sometimes has *a dig* at women: never men?'

This question from Templeman jolted Yvonne as surely as if she'd stumbled over something unforeseen.

'I've never thought about it like that. Anything disparaging has been mainly about women, but, then, most of the people who bring their pets for treatment are women ... or teenage girls. We see very few males in the surgery, except those with four legs.'

Templeman decided he'd exhausted a line that had finally borne fruit. So he took a step back before continuing forward. 'This seems such a big property just for one person. It must have been built to house a large family.' There was a question in that observation which Yvonne addressed without a further prompt.

'If Mr Carey lived here at any time with a family of his, it's news to me.'

Now came the googly, bowled with maximum camouflage. 'When were you last in the basement?'

'I've never been in the basement.' Her reply was as spontaneous as an echo. 'Why do you ask?'

'We couldn't find a key to the basement door.' This wasn't an answer to Yvonne's question, of course, but it was a means of initiating further exploration, testing her veracity.

'Mr Carey is the only person with a key to the basement. He carries it with him at all times.'

'What's so important and private down there that it's a no-go zone for you, his trusted employee?'

'No idea. But many areas of the house are out of bounds to me.'

'Such as?'

'All the domestic quarters. That's natural enough to me. With roles reversed, I wouldn't want an employee of mine tramping through my home. There have to be boundaries that can't be breached. For all I know, he may have priceless paintings and heirlooms of sentimental value stored below deck. Now, would you please tell me what this is all about?'

Templeman handed over to Hardman.

'Sorry, can't go into that at present, but you can take it from me you won't be working today. I'll have an officer take a proper statement from you later, so we'd better have an address from you and a contact phone number.'

Yvonne blanched as she gave the information asked for, after which Hardman said, 'I don't suppose you know where we could lay a hand on a photo of Mr Carey?'

'You're right, I don't,' she replied, slightly nettly now.

'He must have relatives.'

'Yes, he must have, but who and where I've no idea.'

'Does he visit people at weekends?'

'What he does and where he goes outside business hours has never been made known to me.'

'So you've no idea where he might be now?'

'If he's not here and has left without warning, then a real emergency must have turned up – or he's ill. Have you checked admissions at all the local hospitals? He could have collapsed somewhere *last night*.'

'I'll bear that in mind. What sort of car does he drive?

'A Volvo Estate.'

'Colour?'

'Green. Dark green.'

'Registration number?'

'No idea, but it's a fairly new car. He bought it within the last year.'

'How would you describe him, physically?'

'Quite tall and athletic for his age. He jogs regularly and belongs to a fitness club, I think, but I couldn't tell you which one.'

'How old would you say he is?'

'Oh, forty-five … ish. '

'Hair colour?'

'Black; a little grey around the temples. Fairly short cut, but not severely so.'

'Concentrate for a moment on his face, will you?'

'Pleasant.'

'I'm thinking more about shape and complexion.'

'Angular, a wee bit high-boned, sallow.'

'Colour of eyes?'

'Blue. Very blue. Riveting.'

'Well done. I might ask you to team up with one of our artists later today to see if we can come up with a convincing likeness of Mr Carey.'

'If you think it'll help …'

'It will.' Hardman closed the subject curtly, then thanked her and moved on, while Templeman sent her a bouquet of smiles with the unspoken message, *Don't worry, he's like this with everyone. You did good.*

Rubbing his hands, Hardman said to Templeman enthusi-astically, 'We'll have him in the net before the day's out.' And then, as if a fisherman, 'What a catch of the day!'

Once again he was wrong – by several thousand miles.

CHAPTER 22

Next day:

The hunt for George Carey had been in top gear for more than twenty-four hours. The Passport Office and the DVLC headquarters in Swansea had quickly supplied the Thames Valley police with copies of convict-style photos they held on file of Carey. The artist's impression, crafted in collaboration with Yvonne Church, injected personality into the still-life of a man who had silenced and stilled so many other lives. The media was feeding off the latest developments like a jungle big cat that hadn't eaten for weeks. Its appetite was insatiable. Templeman's advice to both Hardman and Badger was to drip-feed them everything.

'Now's the time to exploit them to our advantage,' he reasoned. 'They have the resources to probe Carey's background right back to conception. Some people may talk to reporters who wouldn't dream of helping us. The tabloids will be scouring the world for relatives and ex-lovers, et cetera. Let's use them as unpaid coolies.'

This appealed to Badger, and Hardman recognized the logic, provided he wasn't expected to be the nursemaid to the hacks.

'You leave *them* to me,' Badger told Hardman peremptorily, luxuriating in the whirlwind of activity and publicity that was sweeping the city. 'You bring in this headbanger – and make it quick, while the momentum is with us.'

It was just before noon that Templeman took a call from

Hardman on his mobile in the News Café, a quaint gem of a place he'd stumbled across in Ship Street, behind Jesus College and next to the ancient landmark of St Michael-at-the-North-Gate, the tower of which is the oldest building in Oxford, of Saxon origin and dating back to around 1000, pre-Norman Conquest.

Hardman's grave tone prepared Templeman for pain, as surely as a nurse warning of a 'sharp prick coming' as she aims a needle at the muscle of your arm. 'I'm at Carey's place. There's been a find.' He drew in air deeply, as if running short of oxygen; running almost on empty.

'A body? Not Carey? He hasn't topped himself?'

'Unfortunately not. If that were the case, we'd be popping corks. No, the remains of a human have been dug up, which rules out Carey! Under a rose bush – red roses, the emblem of love – at the bottom of the garden, at the rear. Old bones. A female, according to our Doc at the scene. There are personal items too, which I think you'll recognize, Luke. You know what I'm saying. I'm sorry.'

Templeman had gone cold, even though it was the hottest day of the year so far. 'You think it's Charley?'

'I *know* it's Charley.'

'I'll be with you in ten minutes.'

'Not a good idea, Luke. Stay where you are. There's nothing for you here.'

'I've got to be sure, Mike, for God's sake! I've got to see for myself.'

'But not *here*; not like this. The professionals have to be left alone to do things their way; everything right, by the book. This is no place for anyone with emotional baggage.'

Hardman was right, of course, though that was something Templeman had difficulty accepting. He had waited so long for this moment. During his police career, he'd tried to comfort many parents of missing children. All of them, without exception, had craved most of all for knowledge of what had befallen their loved one. *It's the not knowing that's the hardest to live with,* was the cliché that united them all. That was a truism with which Templeman had identified ever since Charley's disappearance, even though the love between them had died of detrition long before her death.

'You don't want to come here just for what even the rats and worms have turned their backs on,' Hardman continued, a tenderness in his voice that was awkward for him, thus underscoring its sincerity. 'The *real* Charley is some other place; whatever you believe in. Take my advice, you keep away from here. I'll catch up with you later, when it's time for you to do something official. When that time comes, I'll drive you up to the Radcliffe. Then we'll have a few beers. Do things right. Draw a line under it properly. This psycho can't go far. Every force in the country's been alerted. So, too, all our air and sea ports. Interpol as well. His mug shot is all over TV and every daily newspaper in the land. He's getting more exposure than Elvis in his stardust days. He's the UK's most wanted man on the run. Someone, somewhere will finger him within the next forty-eight hours. If they don't, we'll offer a jackpot reward. That'll do the trick. Greasing palms never fails. You know the statistics. The odds are stacked against him. In fact, the odds in his favour are zero. He may think he's running, but he's on a treadmill. He ain't getting anywhere.'

'Keep in touch,' said Templeman, hitting the kill button as tears filled his eyes, but remained contained within their darkling sockets. He was too choked up for any more of this.

A concerned waitress, having observed Templeman's overt distress, touched his shoulder solicitously. 'Are you all right, sir?'

He looked up forlornly, his sightless gaze seeing only images of years gone by, another woman's face superimposed on the waitress. 'It's kind of you to ask. I've just received some unpleasant news, but I'm OK.'

'Well, if there's anything else I can get you, just shout.'

As his eyes dried out, he was drawn, as if by the power of a magnetic field, towards a TV that was angled towards him from an eyrie-position on a wall opposite. Momentarily disorientated, he thought he must be staring into a mirror as his own face filled the screen and stayed there for several seconds, before being replaced by a reporter, stationed outside Carey's house. The reporter was saying into his mike, 'Police officers, who have been digging in the grounds of the veterinary practice for the past twenty-four hours, have unearthed the remains of a human body, believed to be missing barrister Charley Templeman, the estranged wife of ex-top cop Luke Templeman.' Luke's picture flashed on the screen again, before the camera on the reporter became live once more. 'This discovery comes hot on the heels of the murder of solicitor Carla North, the feisty campaigner on women's issues, who has been identified as the Oxford serial killer's fifth victim. In a major breakthrough, the police have named Oxford vet George Carey as their chief suspect.' Now it was the turn of Carey's mug shot to dominate the screen. 'Mr Carey hasn't been seen since closing his surgery early the day after Miss North was apparently lured to her death, after leaving Ruskin College around 10 p.m.'

Templeman couldn't take any more. He paid his bill, forced out a smile, and hurried into the baking sunshine, allowing himself to be swept along by the tide of tourists in Cornmarket Street, riding the waves of people, going wherever taken.

By six o'clock, Hardman's boiler-room team – the deskbound grafters on phones and computers – had tracked Carey to the USA. He had purchased a ticket at Heathrow for American Airlines' last flight of the day to New York on the day that his voice had been broadcast nationwide on all TV and radio networks, leaving his Volvo in the long-stay multi-storey car park. He passed through Immigration into the USA at 10.10 p.m., just hours before he was listed internationally as a fugitive. He had given 'vacationing' as the reason for entering the USA and the Waldorf Astoria as the address where he would be staying in New York for 'two weeks'.

FBI agents went to the Waldorf, but there was no-one registered under the name of Carey. All registration cards were examined of those residents who had checked in during the last forty-eight hours. The names on the registration cards were authenticated by credit cards, which had been swiped by staff on the guests' arrival to guarantee payment.

Hardman was now ready to catch up with Templeman. Inevitably, the meeting place was a pub: this time the Turf Tavern, another historic monument to Oxford's past, reputed to be more than eight centuries old and renowned for pacifying every conceivable palate with a selection of eleven different traditional ales. But Templeman wasn't altogether comfortable here, for one obvious reason. After all, this was the place to which he had been tempted under false pretences on the evening of his wife's disappearance.

Both men took considerable precautions to ensure that they weren't followed by the press corps. As solemn as pallbearers, they carried their beers outside to a bench-table on the paved patio, enclosed within wrought-iron railings and under a overhanging tree that served as a natural parasol, protecting them from the still mercilessly roasting sun.

Although the Turf was at the heart of Oxford's throbbing anatomy and was as popular with students as with tourists, it was also something of an oasis, invisible to the casual passer-by, who could tread the hallowed pavements of Holywell Street, along the city wall, for a lifetime without ever being aware of the sacred watering hole closeted in Bath Place, among a labyrinth of shaded alleys.

They both folded their jackets on the picnic-styled wooden tables, having already loosened their ties, popped shirt collar-buttons, and rolled up sleeves. Summer had reached its blistering peak, but for these men the salad days remained elusive.

'Florida weather, huh?' commented Hardman, in a typical British way of kick-starting a conversation. Talk about the weather!

'Almost,' said Templeman, the weather rating low on his priorities.

They both drank thirstily. Hardman dabbed his sweaty forehead with a handkerchief. Templeman was still frozen inside, despite the outside heat.

'I've decided there's no point dragging you up to the Radcliffe,' said Hardman, at last tiptoeing on to the sensitive business agenda. 'All they have there is a bag of bones. You don't want to see all that stuff. Won't do you any good. Me neither.'

'I have a duty,' Templeman protested, stiff-lipped.

'It'll be a pointless, though painful, exercise in terms of IDing. We'll do it from dental records and DNA. Leave it to the boffins. We have the clothes at the nick. You can come look at them whenever you're ready. It's nothing more than a formality. There's no doubt. I know it's Charley. You know it's Charley. The scientists will do the rubber-stamping. As for Carey, he's running down a dead end. He can't possibly have a bottomless pit of cash in dollars and that means sooner or later he's going to have to use credit cards. And plastic trails are even better than paper trails. Within minutes of his paying for a meal, a rental car, an airline ticket, or a bed for the night, the FBI will know exactly where he is. Bingo!'

'I don't get it.'

'What don't you *get*?'

'He kills Charley, a visitor to Oxford, here on business, a mere transient. He takes her back to his home. Does he kill her there or is she already dead?'

Hardman shrugged and drank some more. 'We should soon have all those answers, for what they're worth.'

Templeman wasn't listening. This was to be more a monologue than dialogue.

'How did he lure Charley into his car, if indeed that's how it began? She wouldn't have voluntarily taken a lift from a stranger. Charley was as streetwise as you or me.'

'She went for a stroll, Luke. There's no telling where she went, maybe exploring. *He* could have been biding his time or maybe it was just a chance encounter. Who knows? Charley was in the wrong place at the wrong time, something we hear about in court every day.'

'He cuts off a hand before burying her. He has a plan, right from the very beginning – even *before* the beginning – don't you see? He knows exactly who she is. She isn't a random victim. She's special, the chosen one. Already he's gone to all the trouble of enticing me to Oxford, to this very pub, setting me up nicely for the murder of my wife; don't forget that part of it. He's not only killing Charley, but also killing off my career, my future, my prospects. The whole plot runs deep, dark and dirty. Why Charley? Why me? He has no criminal record. Charley wasn't responsible for putting him away. Me neither. So why the grudge?'

'You probably need to be as deranged as he is to appreciate that one.'

'Having murdered Charley, he lies low while I'm arrested, tried and convicted.'

'That was probably orgasmic for a creep like that. I expect he got off on it.'

'But then he's able to suppress any urge to kill for another two years. He could have left me to rot, but that would be to rewrite the script because Charley's hand had been preserved for one purpose only. Then, by ensuring I was exonerated, he put his own freedom and future on the line. From that point, he kills again, and again, and again; suddenly more like the classic psycho, except his victims are atypical. They're all successful professionals with strong personalities, as far from the fragile demimonde as it's possible to get. Not a mini-skirt or fishnet stocking between them. All Oxford-based, unlike Charley.'

'Which makes almost all of them of a kind.'

'Homogenous.'

'Whatever.'

'No sexual motivation.'

'Nothing obvious, though we don't know what's going on in his addled head, Luke.'

'He kills four times without making a single mistake.'

'He was lucky.'

'Then after the fifth, he blows it completely.'

'His luck ran out, simple as that, as we said it would. It always does.'

'This was deliberate, Mike. Remember the game, the cat and mouse, the taunting; his *need* for my participation. And as soon as he has me here, he appears to fluff it.'

'Forget the *appears*, he has fluffed it. Big-time. Period.'

'But has he?'

'Of course he has! He's identified himself. He's uncovered.'

'But we haven't got him.'

'The sand in the egg-timer's running out. He's cooked!'

'I can't help thinking he still has us dancing to his tune.'

'If he has, it can only be the last waltz.'

Templeman was ruminating over Carey's last jeering note, which had been left for them to find in the basement freezer. *Sorry I missed you, but, as always, you're at least one step behind. Think about the game plan, then you might just anticipate my next move ...*

The more Templeman reflected on that note, the more certain he was that if anyone was on the run, it was them. Carey hadn't fled, he had merely made his next move.

Imagine we're playing chess, he'd written. *Try to fathom how I might be seeking checkmate. Contemplate the kind of sacrifice I might be prepared to make if it presented me with the ultimate prize.*

'It's as if he's pulling our strings, yanking our chain,' Templeman said, ruefully.

'Like heck he is! The only string attached to him now is in the shape of a noose, and it's tightening.'

They drank up.

'I reckon your job's just about done here,' said Hardman, slapping Templeman on the shoulder heartily as they headed back into mainstream Oxford.

Templeman didn't respond. He saw no point in spoiling Hardman's cosy sojourn in fool's paradise, purely on a hunch.

They walked together in contemplative silence, jackets over

their damp arms, until they reached the western end of Holywell Street, where they parted; Hardman cheerily, Templeman more reserved.

Hardman continued straight ahead into Broad Street – as wide and imposing as its name suggests – while Templeman took a left into Catte Street and then into the High, which he crossed by All Souls College. Fumes from the traffic were trapped in the humid heat like a miasmic, London smog of the 1950s. There wasn't even a whisper of a breeze to freshen the sultry air. The only scent was of sulphur.

From the south side of the High, he made down a comparatively cool alley – completely hidden from the sun and indeed any sky-light – into Magpie Lane alongside Oriel College, following a path around Merton College until he was on Deadman's Walk, with Christ Church behind him and the Botanic Garden and the River Cherwell ahead. Centuries ago, this was the route of Jewish funeral processions to a synagogue that stood on the site of Christ Church's Tom Tower.

Deadman's Walk: how apt this should be the way I go! he mused to himself.

He needed this space and solitude, plus detachment, to give him the chance to crack the code. Hardman, Badger, and the rest of them, dismissed Carey's farewell missive as nothing more than the maundering machinations of a madman. True to a point, but they were confusing deranged with dim. The two weren't necessarily the same. Carey was intelligent, proved by his academic qualifications, a prerequisite for acceptance into his chosen profession. Hence the IQ of the quarry was probably far higher than that of any of the hunters, including Templeman. Cryptography would be well within his grasp.

And it was while in the idyllic, sleepy peacefulness of Christ Church Meadow, as he approached the weeping willows slumbering along the ragged bank of the Cherwell, that the baleful coded message dawned on him, like a spiritual revelation, paralysing him mid-stride.

But was it too late to deny this erudite demon his *coup de grâce*?

There was only one way to find out.

CHAPTER 23

The ringing tone, like a healthy heartbeat, was steady, regular and strong.

One, two, three … Templeman was counting, as if listening to the pulse of his own life. *Come on, pick up, Simone. Please be there. Please be OK.*

Six, seven, eight … *The answer-machine will soon kick in. Then what shall I do? Dammit, Simone! Where are you?*

The ringing tone stopped, as suddenly as a cardiac arrest. And then, 'Hello?'

'Simone!'

'Who else did you expect?'

'Are you all right?' Templeman's voice was dripping with unease.

'Yes, of course, why shouldn't I be?'

Something was wrong, Templeman knew it. There was such an affinity between them that they could communicate by telepathy, the nuances of body language and verbal shorthand. And at this moment Simone was transmitting bad vibes.

'No reason,' said Templeman, playing safe. 'I just thought you sounded rather strained. You have every right to be, mind you, after your manic last few days.'

'And how about you?'

This wasn't the *real* effusive, animated Simone Tandy. This was an iceberg. A stranger to Templeman. This was Simone sending out an SOS signal with every constricted breath.

'Things are happening this end, too. We now know the identity of the serial killer. We got the breakthrough.'

'Oh, good.'

Oh, good! What kind of reaction is that? If there wasn't something – someone – stopping her, she'd be doing cartwheels.

'Trouble is, he's given us the slip.'

'Too bad.'

Too bad! This is ridiculous, like trying to have a conversation with a flat tyre.

'But he won't get far. We've got his car reg and a photo. The police are watching all ports – sea and air. If he's managed to slip through the net and is already out of the country, we'll soon know where he's flown.'

'So it's almost all over.'

'Almost. Look, you sound bushed, so I'll leave you to rest and catch up on your sleep. I'll call you again tomorrow. If you need me, I'll still be at the Randolph in Oxford for the next two or three days. I'll let you know when I'm flying home. My job's almost done here.'

'Oh, Luke, do me a favour: call my parents and let them know I'm OK, will you? I don't want them worrying about me, but I'm not in the mood for the inevitable inquisition from them yet.'

Templeman hardly missed a beat before saying, 'Of course, darling, I'll do it right away.'

That was the confirmation. He hung up knowing that Simone was in mortal danger.

Simone's parents had died several years ago.

'Good girl,' said Carey. 'We know now that your beloved Luke is still in Oxford. Despite what he said, the police must know that I'm in the States, but in New York. Luke is either out of the loop now or has been told to keep his mouth shut, even to you. But the one place they'll never dream of looking is *here*, especially as Luke has just talked with you and you're OK; fine and dandy. By the time your beloved puts it all together – if ever – it'll be far too late to prevent the *coup de grâce*.'

Carey cuffed Tandy's hands behind her back. Her ankles

were clamped in irons and chains, allowing her to walk only at a shuffle, a condemned prisoner on Death Row, as Carey was to delight in reminding her *ad nauseam.*

Now she sat deflated on the end of her bed, her aching bare feet resting on the beige carpet. Her ankles were bruised and swollen from the tightness of the metal clamps. The handcuffs were biting into her wrists, chafing her flesh to such an extent that blood had been drawn. The hooded lids of her emerald eyes felt as large as oyster-shells and just as heavy. She was fighting to stay awake, having been constantly sedated with medication Carey used to drug sick animals. The handcuffs and ankle clamps, with chains attached, linking legs, had been bought in advance at an Oxford sex shop.

Carey, as relaxed as a holidaymaker, was slouched in a wicker chair a few feet away from the foot of the kingsize bed, his back to an ivory-coloured pair of wardrobes, with sliding doors and mirrors, that covered the entire wall behind him. He wore a crisp, freshly laundered, sleeveless white shirt, light-weight grey trousers and fake crocodile loafers. He had showered and shaved, and the redolence of an expensive aftershave was so heady that it was almost as soporific for Tandy as the tranquillizer she'd been administered.

In contrast, Tandy was still wearing the same business clothes she'd worn when rendezvousing with Carey the previous day in a parking lot near Naples beach. Advertisements for the PI agency, called T for Two, run by Tandy and Templeman, gave only their mobile numbers. Initial meetings with prospective clients were always conducted in public places, for security reasons. In the past, private detectives, like most small businesses, needed a public presence, a visible base with a name on a door and perhaps even a brass plaque. That was no longer necessary and it had been Templeman who had pointed out the advantages of not being anchored to an office base, but rather operating as 'floaters', like ships that were always at sea, rarely docking.

'All we need are mobile phones, a post-office box number, and an apartment spacious enough for an office for two, with room for filing cabinets,' Templeman had said. Too many premises of private detectives in the USA had been torched. Neither was it uncommon for private sleuths to be the dead victims of vendettas. There was safety in invisibility. Well, that's what they had thought.

Carey had introduced himself on the phone as a Brit married to an American and living 'Naples way', going on plaintively, 'I'm concerned my wife's having an affair and is planning to run off with her lover, who's nothing more than an opportunist, on-the-make toyboy. I know he's only after her money – *my* money! – but my wife can't see that because she's so besotted. She's at that *funny* age, trying desperately to cling to her youth. I have to know the truth. And if my suspicions are correct, I want to know as much as possible about the young stud.'

He had pressed the point that 'money was no object'. He would 'pay whatever it costs to get at the truth', adding, 'Of course I expect to have to cover all expenses. Whatever you charge upfront will be fine by me. Just name your price and I'll pay in cash: no cheques, no plastic, if that'll induce you to drop everything else and just give my case your undivided attention'. He had stressed the urgency, saying he would give the assignment to someone else if Tandy was unable to offer him an appointment 'within the next couple of hours'.

Tandy had suggested they meet for a coffee in the Registry Hotel, but Carey had replied, 'I'm too well known there. Sonia – that's my wife – is frequently there with clients. She's in real estate. In fact, she's into *everything*. We both play golf and tennis and, therefore, we have a wide circle of friends. There are so many places we could bump into her, such as the Registry.' He had then proposed the parking lot. 'We can sit in your car or mine and I can show you photographs of Sonia, our kids – such lovely kids! – and give you other important info, like the make of her car and registration number, and her daily routine.'

Tandy had been disarmed by his English accent and aura of stuttering vulnerability.

After Carey had climbed into the front passenger seat of her Oldsmobile, Tandy found herself with the twelve-inch-long blade of a hunting knife pointing at her throat.

'I know everything about you,' he'd boasted, his calculating eyes concealed behind reflector shades. 'I know you're physically capable, but even you are no match for *this* at close quarters, especially in such a confined space.' He'd nicked her pulsating neck with the tip of the blade. There were several other cars in the parking lot, but no people. In the driving mirror, Tandy saw a police cruiser idle past on the main highway behind, then was gone.

'OK, what do you want?' she'd said as positively as possible in the circumstances, resigned to playing along with this crazy, whom she was confident of being able to 'take' at some opportune, off-guarded moment.

'You.'

Well, at least that had the merit of being unequivocal.

OK, he plans to rape me, then what? she said to herself philosophically, determined to be sangfroid to the end. Will he dare let me go? Will he dare kill me? Killing someone didn't take a lot of courage these days, especially if on drugs, was a consideration that did little to console her. All hostages quickly adapt to the survival game.

Reading her thoughts through the transparency of her eyes, Carey had said sneeringly, 'So typical of your gender! You automatically assume I'm lusting after your body. God, you disgust me! Well, let me make this clear: I'd throw up if I had to touch you. In fact, should you force me to touch you, that will make me very angry, very dangerous. I cannot imagine anything more distasteful than having a sexual encounter with someone like you.'

Tandy had been shaken by this outburst, not because she was offended by his lack of carnal interest in her, but because now she had no notion of what was driving him and that was more disturbing than the act of abduction. If you knew the motive, you always had a chance to manipulate. Without that knowledge, you were bereft of bargaining power; helplessly adrift. Anchorless had seemed an asset. Rudderless was something very different, especially when a psycho pirate had jumped aboard and taken over.

'Drive,' he'd ordered.

'Where to?' she'd asked, still spirited and defiant.

'Your place, of course. Don't try anything silly. You wouldn't have a chance. I'm an expert with knives. I use them every day of my working life. I know just where to stick them to bring about closure.'

Her place, which she shared with Templeman, of course, was a top-storey luxury apartment. The living room and the bedroom both had spectacular views of the ocean to the west and the inland waterway to the east. Tandy hadn't tried anything silly. She had been obedient, if not meek. Now she was incapable of trying to escape, even if she was prepared to gamble against all the odds.

Outside the east-facing windows, pelicans perched on a pontoon. Flamingos gathered on a small, green island about 200 yards offshore in the backwater. Lots of residents preferred boats to cars for transport. Hence the inland waterway was as much a busy highway as the roads.

A couple of small motorboats, heading for a slipway, were overloaded with shopping bags. Beachside, the ocean shimmered in the mid-morning sunshine, but an ominous black awning in the sky to the south warned of the approach of the hurricane season. An electric storm was on a roll from Mexico and the pyrotechnics were forecast to light up Naples that evening. Oblivious to storms on the horizon, groups of men and women fished from the pier. Tourists splashed playfully in the sea, even though only two days previously a teenage surfer had been snapped in two by a rogue shark in the shallows. Danger was all around – indoors as well as outside. The knife was on the floor, between Carey's feet, as he gripped a mug of coffee with both steady hands.

'I'm thirsty,' Tandy mumbled, dead-eyed.

'So you keep saying.'

'Then why won't you get me a drink?' Her head remained

dipped, like that of a slave who knew she'd be in for a whipping if she dared to look into the eyes of her master.

'Because a little dehydration will help to keep you disorientated and immobilized.'

In the hours since she was kidnapped, Tandy had been allowed only the occasional sip of water and no food. This was to ensure that she remained weak and dysfunctional.

'Why are you doing this to me?' Tandy was forcing herself to ask questions in an effort to stay awake and as alert as possible.

'You really don't get it, do you?'

'If I did, I wouldn't be asking.' Sweat was making her brunette hair tacky and she was itching all over. Although Carey had never mentioned his name or specifically identified himself as the serial killer being hunted in England by Templeman and the Thames Valley police, Tandy had quickly pieced it all together.

'Your partner is a smart detective.'

'The best.'

'I admire your loyalty.'

'But not much else, it would seem.' Her suntan seemed to have been peeled off overnight, leaving her like a skinned banana. Not ripe, though, but gaunt and slightly disfigured with an unmistakable haunted look. Even her normally unblemished teeth had turned yellow with the fever of fear.

'Your lover was married to scum.'

'What has that to do with me? I never knew Charley.' Her lips were parched and the scar on her head, hidden by newly grown hair, marking the area where surgeons had operated successfully on a brain tumour, felt as if it had become raised in a reaction to the stress.

Carey allowed himself to slide lower into his chair, not answering her immediately. Instead, he drank some more coffee, slurping noisily while the windmills of his mind were spinning.

'Charley Templeman was scum. Her entire life was dedicated to representing the lowest of the low, sewer creatures, the sediment of society, and she rejoiced in seeing her rodent clients cheat the justice system. She became an icon of idolatry, a symbol of a truly sick society, in which the highest rewards are commensurate with the highest infamy. She was a disgrace to womanhood. She debased the human race.'

'She defended people. Juries acquitted or convicted them, not Mrs Templeman.'

Logic was a loser.

'She beguiled and bewitched. During jury selection, she'd object to anyone who looked half-respectable. She always went for a full house of men jurors. With her flighty eyes and suggestive mouth – her dirty mouth! – she'd seduce them, one by one, across the courtroom. They'd go to bed with their wives wet-dreaming about Charley Templeman.'

'How can you possibly know that?'

Reasoning with this man really was bad tactics.

'Because I saw the bitch in action.'

'In court?'

'In court, for three weeks, on the jury, listening to her filth as she defended a rapist.'

'But she didn't seduce you?'

'I was the only one she didn't. It was eleven against one for acquittal. He was as guilty as hell. He raped a seventeen-year-old church-goer. Not many of those around these pagan days. A devout Christian child physically and mentally destroyed by a barbarian, a leering lager lout, who walked, not because of his innocence or any genuine doubt, but because of his barrister's own ungodly guilt, her pact with the devil. Faust got to her first, but I was quick on his heels. She was a sorceress, endowed with the black art of casting spells over men.'

'But you weren't taken in.' Tandy tried to bond spiritually with him, but it was too late to tamper with the template.

'I went ballistic in that jury room. Those morons couldn't talk about anything other than how desirable that cow was. In three weeks, she'd become their pin-up and she knew it. Loved it. Lapped it up. She knew she had them hard for her, in a trance, salivating. It was pathetic. Grown men, infatuated like adolescents! And she teased them all the way to a not guilty verdict, allowing the rapist to go free to do it again.'

'Did he – do it again?'

'What do you think? Of course he did. Next time, though, he killed. The bitch didn't have the guts to defend him second time round, though. She knew she'd be on to a loser. She wasn't prepared to face the heat of hate that would have been conducted her way.'

'So you decided to kill her? To play God?'

'I don't *play,* in the manner of a dilettante, at anything!'

His eyes – and hers – were sucked towards the knife, as if in acknowledgement of the seriousness of his intent and her plight.

'You saw your chance when you read that she was going to be the defence counsel in a forthcoming trial at Oxford Crown Court. But why did you want Luke to be blamed?'

'To see if it was possible. Just as rational as the reason why people climb mountains: because they're there. The joust with your beloved has been the sub-plot, a sideshow really, an element of light relief to make the main agenda more interesting and less of a chore.'

Tandy decided it made sense to engage with him, rather to confront and trash his untenable crusade, what amounted to a personal holy war against warrior women.

'I can understand your outrage.'

'You *can?*' he said doubtfully.

'Often, when I was in the police, I had to restrain myself from harming people I arrested if I thought they were truly evil, without redeeming features.'

'Were you always able to suppress your gut instincts?'

'Always, because it was a learned discipline, a demonstration of strength. To have been physical would have revealed a crack in my character, a weakness.'

'That's where we differ, you see. I believe you should stamp on maggots and cockroaches. Extermination is the only solution. Anything less is to enable them to continue to infect and to breed. Appeasement is a bigger sin than the evil others do.'

'I see why you hated Charley Templeman so much, but what about the others? How did they offend you?'

'Do you really want to know or is this a pathetic attempt to negotiate for your life? If it's the latter, then forget it, it's futile.'

'I *really do* want to know.'

Carey stood up, stretched, and ambled with his now tepid coffee to the ocean-facing window, part of a sliding door that led on to a balcony, where there was a glass-topped table and a couple of white, plastic garden-type chairs. 'Such a glorious day, but spoilt by the shit looming in the distant sky. That's the point, you see, the answer to your last question: there's always some little shit spoiling what could otherwise be such a beautiful planet.'

'And the other women fell into that category?'

'Every one, without exception, a pushy, bigoted big mouth. I knew them personally. They trusted me; felt safe with me. Cretins! They weren't championing sexual equality, they were fighting for female dominance. The eunuchification of the world! Every word they ever uttered grated with me. They fitted the bill.'

'What *bill*?'

'The status of human maggot, cockroach and parasite. They reminded me of my own mother, may God curse her soul!'

'You didn't get along with your mother?'

'She was one of *them*.'

'A formidable woman?'

'A coward. Another bitch! She even admitted to me that I only got born because abortion hadn't been legalized and she didn't know how to go about getting one on the back street black market.' He stood with his back to the bed, still gazing desolately out to sea, though his sight was unfocused. 'She was one of those who lobbied for even more liberal abortion laws right up until her long-overdue death. What she was really doing was making a statement that she wished me back among the unborn. From the age of fifteen, I wished her

dead every day of my life. No exaggeration. She was the catalyst.'

'How did she die?'

'Not painfully enough.'

'Did you have a hand in it?'

Now he turned slowly to face her, a sly smile creasing his
pained face.

'If only!' he said wistfully. 'Unfortunately, I hadn't yet
found my true calling. The way ahead for me hadn't crystal-
lized. Anyhow, cancer did a pretty good job on her. Cancer of
the breast. How apposite! Cancer of the bosom that had never
embraced her son. Good riddance! She was eaten away long
before Big C got its teeth into her. Now she rots in hell.'

'Can you be sure of that?'

'If she doesn't, then there is no hell. Without hell, there can
be no heaven. You can't possibly have one without the other.
To appreciate what is good, you need the bad. Paradise is a
place where decent souls are no longer plagued by degener-
ates.' And then, 'At one time I wanted to become a doctor
rather than a vet.'

'What changed your mind?'

'I couldn't bear the thought of having to help cure people
I'd prefer dead. You see, if I'd become a doctor, I'd have
expected my patients to be able to justify their right to
continued life, to prove they'd earned it by their contribution
to morality. I suppose I could have always become another Dr
Harold Shipman.'

Shipman, of course, was Britain's most prolific serial killer,
with his tally totalling hundreds, defying a definitive count.

'He took his reasons to the grave, when he committed
suicide,' commented Tandy, succeeding in siphoning out more
from Carey.

'And that's something I understand; that's my intention.
That's one of the reasons why I cannot allow you to live,
because you have the answer to the question the whole world
will want answered – why? You see, without the answer to
why universally known, I am the winner and your super-

sleuth partner, and all the brains the police can muster, are losers. They won't even get to parade me as their prize catch.'

'You've explained your reason for killing the four Oxford women and Charley, but what's *my* crime?'

Carey began cracking his knuckles, wrestling with his own demons. Despite his external composure, he was becoming knotted inside with tension.

'For a start, you're a high-profile marriage-breaker.'

'Charley was already having an affair,' Tandy defended herself, as if in Oliver Cromwell's moral dock, with purity to be proved.

'The fact that Charley Templeman was a bad lot isn't in dispute. Nevertheless, she was married to Luke and it was not for any other woman to come between them, to put asunder. There's more to it than that, though. Much more.'

Tandy was kept awake by the need to know the absurd reason for her death sentence.

'Two names. Lynn Morton and Gregory Spencer. Two young people destroyed by you.'

Cognition came creakily from pulling a dusty file from a back-room depository of her brain. 'They torched a house in north London, Hampstead. Middle of the night. A couple were cremated in their beds in that arson blaze. Their six-year-old daughter also died.'

'The little girl's death was unfortunate.'

'It was the premeditated murder of a young family.'

'Carl Linberg ran a laboratory that conducted cruel experiments on animals – blinding them pitilessly, not even for medical science but purely for women's vanity, for cosmetics.'

'Jennifer Linberg was a housewife and mother. She didn't work at the laboratory.'

'She was a shareholder; she reaped the reward and pocketed the profits from institutionalized cruelty.'

'The daughter, Lilac, was an innocent.'

'She was infected with her parents' blood. The devil was in her, but, I agree, her death was an unfortunate necessity.'

'*Necessity?*'

'Morton and Spencer were terrestrial angels, God's saboteurs on earth. There was more work to be done, more savages to be silenced. But you had to spoil everything. Wrecker!'

'They were caught through forensic evidence, the myopic plods with microscopes.'

'You arrested them. You ran errands for the devil. You were his factotum. If you'd been half-decent, you would have turned a blind eye. Morton and Spencer deserved deification, not persecution.'

'What part did you play in their actions?' Tandy fished in deep, murky waters.

'I was simply a distant admirer, one of the spineless in the gallery, leaving others to rattle the sabres in the cause of probity. There's a Jekyll and Hyde in every one of us. The trick is to be able to utilize those conflicts for overall good.'

'And you think you've achieved that?'

'I know I have. J and H became my own personal logo: I'm sure I fooled your dear partner with that little conundrum.'

'But not me.'

Now it was Carey's turn not to understand, but he didn't intend squandering any initiative by being sidetracked.

'Animals have much nicer natures than humans,' he continued with his diatribe. 'I could never stand by while an animal – any animal – was being ill-treated. My blood would boil over. I would never be able to control myself.'

And then the haunting warning, 'Here is where it's going to end for all of us.'

The captain of the British Airways 747 decided to update passengers on their progress towards Miami.

'We're currently skirting the Carolinas. Sorry about the bumpy ride so far. Unfortunately the weather's one thing we can't yet control. The good news is that the rest of our passage to touchdown should be boringly uneventful. For those who would like to synchronize their watches with Florida time, it's 1.30 p.m. We shall be continuing down the eastern seaboard, passing Palm Beach on the right-hand side, before beginning our descent. We expect to be making our final approach over Miami Beach and should be on the ground by 3.30. The temperature at Miami International Airport is now ninety-two degrees Fahrenheit and very humid. Prepare to sweat. I'll talk to you again when we're over Palm Beach.'

The movie, the latest Harry Potter film, had just finished. Window blinds were popping up, allowing undiluted sunshine to flood back in with a dazzling gold-rush all of its own. Flight attendants prepared to serve a light afternoon, pre-landing meal. There were queues for the toilets; men with their electric shavers and bottles of cologne, women with recently purchased duty-free perfume, and cross-legged, crying children desperate to empty over-filled bladders. Others, fully paid-up members of the fear-of-flying fraternity, were pressing their call buttons, eager for another transfusion of alcohol to further lubricate their ragged nerves during the final leg of the long haul.

Templeman, with a window-seat on the left-hand side of

the plane, had been nursing a whisky on the rocks for the last two hours. He had declined lunch and had missed the movie, preferring to be soothed by easy-listening music, playing the same track on the stereo system endlessly. He would say no to the snack that was about to be offered. An elderly woman next to him had tried several times to initiate conversation, but he'd made sure each attempt was stillborn. He'd spent almost the entire flight, so far, staring out of the window, seeing more through his mind's eye than what was within his arc of vision. Fluffy, flimsy white clouds floated by, several thousand feet below, like bubbles in a baby's bath.

He hadn't a plan. He hadn't even formally checked out of the Randolph. He'd simply packed his bags the previous evening and walked out, catching the shuttle to Heathrow. On reaching the airport, he'd transferred to a hotel courtesy coach to the Sheraton Skyline, where he'd stayed overnight. On re-entering the USA, he would hire a car and drive the Tamiami Trail northwards to Naples. He wouldn't call Simone until he was within a mile of their apartment, purporting to be phoning from Oxford, as promised.

Templeman hadn't a single doubt that Carey was the cuckoo in their Naples nest and Simone was lined up as the next victim. First Charley, now her successor in Templeman's life. This was persecution beyond endurance for any man. But for the sake of Simone, he had to keep his nerve. Most of all, he had to keep Carey guessing. It was another gamble, of course. There was always the danger that uncertainty might spook Carey into premature, irrevocable action. In these circumstances, there were never any guarantees. He could do no more than play the percentages and trust his empirical intuition, which had prompted his impetuous evacuation of his hotel and Oxford, without consulting Hardman.

Templeman had also quickly dismissed any notion of calling FBI agent Joe Parmitter. Firstly, he doubted whether Parmitter would take him seriously, dismissing the approach as a publicity stunt. He expected the response would have been something like, 'You've got a nerve!' If Parmitter did do anything, Templeman suspected it would merely be going through the motions, sending a local cowboy banging on the apartment door, calling out: 'You OK in there, Ms Tandy? We had a call from some guy in the UK claiming you're being held by some moonstruck fugitive.' Goodnight and goodbye Simone!

It had all come together for Templeman in a flash: the last taunting message from the killer, Simone's SOS by asking for Templeman to contact her dead parents, and the fact that it was known that Carey had fled to the USA.

The irony of the parallel with the bogus kidnapping case, in which Tandy had become embroiled, purportedly as a mediator, hadn't escaped Templeman. He had tried to cajole Tandy into involving the police, but here he was flying in the face of his own earnest counselling. Detachment had its virtues, but emotional involvement could lead to the kind of blind passion and reckless valour that made heroes out of fools. Life was like that; nothing more choreographed than the spin of a coin. Heads or tails. Heroic winner or foolish loser. Capricious destiny.

In Oxford, Hardman had tried to reach Templeman several times. He'd left three voicemail messages for him at the Randolph and on Templeman's mobile. The skeletal remains of Charley Templeman had been positively identified by her dental records. Now it was time for Luke to examine the items lifted from the shallow, makeshift grave in Carey's garden and to make a statement.

'Lost someone else!' Badger jibed.

'He's probably taken himself off somewhere for a couple of days' solitary reflection,' Hardman had said, ignoring the bile. 'I can understand that.'

'What you *understand*, I flush down the toilet every day of my life, except when constipated. Find Carey. Find Templeman. In that order.'

Nothing changed between those two. Such was the rapport, they could have been a married couple.

CHAPTER 25

On arrival at Miami, Templeman hurried out of the airport, helped by the fact that he had no baggage to collect and negotiate through Customs, and rented a car from Hertz.

For an hour and a half he broke all speed restrictions through the Everglades along the Tamiami Trail as he drove towards the sunset – perhaps his own and Simone's.

The sun, like a massive crimson balloon on the ocean's horizon, was sinking fast, as if being brought down by a slow puncture. The crickets had already begun their dusk chorus. A sticky day was to be followed by a sultry night. Palm trees were as still as sentries. The flags at the top of long white poles, outside a hotel, were as limp as the symbol of impotence. Suntanned women, still in bikinis, were sauntering from the beach, their arms looped around the hard torsos of their men, all of whom seemed built in the image of muscle-pumped lifeguards. Cadillacs cruised by with the lack of urgency that went with people free from deadlines, the whole night ahead to be enjoyed at leisure. The air was already buzzing with squadrons of mosquitoes – airborne vampires – preparing for blood-raiding missions. The fragrance of jasmine reminded Templeman of barefooted evening strolls along the beach with Simone, allowing the gentle waves to lap over their feet, the sea feeling as warm as bath-water. In fact, every scene, sound and smell triggered a memory associated with his life with Simone. Emotion had him by the throat, making his eyes water. Like a drowning man, all the good times flashed before his eyes. If only the clock could be turned back. If only he had rejected the offer to return to Oxford. If only he'd been able to resist vanity's beguiling, though meretricious, charms. If only … Templeman was no different from anyone else when it came to mawkish self-analysis beyond the rubicon.

Just after crossing the urban boundary into Naples, Templeman made a call from his mobile to his apartment. After six rings, the answer-machine kicked in.

As patiently as possible, he waited for Simone's recorded message to finish. Then, staying as calm as possible in the circumstances, he said, 'I guess you're out on an assignment earning us lots of lovely lolly. It's nothing urgent. I just wanted you to know I've called your parents and spoken with your mother. She was grateful for the call and sends her love. I'll probably be on my way home tomorrow. Talk to you before then, hopefully. Sweet dreams. Bye.'

Templeman hoped that Simone was being prevented from taking calls by Carey, rather than any of the alternatives, such as her captor having decided to transfer his 'prize' elsewhere for safety or, worse still, having already killed her.

All he could do was to keep going and play the percentages. At least if Simone was still there and conscious, she would know from Templeman's message that help – if not exactly the cavalry – was on the way.

When Templeman was within a hundred yards of his apartment, he parked in a side road out of sight and began walking stealthily, keeping close to the buildings, an embryo plan spurring his stride.

At that moment, there was a tap on his shoulder. Templeman spun round, not knowing what to expect. But certainly not expecting to come face-to-face with FBI Agent Parmitter.

'Where you going in such a goddamned hurry?' demanded Parmitter in his deep, measured tones.

Templeman had frozen and blanched, with his mouth hanging open and nothing coming out, however hard he tried.

'Don't say anything,' said Parmitter, an instruction with

which Templeman had no trouble complying. 'We know a lot about what's going on. Not all, not by any means. You'll have to fill in the gaps.'

Regaining some composure, Templeman said, 'Where's Simone?'

'In your apartment?'

'Is she all right?'

'I wouldn't think she's *all right*, but if you mean is she still alive, then the answer's yes – as far as we know.'

Shaking his head, Templeman stammered, 'But what are you doing here? I don't get it.'

'You could sound a little more pleased.'

'Don't get me wrong, of course I'm glad, but ...'

'All in good time. After we've got Simone outta there.'

'I don't want you rushing the place like stormtroopers.'

'No intention, Luke. We left the cowboys at home on the ranch. Strictly sophisticates for this mission.'

Templeman managed to meet Parmitter's smile halfway.

'You got any ideas?' added Parmitter.

'As a matter of fact, yes, but I'm going to need help.'

'We're here for the action. Wouldn't miss it for the world. Come with me.'

Parmitter led Templeman about fifty yards the way he had come and into a pebble track that led to the beach. Just inside the lane was a vehicle that appeared to be a camper van. Inside, however, it was equipped with all the latest high-tech electronic surveillance equipment, including screens for receiving film from cameras. Sitting around the interior was a team of five operatives, including one woman agent. On a shelf beside the command post were stacked the mandatory six-packs of Budweiser.

After introductions, Parmitter said, 'OK, Luke thinks he has a plan that might work.' Turning to Templeman, he said, 'Let's hear it.'

'When I tell you to sit, you damn well sit, you ugly pooch!' the woman yelled. 'Do as I say or you'll get another taste of this stick.' This was followed by a resounding thwack, like a cane cutting into flesh. 'I'll teach you to pee on my new carpet. Just you wait till I get you outside. You want the sharp end of my stiletto up your butt, too? Stop cowering! What's a choke chain for if not to throttle worthless pugs like you?'

Carey's blood surged headwards, like the molten larva of an erupting volcano. Nothing enraged him more than the sound and sight of an animal being abused, as his young assistant in Oxford had related to Hardman and Templeman.

Acting on impulse, he pushed back the bolt on the outer door, turned the key and released the chain. Driven by the reflexes of his brain, he propelled himself into the corridor, where directly in front of him was a woman in jeans and a T-shirt, with a bamboo stick in one hand and a leather-bound book in the other, but no dog.

On seeing him, the woman's face flowered into a triumphant grin. Then she uttered just one ecstatic word: 'Gotcha!'

Carey's uncomprehending eyes were too transfixed on the dogless woman to notice Templeman and the other agents with their backs pressed to the wall.

The frame froze for Carey and in that instant it was all over. He was on the floor at the bottom of a scrum, trapped and soon to be tethered. His knife was still under the chair at the foot of the bed. And Simone, who had been drugged, had slept through her rescue, Carey's capture, and even the message on the answer-machine that was designed to give her some comfort.

CHAPTER 26

Paramedics checked over Simone Tandy's comatosed body, the senior of the emergency team declaring, 'Looks like she's going to be OK. Vital signs no problem. We'll take her in for proper resuscitation and a full medical. But this one's going to make it. I'd stake my own life on it.'

'I'll come with you,' said Templeman, naturally enough.

'No, you come with me,' dictated Parmitter. 'You can catch up later with your partner in folly – if not in crime. She'll keep. You won't.'

The FBI agents had a fleet of cars in addition to the converted camper. Parmitter commandeered one of them to drive a mile to the Registry Hotel with Templeman, still traumatized, beside him, then led the way to a circular, thatched-roof outside bar.

They found seats at a poolside table, away from the serious drinking action. Their first Budweisers went down like nectar, their Adam's apple regulating the flow, like a valve on a plumbing system. The crepuscular light would be short-lived. Darkness tended to descend like a guillotine in the sub-tropics.

'I could easily get used to life on this dried-up swamp,' said Parmitter, thick-set legs apart, his waxed and polished black shoes planted firmly on the concrete. His sharp-cut Bureau suit, wedding-white shirt and shorn hair made him transparent for what he was.

Everything about Templeman's body language was screaming for explanations and even Parmitter couldn't bring himself to prolong the tension.

Templeman allowed Parmitter his rites of tribal triumphalism. He had little choice. Stoicism was at least preferable to overt bluff or comic denial.

'OK, here's the narrative,' Parmitter began, like a book-at-bedtime storyteller. 'After your partner's monumental cock-up over the Tammy Carter kidnapping charade, we considered it advisable – how should I put this? – to take a closer look at your agency.'

Templeman flinched, but held his fire.

'I, for one, wanted to be sure that your set-up was operating ethically. I could use stronger language, but I think you get the drift.'

'Are you saying that you suspected Simone of being part of the scam?'

'I'm saying I wanted to exclude the possibility. We had a small, elite team stake out your place. Very unobtrusive. Very hands off. Invisible. Top mechanics, mainly relying on electronics.'

'You mean phone-tapping?'

'Very passé, Luke. It's phone-scanning these days. Has been for several years. Using scanners, they were able to sit out of sight in cars and monitor every goddamn call within a quarter-mile radius. Plus every word spoken in your apartment. Fun, huh?'

'How did Carey get into the apartment?'

'Conned his way in, I guess. The nuts and bolts will have to come from Simone, but we observed them entering together. There could have been a weapon being held out of sight. Remember, as I've said, we were keeping well back. We were videoing comings and goings, but we didn't get to grips with what was really going on until the guy was ensconced. At no point were we going to play cowboys. Rushing the place was never going to be an option unless as a last resort to try to save Simone's life. Brain before brawn, the Bureau's new motto! What became apparent was that Carey was hoping to be able to await your return, taking you all down together in some weird and whacko grand finale. You played it cool, I'll grant you that. At first I didn't catch on to the coded cry for help. It was only some hours later that it dawned on me. In one of our drinking marathons you'd mentioned that your partner didn't have any parents, that they'd died long before you met.'

'That's right, I did tell you.'

'And when you said you'd contact them and wouldn't be on your way home for two or three days, I knew you were hotfooting it back pronto. We checked flight lists with all the transatlantic carriers and soon knew which flight you were on. Hence our little welcoming party. We had to bank on being able to lure Carey into the open long enough for a marksman to squeeze off a round. But we didn't know how we were going to do it, until you came up with that damned absurd idea of yours!'

The insult lacked bite.

'Our electronic wizards fixed limpet mikes to the external walls of the apartment. You must have seen 'em many times before: they stay in place through suction and latest technology enables the operators to record every word spoken inside premises. As a result, we have a recording of Carey admitting the homicide of five women, including your wife. It's all there. Bingo! To be honest, I warmed to your ruse the moment you spelled it out. You see, during his rant to Simone he revealed that the ill treatment of animals made him more mad than anything; whatever the consequences, he couldn't just stand by and let it happen.'

'What now?'

'We'll charge him with kidnapping and attempted homicide, but it's most likely that our attorneys will allow the UK slayings to take precedence. Extradition will be a formality.'

'Have the Oxford cops been informed yet?'

'No, I reckoned that might be something that'd give you a kick.'

'You bet!'

Then came the big one.

'Did he *touch* Simone?'

'Only to shackle and drug her. He's no stereotype serial junkie, for sure. As weirdoes go, he's really weird!'

TV programmes in the UK were interrupted for news of the arrest of Carey in Florida. The press release from Badger's office was doctored to glamorize Templeman's role in the dramatic showdown, saving his lover from the dragon's den in true St George fashion, with only minutes to spare. This spin enabled Badger to further congratulate himself by highlighting the fact that Templeman was *his* man, brought in through his initiative to revive an investigation that had become 'depressingly bogged down'. Badger added, 'Cometh the hour, cometh the man. *My* man! Good leaders are like world-class football coaches. Instinctively, they know just when to make a substitution; which player to take off and which one to replace him with. The game turned in our favour the moment I sent on Templeman.'

'Does that mean you took off Hardman?' asked a canny TV reporter.

'No comment,' Badger replied, impishly, which was confirmation enough.

Hardman was doing what he always did best when he saw Badger on TV. He quickly finished his beer and ordered another pint. There wasn't anything new in a boss thieving glory from subordinates with the shamelessness of a common poacher.

Hardman bore Templeman no grudge because he had been instrumental in wooing him to Oxford, not Badger. He and Templeman knew the truth and that was all that mattered. '*We* did it, bless you!' he murmured, made maudlin by the booze, not loud enough to be overheard by any of the other tipplers in the Lamb and Flag, in a symbolic toast to Templeman.

Templeman collected Tandy from the Naples Downtown Medical Center at 9 a.m. the next day. She was still groggy and unsteady on her feet, and Templeman had to support her physically all the way to his car. She had only a sketchy recollection of the apocalyptic events of the last forty-eight hours because the sedatives she'd been administered by Carey had an amnestic side-effect.

'I've told Agent Parmitter that Simone is unlikely to be of any help to him, so I doubt that you'll be harassed,' opined Dr Jennifer Blake, as she spoke with Templeman, after he'd helped Simone into the car.

'Thanks, but that's something I won't be counting on,' he said.

Throughout that morning, Tandy blitzed him with questions, most of which he parried, saying, 'I'll tell you everything in a day or two, but for the time being just rest.'

The following day, Tandy was awake by seven and as skittish as a spring lamb. She showered, made coffee and breakfast, refusing to allow Luke to do anything for her. She had something to prove.

'We're going for a swim in the ocean later this morning, then we'll go for cocktails and that'll be the cue for storytime,' she announced friskily. 'No more stalling.'

'OK, you win.'

'Just like old times!'

They kissed, also on cue – and returned to bed, putting the ocean on hold until the afternoon.

Around noon, as they lay naked on the bed, holding hands, bathed in a suffusion of sweat, gently blow-dried by the air-conditioning, Templeman said, 'I think we should take a week's holiday. Drive down to the Keys. Leave our mobiles behind. Make ourselves uncontactable. Beyond reach. Beyond recall. Just fish and ...'

And that's when the phone rang, with a frantic woman dictating a message to the answer-machine, 'I need your help. I'm frantic. My teenage daughter's gone missing and I fear the worst ...'

Templeman and Tandy looked at one another and instantly cracked up.